THE END OF ACT THREE

Other Dani Ross Mysteries

One by One

And Then There Were Two

A Dani Ross Mystery

THE END OF ACT THREE

GILBERT MORRIS

CROSSWAY BOOKS • WHEATON, ILLINOIS
A DIVISION OF GOOD NEWS PUBLISHERS

The End of Act Three

Published by Crossway Books
A division of Good News Publishers
1300 Crescent Street
Wheaton, Illinois 60187

First published by Fleming H. Revell, a division of Baker Book House, 1991 as *The Final Curtain*

First Crossway edition, 2001

Cover design: Cindy Kiple

Unless otherwise noted, Scripture quotations are taken from the *King James Version.*

First Crossway printing, 2001

Printed in the United States of America

Library of Congress Cataloging-in-Publication Data

Morris, Gilbert.
[Final curtain]
The end of act three / Gilbert Morris.—1st Crossway ed.
p. cm. — (A Dani Ross mystery ; bk. 3)
Originally published as: The final curtain.
ISBN 1-58134-245-4
1. Ross, Danielle (Fictitious character)—Fiction. 2. Women private investigators—New York (State)—New York—Fiction. 3. New York (N.Y.)—Fiction. I. Title.
PS3563.O8742 F56 2001
813'.54—dc21 00-011654
CIP

15 14 13 12 11 10 09 08 07 06 05 04 03 02 01
15 14 13 12 11 10 9 8 7 6 5 4 3 2 1

To Kay

*We've come a long way, and we've got a way to go—
so let's stick together and make it count, Sis.*

CONTENTS

One

A NEW CLIENT

For the hundredth time Dani moved out of her new office to stand on the small balcony framed with wrought iron. Staring down at the passing parade of traffic on Bourbon Street, she wondered if she had done the right thing in moving Ross Investigation Agency to new quarters. She loved the busy activity of the area and knew that she'd signed the lease mostly because of the small balcony, from which she could take in the scene below—the rough, irregular bricks that made up the narrow street, the black, ornate ironwork framing the balconies that had become the symbol of the French Quarter in New Orleans, and the row of shops and restaurants below, designed to snare the crowds that packed the street, especially during Mardi Gras.

This February was even milder than usual in New Orleans. The humid air rose from the cobblestones, bearing the odor of fresh boudin from the cafe below. Suddenly a man's voice heavy with a French Cajun accent rang out. "Hi, Dani! Let's me an' you go pass a good time!" She looked down with a smile at the tall man who stood staring up at her and shook her head. "Aw, it's only three or two hours till time to quit. Come on, Cher!"

"I have to make a living, Rene," she called out. "Besides, Lucy would kill us both if she caught us together."

Rene LeBlanc, who played fiddle in a Cajun band, made a sour face, then raised his hands in dramatic fashion. "You got dat right, Cher! Me too. I see you sometime."

Dani watched as he almost danced down the street. A cloud crossed her face, and she moved back inside to consider the new office. It was a narrow room with a large, mullioned window in the center of a long wall. Pale afternoon sunlight filtered through, giving the dark, polished wood of her antique desk a glow. A walnut chair, newly re-covered in mauve leather, sat behind it, with its mate squatting squarely in front of the desk. Angie Park, her secretary, had argued for more chairs, but Dani had said, "People want privacy when they hire a detective. And three's a crowd." She had finally compromised by adding two antique oak chairs, directly under the single painting on the wall.

That painting showed her great-great-grandfather, Daniel Monroe Ross, dressed in his Confederate colonel's uniform. She loved the way his piercing eyes stared at her. He had led his company in Pickett's Charge at Gettysburg, had been wounded three times at Chancellorsville, and had refused to surrender his men and his flag at Appomattox, choosing rather to flee to Mexico. The flag was her father's most cherished possession, and more than once he had said, "Dani, I think some of the colonel's stubbornness filtered down to you!"

Staring at her ancestor, Danielle Ross felt a sudden touch of fear. Since her father's heart attack, she had tried to bring the agency back into full swing, and it had been her decision to spend a considerable amount of money on a new office and a new advertising campaign. They had been in the new offices for a month. So far the tactics had not brought a significant increase in business. As she had secretly told her right-hand man Ben Savage, "You might say we're a bit underwhelmed, Ben."

She had smiled, but it had not been a convincing smile, for no matter how confident she tried to sound, Dani was worried about the agency's future.

Looking up into the piercing eyes of the colonel, she shook her head and wistfully remarked, "I'll bet you wouldn't be worried, would you, Colonel?"

Angie's voice suddenly came through the intercom. "Miss

Ross, a Mr. Montgomery Stone would like to see you. He doesn't have an appointment, but I thought you might give him a few minutes."

"I think that will be possible," Dani responded quickly. "Give me a moment." Turning to her desk, she quickly took some papers from the side drawer and scattered them over the top. Pulling a pen from its marble and gold holder, she chose a fresh sheet of new stationery and began writing. A smile pulled at the corners of her lips as she thought of what she was doing, both irritated and entertained by her own foolishness. She wrote carefully on the pad in a neat script: *Lord, let Mr. Stone become a paying client—and let him be very rich!* She nodded, then added, *For You know, Lord, that I am broke!* She flipped the intercom switch, briskly commanding, "Send Mr. Stone in please."

The man who came through the door was in his late sixties, Dani judged. He was tall and bent, wore a brown suit that was out of style, and held a narrow-brimmed plaid hat in his hand. His face was narrow and hidden behind a short salt-and-pepper beard. As he headed toward her, he gave Dani a penetrating glance from a pair of large, deep-set blue eyes.

"I'm Danielle Ross, Mr. Stone." Dani rose and moved to offer him her hand. The hand that took hers was surprisingly firm and muscular for a man his age. "Won't you sit down?" she offered.

"I suppose so, but my business won't take long," Stone answered in a high, thin voice. "I won't take much of your time."

"Oh?" Dani said, hoping her disappointment didn't show in her voice. She waited until he was seated, then sat down behind her desk. "What can I do for you?"

Stone regarded her carefully, and his lips grew thin. "Nothing. You've done enough for me already. But you won't do any more for me and my family—or for anyone else, Miss Ross."

Dani studied him, noting the fixed, almost rigid expression. "Have we met before, Mr. Stone?" she asked. "I'm afraid I don't remember you."

"We've never met, but I'm sure you recall a certain member of my family." Stone's lips suddenly turned up in a grim smile, and a thin, humorless laugh came from his throat. "Surely you haven't forgotten my brother."

An alarm went off in Dani's head. After some hesitation she commented, "I assume you're Maxwell Stone's brother."

Again the thin laugh, and then the man prompted her, "So you *have* done something for my family, haven't you, Miss Ross?"

If he's as crazy as his brother, I'm in trouble! Dani thought. She studied the man, thinking there *was* a resemblance. The memory of Maxwell Stone swept over her. Stone had been a very wealthy man who had become dangerously unstable. He had formed a right-wing organization in the Ozarks, a paramilitary organization complete with practically every weapon except tanks. Dani and Ben Savage had been lured into his mountain lair and had barely escaped with their lives. For months afterward Dani had had nightmares over the terrible incident.

Maxwell Stone had been tried on charges of kidnapping and murder and was convicted of both. He committed suicide only two weeks after beginning his term at a federal prison. As she stared at the man before her, Dani remembered how she had been forced to struggle with her hatred for his brother. Carefully she said, "Yes, I remember your brother. He was not himself, Mr. Stone, as I'm sure you know. No sane man would have done what he did."

Stone nodded. "You must have been glad when Max killed himself."

"No, I didn't enjoy hearing of that." Dani shook her head. "I was very grieved. I pitied him."

Stone hesitated, then went on, "I heard you were some sort of a minister. Well, that makes what I've come to do much easier."

"What do you want, Mr. Stone? Why *have* you come here?"

"I've come to kill you, Miss Ross." Stone suddenly reached inside his coat and pulled out a gun, aiming it directly at Dani. "It's only fair, isn't it? I mean, you killed my brother, so now I'm going to kill you." The thin laugh sounded again, and a note of hysteria rose in his voice. The gun wavered as if it were too heavy, and he taunted her. "But since you're a Christian, you're not afraid to die, are you?"

The sight of the blunt-nosed revolver aimed at her heart chilled Dani, but she did all she could to hide her fear. Her mind raced madly as she took in all the details. Even under the threat of death at the hands of a madman, she noted that the gun he had trained on her was a .38. Aware of the eyes of her ancestor fixed on her, she thought, *You would know just what to do in a situation like this, wouldn't you, Colonel?* Glancing up at the stern-faced Confederate soldier, she thought wryly that he had faced thousands of guns when he charged up Little Round Top.

Well, this is only one man with one gun, she decided. *A dangerous man with a loaded weapon. Lord . . .*

"You don't really want to do that, Mr. Stone," Dani responded calmly. "In the first place, I'm not responsible for your brother's death. In the second place, even if I were, you wouldn't want to spend the rest of your life in prison for shooting me, would you?"

Stone's blue eyes widened, and he shook his head. Admiration was evident in his voice as he said, "I heard you were cool and collected." All warmth left his tone as he continued, "But I don't care about going to prison. I can't let you get away with killing my brother. I have too much pride for that."

He lifted the gun, now aiming it at her head. "I guess I should at least give you time to say a prayer before you—ah—go to glory, shall we say?"

Dani shook her head. "I don't need time to pray, Mr. Stone."

"You don't?" Surprised, Stone lowered the gun a few inches. "I'd think even someone like you would want to get ready to meet her Maker in a situation like this."

Dani knew her only hope lay in getting the man to use reason; she would have to keep him talking. "I'm ready to meet God right now," she explained. "You see, I belong to Him because of Jesus' death on my behalf. So when I die I'll be going home. That's the way it is with all real Christians."

He studied her and asked curiously, "But surely you have a few sins you need to confess. You wouldn't want to carry them with you, I'm sure?"

"Oh, I'm not perfect." Dani shrugged. "But I don't have to be to go to heaven—Jesus paid the price for all my sins. That's why I want to serve Him every day. So every morning when I get up I ask God to help me obey Him all day long. And I ask Him to let me know at once if I do anything that offends Him. So when I do something wrong, He lets me know, and I ask Him to forgive me."

"Ah, you talk to God, do you, Miss Ross? I've always admired the great mystics of the church. Unfortunately, I've not been one of those who have been privileged to hear God's voice. What does God sound like—Charlton Heston perhaps?"

Dani refused to react to his sarcasm. "I haven't heard an audible voice either. But when Jesus went away after His resurrection, He promised that He would never leave those who believe in Him alone. So when I became a Christian, I began to pray and to read His Word. Before long I began sensing that God was speaking to me—in my spirit, not with an audible voice, you see."

Stone listened carefully as Dani went on for five minutes, explaining how her Christian life worked, showing no sign of fear, surreptitiously flipping a special switch underneath the desk.

Finally Stone interrupted. "All this is very interesting, I'm sure, Miss Ross." He smiled grimly. "But I didn't come here for a lecture on God. I'm afraid I must end our little meeting."

He raised the gun, and Dani looked past the wide muzzle and into his eyes. She said nothing more, but her hands began to tremble. *God,* she prayed silently, *if this is my time to die, let me die in a worthy fashion—with Your name on my lips!*

She glanced up again, meeting the eyes of the colonel, then looked back at Stone. "I don't want to die, Mr. Stone; but if I must, at least let me tell you that I refuse to hate you for what you are about to do. Since Jesus Christ came into my heart, I find it difficult to hate anybody. And I hope that before you die and go to meet God, you'll receive Him as your Savior."

Stone's brow wrinkled. He hesitated before admitting, "I must say, Miss Ross, you've—"

He got no further, for a sudden flurry of movement to his right caught his eye. He turned his head just in time to feel the hard edge of Ben Savage's hand strike his temple. The force of the blow snapped his head to one side, and he collapsed silently on the carpet.

Savage picked up the gun, then turned to Dani. A slight smile crossed his wide mouth, and his hazel eyes contained a hint of relief as he greeted Dani. "Good morning, boss!"

"Ben!" Dani exclaimed. She moved toward him, but suddenly, now that the danger was over, her knees seemed too weak to hold her, and if he hadn't caught her, she would have fallen. Her breath came in shallow gasps, and her head was spinning. She'd had the same reaction after nearly running head-on into an eighteen-wheeler. That time she had pulled over to the shoulder and promptly fainted!

For a few moments she leaned against Savage, who said nothing. When the trembling finally stopped, she lifted her head to look into his eyes and pulled away, embarrassed that he had seen her reaction.

"Danger affects a person like that," he whispered. "It always hits me *after* the trouble is over."

Dani stared at him, taking in the deep-set eyes, the coarse, black hair, unruly and in need of trimming as usual. He had a thin upper lip and a fair complexion. A scar on his forehead ran into his left eyebrow, which he touched whenever he thought hard about something. He was her chief operative, and they constantly carried on a subtle war of words. Times without number she had been ready to fire him, but he had the physical skill and toughness she knew the agency needed, though that fact also irked her no end. Savage *knew* it bothered her too, though he seldom alluded to it. "Every detective agency has to have one hard nut," he had said once. "I know it eats at you that you need to have a man around, that there are some things a woman can't do. But that's just the way it is, boss."

Dani threw her long, auburn hair back with a sudden gesture of relief. "Ben, thanks." She smiled, and he took in her face, a bit squarish and yet perfect, and the large, almond-shaped, gray-green eyes and thought again how she would never be a winner in a beauty contest, unless he was the judge! Her nose was just a little too short, her face too square, and she had a small mole on her right cheek. *She'd never make it as a model either*, he thought. At five feet eight she was only two inches shorter than Savage and often wore high heels in an attempt to intimidate him, a tactic that never worked.

"I—I guess you were right about that switch under the desk," Dani offered unsteadily. He had insisted on installing it. "Might get a rough customer for a client someday," he had explained, shrugging. "With this little gadget, you can let Angie know you need some help."

Dani had argued that she could handle any client, but he had simply ignored her and installed the switch. It had angered her at the time, but now she said, "Guess you have a bonus coming for that one, Ben."

"Put it in my Christmas stocking," he responded easily. He moved to her desk and flipped the switch on the intercom. "Angie, all is well. We'll talk to our little friend before we call the cops." Reaching down, he grabbed Stone and pulled him into a sitting position, then plopped him into a chair. "I saw him at the trial," he remembered, studying the face before him.

"So did I," Dani agreed. "But he didn't have a beard then." She came around to look carefully into the man's face. "Seeing him brings back some bad memories, Ben."

"Yeah, like Yogi Berra says, 'It's déja vu all over again.'"

As Stone's eyelids began flickering, Dani and Ben both thought of the weeks spent in Maxwell Stone's grim prison, especially remembering those who had died there at the hands of their captor's paid assassin. Their eyes met, and Dani whispered, "I still think about them a lot—Rosie and Alex and Candi."

"Me too," Ben said, and she saw that he meant it. He was so

tough that she often found it difficult to know what he was thinking, but he had momentarily allowed his iron control to slip. He smiled and added, "Yeah, boss, I have a few soft spots." But when he glanced at Stone, the gentleness disappeared. "Welcome back, Stone."

"What . . . ?" The man was pawing at the air. As they watched, his eyes cleared. He sat up straight in the chair, touched his right temple, and winced. "Well, sir, you didn't leave a scar. I'm most grateful for that."

Dani stared at him, for the voice was suddenly different—deeper and more resonant. "I don't believe your fellow inmates will be very concerned with your appearance, Mr. Stone," she commented as she picked up the phone. "Get me the police, Angie." Moving back to their captive, she warned, "Assault with a deadly weapon is a serious offense. But with good lawyers, you might get off with a year's actual prison time. I suppose you received quite a bit of money from your brother?"

"Why, no," the man said with a deep chuckle. "As a matter of fact, I don't have any of Maxwell Stone's money. Why should I? I'm no relation to him—thank God!"

Dani stared at him. "But you said—" Over the phone a voice answered, "Police station," and she requested, "Let me speak to Lieutenant Spears please. Yes, I'll wait."

"Just give me five minutes, Miss Ross. Then you can make all the calls you want, please."

The man's final words convinced Dani to give him a chance. She hung up the phone and returned to her chair. Sitting down, she leaned back. "You have five minutes, Mr. Stone, but no more."

The man straightened up. With both hands he reached up and began pulling at his beard. "This thing itches like crazy," he remarked, laughing at the expression on Dani's face as the beard began to come off. "Oh, it's not real, Miss Ross," he confessed cheerfully. "And my hair isn't white either, but I'll have to wash the dye out to prove it. There, how's that?"

"It doesn't keep you out of jail," Dani said. "Did you disguise yourself so it would be harder for the police to find you?"

"Indeed not! And my name is not Stone, by the way." Ben hefted the .38 in his hand and questioned idly, "This gun registered in your name?"

"No, it's not. And it isn't loaded, as you can see."

Ben pulled the cylinder out, stared at it, then told Dani, "He's not lying about that anyway. But, Mr. Whoever, you can do time for just threatening a person with an unloaded gun."

"May I stand up?" The man rose and reached into his back pocket. "Oh, don't worry, I'm just getting out my wallet." He smiled as Savage tensed. "Here, Miss Ross, please check my identification."

Dani took the billfold, noting that it was made of very expensive eel skin, and looked at the driver's license, then at the credit cards. "Jonathan Ainsley," she read, darting a look at Savage. "We have a celebrity in our midst, Ben."

"Yeah," Ben nodded. "Can I have your autograph?"

Jonathan Ainsley was more than a celebrity. He was one of the top names in the theater. He had been the boy genius of the stage. At twenty-four he had written, produced, and starred in a modern drama, *Climax,* and it had won every award the world of drama offers. It had also been made into a movie, starring Jonathan Ainsley naturally. The film had won the Academy Award for best film, and Ainsley had won the award for best actor.

Dani leaned back, realizing that the man actually was Jonathan Ainsley. She had seen him in the play and had seen the movie many times. *He must be about thirty now,* she thought, admiring the sensitive face. *He's beginning to show a few lines around the mouth, and his neck is thickening just a bit, but he still reminds me of Olivier!*

"What's this all about, Mr. Ainsley?" Dani said with quiet admiration. When the other girls had been squealing over rock stars, she had been poring over every detail of Ainsley's life. She felt elated just looking at him but could think of no reason for his coming to her office, especially under such bizarre circumstances.

"Why, Miss Ross . . ." Ainsley smiled. "It's really very simple."

He paused, pulled a gold cigarette case from his inner pocket, and made a business out of removing a cigarette and lighting it. It was a theatrical thing, Dani recognized. *He probably acts for himself in the shower*, she thought wryly. The man certainly had a knack for drawing attention to himself.

"I want to hire you, Miss Ross," Ainsley explained, smiling again at the look of incredulity on Dani's face. "Oh, I apologize for my overdone approach. I've been in the theater so long, I can't scratch my nose without making a production out of it! But this time there was method in my madness."

"Mr. Savage and I would like to hear about that," Dani invited evenly.

"Ah, your name is *Savage*?" Ainsley touched his temple and, giving Ben a half-angry glance, said, "You are well named, sir! A very sanguinary fellow indeed!"

Savage had gone to lean against the wall, his eyes studying a young woman standing on the balcony across the street. He tore his gaze away. "Me sanguinary?" he queried sarcastically. "I don't believe I've ever heard anyone use that word for me."

"It means—" Ainsley began.

"He knows what it means," Dani cut him off. Savage, who was usually polite to waitresses and clerks, seemed to delight in sinking verbal barbs into those in high places—a habit that had gotten him and the agency into trouble more than once. "Ben, behave yourself. Now, Mr. Ainsley, I take it you have a problem, but why all this business with the fake beard and the gun?"

Ainsley flushed slightly, then gave a rueful laugh. "Well, I have to admit it wasn't one of my better ideas. Yes, I have a problem, and I have to be sure that I get the right people to help me. Your encounter with Maxwell Stone was all over the papers, and it fascinated me. But no one knows better than I how much the papers lie. So although I was inclined to ask you to help me, I wanted to make sure you'd be the right one. It just happened that I had to make this trip to New Orleans on business, so I decided to give you a little test."

Dani stared at him. "Well, that was foolish. If you'd pulled that gun on Ben, who knows what he might've done. But at any rate, you have a problem, you say?"

Ainsley's lips suddenly grew tense, and he spoke soberly. "I have indeed. Will you look at these, Miss Ross?" He pulled an envelope from his pocket and pushed it across the desk. Dani pulled two sheets of paper from the envelope and read each in turn. Both were printed in capital letters on a worn typewriter, obviously a very old one. She noted at once that the letters O and E were half raised. One message read:

AINSLEY—I AM GOING TO DESTROY YOU. A MAN SUCH AS YOU DOESN'T DESERVE TO LIVE. YOU HAVE RUINED MY LIFE, SO NOW I DO NOT PROPOSE TO LET YOU LIVE. YOU ESCAPED THIS MORNING, BUT YOU CANNOT ESCAPE FOREVER.

The other message said:

AINSLEY—YOU HAVE HAD TWO CLOSE CALLS. SURELY YOU KNOW BY NOW THAT I AM SERIOUS. HOWEVER, I HAVE DECIDED TO LET YOU LIVE, IF YOU WILL DO AS I SAY. YOU MUST NOT APPEAR ON THE STAGE. I KNOW YOU. YOU LOVE ACTING AS MUCH AS YOU LOVE LIFE, AND IT WILL HURT YOU WORSE TO LEAVE ACTING THAN TO DIE. I HAVE READ THAT YOU ARE GOING TO DO A PLAY. BUT YOU WILL NOT SUCCEED. I WILL KILL YOU IF YOU GO ON THE STAGE. I MEAN THIS!

"Not a very literate sort of threat, I'm afraid." Ainsley shrugged as Dani looked at him.

"Do you take these seriously, Mr. Ainsley?" she asked.

"I have to, Miss Ross," he answered, "since two attempts have been made on my life."

Dani considered this, then requested, "Tell me about these attempts."

Ainsley moved nervously in his chair. "I get a certain amount of crank mail, of course," he admitted. "That's what I thought these were at first. I had received two others earlier but threw them away. Then, the day after I got the second, I was nearly run down while crossing a street.

"It was quite deliberate," he exclaimed, shaking his head. "I was crossing the street in front of my hotel. It was very early, and I heard the car start up just as I came out of the hotel. There was no other traffic, so I wasn't paying too much attention. When I heard the engine racing I glanced up to see the vehicle bearing down on me. I jumped, and the driver swerved to hit me!" Ainsley took a white silk handkerchief from his pocket and passed it over his face. "The fender of the car tore my overcoat."

"I see," Dani said. "Did you call the police?"

"I couldn't prove it was deliberate." Ainsley shrugged and put the handkerchief back in his pocket. "And no one else saw it happen. I told myself it was just a wild driver, someone who just wasn't paying attention. But when I got another threat, I knew the danger was real." He leaned back and stared at Dani. "If I had any doubt at all, I lost it the next day. I was jogging early that morning in Central Park, and someone shot at me."

"But he missed?" Ben inserted suddenly.

"Obviously!" Ainsley snapped. "Otherwise I would be dead."

"What kind of gun?" Dani asked. "Did you see the man who shot at you?"

"Yes to the last question. I heard a sound—a sort of whizzing noise. The bullet must have been close to my head. I didn't know it was a bullet, of course. Not at first. Then I looked up and saw him. He was wearing a long coat and one of those Russian-style fur hats."

"Could you see his face?" Dani wanted to know.

"No. He was too far away, and anyway I didn't look too hard." Ainsley laughed. "He had a gun in his hand, and he was taking aim at me again. I ducked behind a tree and started calling for help."

"Was it a rifle or a revolver?" Ben asked.

"Oh, some sort of handgun, but with a funny barrel. It had a knob on the end of it."

"A silencer." Dani nodded. "That was all you saw?"

"Yes, and that was enough!" Ainsley said sharply. "Now I knew I needed help. I'd read about your 'adventure' with Maxwell Stone, so I decided to try you out. I could have gone to any detective agency in New York, of course. But you must understand—" Ainsley paused and gave both of them a careful look. "Is there such a thing as privileged communication among private detectives like there is among lawyers?"

"Nothing you say will go any further," Dani assured him.

"Well then, I must tell you that despite all you might think, I am in a fairly desperate position professionally." He smiled grimly at the look of surprise on Dani's face. "That does surprise you, I think."

"Yes, it does. You've done several plays and a movie or two."

"But none lately, and none anywhere as successful as *Climax*." A worried look came into Ainsley's eyes. "Oh, I can still have just about any role I want in Hollywood, but I'm not sure I want the stress and strain. Every time I think of Hollywood, I think of what S. J. Perelman said about it: 'A dreary industrial town controlled by hoodlums of enormous wealth, the ethical sense of a pack of jackals, and taste so degraded that it befouled everything it touched.'"

"What about the stage?" Dani suggested. "Surely there are many good roles for you there?"

"Well, to be truthful, Miss Ross—may I call you Dani?—thank you, there is one good role every year or so, but Broadway is controlled by people with whom I have had, well, difficulties. The only way I will return to the stage is in a play of my own design."

"I see. What play is this letter about, Mr. Ainsley?"

"Jonathan, please." Ainsley grew animated as he spoke, and both Dani and Ben saw that she had mentioned the one subject he was excited about. "It's a new piece, one I wrote myself," he told them. "I call it *Out of the Night*. Can you guess where the title comes from, Dani?"

"Oh, I'd guess from '*Invictus*' by William Ernest Henley," Dani suggested quickly.

"I thought you might know it." Ainsley smiled. "Well, that poem is the spirit of my play. I know you are a Christian, Dani, and I fear you will not agree with my point of view, but I am a humanist. I believe that man is his own god and must make his own destiny. Traditional morality means nothing to me. I feel very strongly that man must pull himself up—and that he *can* do so. That's what Henley meant in the last verse of his poem:

"It matters not how strait the gate,
How charged with punishments the scroll,
I am the master of my fate:
I am the captain of my soul."

He quoted the lines triumphantly, and Dani felt a thrill as his marvelous voice filled the room. "This play is as good as *Climax,* Dani," he assured her. "It will bring me to the top of my profession again. It is a statement that I want to make. Man is making a mess of his own nest, and I want to protest that we are capable of better than that!"

Dani studied Ainsley, then asked, "You want protection, I assume?"

"I want more than that," he demanded. "I want this maniac apprehended, Dani. I can't live my life with the possibility of his being behind every tree just waiting to take a shot at me. Oh, I want to be protected, of course, but this madman must be put away."

"If someone is determined to get you, Mr. Ainsley," Ben interrupted, "and if he doesn't mind paying the price, there's no way to stop him."

"Yes, Savage, I've been told that. But I am assuming that he can be found—and that Dani is the one to do it."

Dani wanted to leap at the chance, but she admitted, "You need around-the-clock protection, Jonathan. Though we have done that before, it was extremely difficult for us—we're really not set up for such a huge operation. And besides, the play is in New York, isn't it?"

"Yes. But I don't want a bunch of big-footed security guards lurking all over the place. That's why I came to you." He moved over and put out his hand. Dani placed her own in his without thinking. "You see, I want someone looking out for me who won't be noticed."

"But your enemies will probably figure out that I'm a detective."

"No, they won't." Ainsley smiled. "Because you're going back with me to New York not as Dani Ross, private investigator, but as an actress. We'll have to come up with another name for you."

"You want me to go undercover?" Dani laughed suddenly. "I can't do that, Jonathan. What would be my excuse for being around you all the time?"

Ainsley's white teeth gleamed. "You'll be Danielle Morgan, costume lady and actress. You probably know that everyone has a part in my plays, even the prop man."

"Me? I'm no actress!"

"Ah, but you are!" Ainsley pulled her closer. "I did some detective work myself, Dani, before I came to see you. I discovered you were in every play at Tulane while you were studying there, and you were good too!"

"Oh, that was just college drama, Jonathan!" Dani protested.

"But you love the theater, don't you?" Ainsley pressed her hands. "And I must add that if this play does one hundredth of what *I know* it can, you'll be paid for your services more than you could make anywhere else. Will you do it, Dani?"

Her hands were held fast in his, and his eyes held her transfixed. She wanted to say that the whole idea was preposterous and absurd. She knew what her father would say. Her head spun as she thought of the many reasons for saying no firmly and at once.

But instead she heard herself saying, "Yes! Yes, Jonathan, I'll do it!"

He leaned forward and kissed her, and she heard Ben Savage remark dryly, "Well, break a leg, boss!"

Two

"JUST ONE BIG HAPPY FAMILY!"

Well, there it is, Dani—the Pearl Theater," Ainsley said. He reached to help her out of the cab, gesturing dramatically at the marquee that proclaimed *Out of the Night* in large, black letters. Underneath in only slightly smaller letters Dani read STARRING JONATHAN AINSLEY. Beneath that she read in very small type, ALSO FEATURING AMBER LEROI.

As Dani stepped out of the cab, Jonathan asked, "Well, Danielle, all ready for your new career on the stage?"

"Not really, Jonathan." A sudden gust of cold air whipped down the narrow street, chilling her face. "I stayed awake most of last night, thinking how crazy this whole thing is." She glanced up at the marquee, then down the paper-littered street toward Broadway. The glitz and glitter there seemed dimmed by bumper-to-bumper traffic and the endless sound of honking horns. "It'll never work, Jonathan. My picture was in the papers when the Maxwell Stone story broke. Someone is sure to recognize me."

"Ah, but they won't!" Ainsley opened one of the glass doors and led her through a darkened lobby and toward the inner doors. "One thing you must know about drama, Dani—it's the art of making people see what you *want* them to see, not what's actually in front of their eyes. That's the way magicians fool people. They move their left hands so emphatically that you forget to watch their right hands, with which they do their real business." He had stopped before entering the auditorium and reached out to grasp her arm.

"And you have no idea how self-centered we actors are! I doubt that any of the cast did more than read a brief story about your business with Maxwell Stone. We were all too busy with *Variety*, wondering who's producing what and so forth. Even if someone did see you on TV or saw your picture, you have a new name and a new appearance now. Why, *I* hardly knew you when you got off the plane last Monday!"

Before he'd left her office in New Orleans they had agreed on the name Danielle Morgan. At first Jonathan wanted her to use a totally different name, but Dani had argued, "People will be calling me by my first name. If we use Helen or something, I might not even realize they're talking to me." They had also agreed that she should change her appearance as much as possible, and Dani had spent considerable time on that.

She had had Merle Baxter, her hair stylist, cut her long, auburn hair very short. A perm created a pattern of curls that framed her face, making it look much less square. The auburn color was transformed into black, which set off her greenish eyes. When Merle handed her a mirror, saying, "A new Dani!" she felt eerie, as if she were looking at a stranger!

This change alone might have sufficed, but she also worked on makeup and bought two new outfits that made her look more slender. When she walked into the office, even Ben had been impressed, though he said sardonically, "Well, I've always said you wanted to be somebody else, boss. Looks like you've done it."

When she had arrived in New York and walked right by Jonathan Ainsley without his recognizing her, she felt a surge of triumph. She reached out to touch his sleeve, and a look of shock ran across his face as he incredulously asked, "Dani? Is it you?" Laughing excitedly, he exclaimed, "Like I said, you were born to be an actress!"

Now, standing in the lobby and looking at her, he insisted, "They'll never recognize you, Dani. You've done a miracle with your looks; now just be a new person *inside*. Think like Danielle Morgan, a young woman determined to make it to the pinnacle of the world of theater, no matter who she has to trample to do it!"

"I can't imagine it's that cutthroat, Jonathan."

He lifted his head, his sensitive mouth tightening. "You'll find out, Dani," he cautioned. "I may as well warn you that our cast is not a happy little family. Most of us are willing to do anything to reach the top. One of the people you'll meet inside just might be willing to commit murder to do so."

"Do you think one of the cast is trying to kill you?"

"It's possible. My world is small, Danielle, and rather vicious. I've had to step on a few toes to get where I am. And don't ask me why I chose people who dislike me to be in my play." He laughed shortly and as he opened the door commented grimly, "If I only worked with people who liked me, I'd have to write a play with one character! Now *there's* an idea!"

He would have said more, but a voice cut in, "Jonathan, we need you in the office before you go inside." Dani turned to see a young man in his late twenties coming toward them. He had a strong face, more interesting than handsome, and wore casual but expensive clothes.

Impatience showed in Ainsley's face. "What is it, Tom?"

"Amber—again."

Ainsley lifted one eyebrow, then sighed. "Oh, well, let's get it over with. Oh, Danielle, this is Thomas Calvin, my business manager. Tom, Danielle Morgan."

Dani nodded, and Calvin smiled. "Glad to meet you. I assume you're our new costume person and prompter. Maybe you'd better come along. That's one of the things Amber's screaming about."

"Yes, come with us, Danielle." Jonathan led the way across the open space and down a short hall, then passed through a door on the left. It was, Dani saw, a spacious office with heavy green drapes and dominated by a large desk. Several black leather chairs flanked the walls, and above the desk was a picture of a horse anxious to jump over the fence to freedom.

Two people were already in the room, standing stiffly and staring at Jonathan Ainsley. One was a small, thin man with dark intense features and a small moustache. This, Dani knew from Ainsley's earlier description, was Simon Nero, the director of the play. He was glaring at Amber LeRoi, whom Dani recognized at once. She had seen her in several pictures and admired her flamboyant beauty, if not her acting ability. LeRoi had dark hair, brown eyes, and the full lips that came as standard equipment on *femmes fatales*. She was at least thirty but still exuded the sex appeal that had brought her from the world of pinups to movies. Dani remembered seeing her on a talk show once. It had been the usual mindless conversation, and Amber LeRoi had run true to form with her passionate outcries of rage against her profession, which had "used" her. She pointed out that she was more than just a pretty face with a magnificent figure and stated emphatically that she would appear in no more cheap and shoddy roles. Only the best of the legitimate stage for her!

"Well, Amber, what is it this time?" Jonathan asked. Dani cast a quick look at Ainsley. "And can you make it brief? We have a great deal to do tonight."

Amber LeRoi lifted her head imperiously. "Jonathan, I'm not at all certain that I can continue with this play. Things have become impossible!" She spoke agitatedly for about five minutes, listing the things that would have to be changed before she would agree to go on. Most of them were minor—such as the size of her name on the marquee and promised improvements in her dressing room that had not been made.

Ainsley abruptly interjected, "Amber, we can talk about all this later!"

"We'll talk about it *now*!" Amber's smooth features changed suddenly, and Dani knew at once that under the actress's beautiful exterior lurked a dangerous person consumed with self. A chilling cruelty invaded her eyes, and her mouth became a steel trap.

"All right, all right, Amber." Jonathan turned to Dani, announcing, "This is Danielle Morgan, but you can get acquainted later. Tom, take Danielle with you. Introduce her to the cast—and stall them until we get there. Simon, you'd better stay."

"All right, Jonathan." Neither Simon nor Amber gave so much as a nod to Dani.

As he led her down the hall, Tom apologized. "Sorry you got caught in the crossfire so soon." He shook his head. "I guess you know about them—Amber and Jonathan?"

"Not really."

"Oh? I thought everyone did. Well, to put the thing bluntly, they were lovers at one time. That sounds like gossip, but it's common knowledge. Neither of them kept it a secret at the time. Now I guess both would like to forget it."

He paused at the door. "It wasn't a very original sort of romance, Miss Morgan. She'd made a hit as Sadie Thompson in *Rain*. She's not really much of an actress, of course, but she's as sultry as a woman can get. She made several movies—awful things! Jungle movies in which she ran around in skimpy sarongs and grunted her lines! But she was hot at the box office. And that's how she got Jonathan."

"How was that?"

"Well, he was unknown until they had a torrid love affair. She put up the money for his first success, a remake of *Jane Eyre*. I guess you saw it."

"Yes. He was the best Mr. Rochester I've ever seen."

Calvin laughed. "And Amber was the worst Jane, wasn't she?" He smiled, then sobered. "Anyway, he climbed to the top and got rid of Amber as soon as he could. I'm sure you could see just now how much she hates him."

"It was pretty obvious, Mr. Calvin."

"Tom, please. Nothing but first names in the theater, Danielle. I suppose you're wondering why he chose her to be his leading lady. That set us all back. But it's quite simple really. Amber's new boyfriend is Charlie Depalma, and guess who's bankrolling *Out of the Night?* Right! But Depalma would only foot the bills if Amber costarred with Jonathan."

"Not a very comfortable situation for Jonathan."

Tom shrugged. "She never fails to make things hard on him—and on the rest of us." He suddenly frowned. "I don't know why I'm telling you all this. You'll think I'm nothing but a gossipy old lady!" He laughed. "I'll let you discover our hidden flaws all by yourself, Danielle. Come along and meet the cast."

They passed through the door, and Dani's first thought was, *It's so small!* The Pearl was a famous theater, going back to the golden years of Broadway. Like much of the theater district, its surroundings had deteriorated, and it had faced hard times. But so many historic dramas had been birthed there and so many acting giants had graced the Pearl's stage that popular opinion had kept it from perishing. A decorating project was near completion, and the smell of paint permeated the room. Painters were touching up the white molding that ran along the buff-colored walls, and the gleam of scarlet plush on the seats matched the half-drawn curtain. A balcony stretched almost halfway down the length of the high-ceilinged auditorium, and Dani glanced up at the arching ribs to see a man peering over the lip, his hand on a cluster of spotlights.

As Calvin walked up the steps leading from the orchestra to the stage, he said, "Everybody, I want you to meet the newest addition to our cast. This is Danielle Morgan. While we're waiting for Jonathan and Amber, let me introduce you, Danielle."

Dani felt self-conscious as every head swung toward her. She glanced at the stage, noting that it was a traditional setting—a richly designed drawing room with a large sofa and several comfortable chairs. The antiques were real, but she had no time to notice any further details. Calvin led her to a young woman and two men sitting around a coffee table. The two men got up quickly as Calvin teased with a sly grin, "I don't know what order to introduce you in. Whoever doesn't get first billing will be mad at me."

One of the men at the table advised him, "Why not take us according to talent, Tom? That way I'll be first." He was a small young man, no more than five foot seven, but his pale-blue knit shirt revealed an impressive set of muscles. He held his hand out. "I'm Mickey Trask, Danielle. Glad to have you with us."

Danielle took his hand, observing that the outside ridge was hard as marble. She knew from Ben Savage what that meant—he was an expert in judo or some other martial art. "It's good to be here," she murmured, noting that though Trask had a baby face, an inner toughness revealed itself in a pair of startling blue eyes that missed nothing.

The other man gave Trask an amused glance, then turned and put his hand out. "I'm Lyle Jamison, Danielle." He was an extremely handsome man of thirty, a *Gentleman's Quarterly* type with capped teeth, brown eyes, and crisp brown hair. He pressed her hand firmly as he shook his head. "I'm not the best actor here, but I'm the tallest."

Dani liked him at once and gave him a smile. "I saw you in the *Jared Sullivan* series quite often. You were very good in that."

Jamison flushed and answered quietly, "Thank you. Not too many remember that one. I hate TV, but in these dark days of the theater it's any port in a storm."

"You have good taste, Danielle. I liked Lyle in that role too." The young woman looked up at Dani and continued, "I'm Lily Aumont. I guess if Lyle's claim to fame is being the tallest here, mine is being the youngest. Doesn't take any talent at all for that, does it?" She was, Dani decided, no more than eighteen, if that, with golden hair, green eyes, and an air of innocence that may have been an act. Dani nodded, murmured that she was pleased to meet them, then turned to the next group.

As usual with her analytical mind, she classified the members of the cast into groups—group 1: two men and one woman; group 2: two men and one woman; group 3: one man and one woman, eight in all. She fixed the names, faces, and personal impressions in her mind as she met the members of group 2, which she deduced at once were of lesser standing than the members of group 1. They huddled together by a fireplace, looking at her carefully.

"This is Carmen Rio, Danielle. She's our makeup lady and plays the part of Rosa Varga in the play." Carmen reminded Danielle of a youthful Dolores del Rio, the fabulously beautiful Mexican star of the thirties. She had the same cool, smooth beauty. Her dark eyes were filled with resentment. "Some role!" she muttered. "A chambermaid!"

"Better than mine," the trim black man standing beside her said, though cheerful humor lit up his thin face. He nodded to Danielle and said in a thick dialect right out of a minstrel show, "I'se de darkie, Miss Danielle, who am de body servant of Massa King. Yessum!" He shrugged and enunciated naturally and perfectly, "Well, I don't do that fake black English as well as Mickey over there. I'm glad to meet you."

Tom Calvin glanced at the black man and said quickly, "I guess if it's raw talent you're looking for, Trey Miller has as much as anybody. He designed this set, which will likely win Best Set Design when the Tonys are handed out next year." He added, "And this is Ringo Jordan. He's the heavy in the play. Looks the part too."

Jordan *did* look like a traditional heavy from an old gangster film. He gave Calvin a brief look out of a pair of the coldest gray eyes Danielle had ever seen, then turned to study her. He was a hulking man of at least six feet two and must have weighed 235 pounds. He had a broad, scarred face, and his nose was flattened and one ear thickened.

Must have been a prizefighter, Danielle assumed.

Jordan made no offer to shake hands but noticed that she was looking at his face. "Linebacker for the Giants," he commented briefly. Then he turned his back, picked up a glass from the mantel, and ignored everyone.

Tom Calvin looked at the huge man's back, an irritated expression in his eyes. "Always a pleasure to have Ringo turn on the charm," he snapped. Forcing a grin, he reminded her, "Just one big happy family, Danielle, but come along and meet the *real* actors in the play."

Dani turned and took two steps, then faltered when she spotted a man and woman sitting together on a love seat, stage left. She spoke their names involuntarily in a whisper. "Why, that's Sir Adrian and Lady Lockridge!"

Both the man and the woman smiled at her response. "I'm afraid we are," Sir Adrian said, rising to his feet. He took her hand and kissed it in an eloquent gesture, then gave his wife a sly glance. "Now, Victoria, my dear, you're going to have to forgive me for being drawn to such youth and beauty."

"I'd send for the mortician if you didn't flirt with this lovely creature, Adrian." Lady Lockridge didn't rise but merely offered her hand to Danielle in the manner of Queen Victoria. "Charmed to have you here, my dear."

Danielle couldn't help staring at the pair, for they were living history. A living history of the theater anyway. Sir Adrian Lockridge was at least sixty but no less handsome, with his regal bearing, aristocratic features, and silver hair, than he had been as a young, dark-haired idol of the stage. He had never achieved the stature of Laurence Olivier or Ralph Richardson, but his stage version of *Macbeth,* when he was only twenty-three, had electrified audiences. Danielle had a video of the film version, which some critics insisted was the finest Shakespearean production ever presented, on or off the stage.

"I never imagined I would have the opportunity to meet you," Danielle whispered. "You've given me so much viewing pleasure!"

Lady Lockridge's cold blue eyes warmed as she looked at the young woman. She had never been a great actress, playing only small roles until she married Adrian. Since then her mission had been, Danielle had read, to help him become the premier actor on Planet Earth. Now she put her hand on her husband's arm, saying with a slight smile, "It's very good to hear such things, Miss Morgan." Her eyes grew cold, and she looked across the room at the other members of the cast. "Some are not so appreciative of *real* dramatic talent!"

A chill fell across the room, and Danielle didn't miss the angry glances thrown by several members of the cast toward the Lockridges. But just at that moment Ainsley's voice broke the silence. "All right, let's get this show on the road!" He came dashing up the steps and took a position at center stage, followed by Amber LeRoi and Simon Nero.

"Sorry to be late," he apologized. He looked around at their faces and waited until the shifting of feet and the muttering fell silent. Dani's gaze moved swiftly from face to face. Jonathan Ainsley was a man who excited strong feelings; others would either admire him or despise him. In Group 1, she noted that Lyle Jamison could not hide his dislike for the man. Lily Aumont, on the other hand, kept her youthful face trained on Ainsley with obvious adoration. It was difficult to read Mickey Trask's baby face.

In Group 2, Carmen Rio stared at Ainsley with an enigmatic expression. The dark-haired beauty seemed to worship the man with her eyes, but anger showed itself in the set of her full red lips. *A love-hate look if I ever saw one,* Dani told herself. When Carmen's gaze moved to Lily Aumont, intense animosity lit her face.

She hates Lily. I wonder why? Dani puzzled.

Trey Miller's rigid face didn't quite seem natural. *He's probably gotten to be an expert at hiding his feelings from others,* Dani decided. *But I think he's frightened.*

Ringo Jordan had turned to face Ainsley. He was a menacing figure with his head held low, his pale-gray eyes steady and fixed. *I'd hate to have been a running back looking across the line at him!* Dani reflected. *He looks like a killer. Then again, killers often look like poets or plumbers. And sometimes the most awful-looking types are gentle as lambs.*

Danielle looked across the stage at Sir Adrian. The frozen expression on his face spoke more eloquently than words of rage. *No love lost between Sir Adrian and Jonathan, and his wife looks as if she'd like to kill him,* Dani thought. Lady Lockridge kept staring at Ainsley with narrowed eyes. Her lips were compressed, and her hands were clenched tightly together.

Well, I guess I'm no Sherlock Holmes! Dani thought wryly. *He'd have taken one look at this crowd and known everything about them and which one of them was out to get Ainsley. I never believed in that old bore anyway!*

"This is the second of March. In three days we must have a dress rehearsal. We open March 14. And we're as far from having a performance on our hands as I've ever seen from a cast in my entire career." Jonathan's deep-set eyes flashed, and his voice, though it never grew loud, conveyed his angry impatience. Going around the room, he pointed out the flaws of almost every member of the cast. He had a satirical gift and used it cruelly, cutting and slashing as if with a rapier. Soon every actor and actress on the stage was white-faced and tight-lipped, though he didn't mention Amber LeRoi, the Lockridges escaped with a slight rebuke, and Lily Aumont got only a nod. Lyle Jamison stood facing Ainsley as if before a firing squad. He came in for the most vicious attacks, though Ringo Jordan, Mickey Trask, and Trey Miller got their share of public humiliation.

No wonder someone is trying to kill him! Dani thought. She'd heard that the man was an absolute slave driver when he worked on a play, but this went beyond being a type A personality.

When Ainsley finally stopped, the silence was thick, no one saying a word in defense of his or her work. Suddenly Jonathan said, "Forgive me—I've been too harsh." His face softened, and he dropped his head. "If anyone's work has been poor, it's been mine." The change in his words and tone seemed inexplicable.

As he continued to speak, Dani found herself feeling sympathetic for Jonathan. Then she realized what was actually happening. *The man's acting, and he's got me believing him!* Irritated with herself for being so easily swayed, she glanced around and saw that several others were accepting Ainsley's repentant mood. *They must be terribly gullible to fall for this!* she decided.

Ainsley, seemingly overwhelmed by his tirade, finally said,

"My only excuse for such abominable behavior is that I'm worried sick about this play. It means everything to me—and I think it does to all of you too."

He paused suddenly and looked toward Dani. "I suppose, Danielle, you're wondering why some of these people are in this play. We aren't exactly one big happy family, are we now? Well, I'll tell you—" He let the silence run on, drawing every eye, then stated flatly, "We're all here for the same reason—we need success, and this play just has to bring it! I chose each of you because you're—how do the football players say it, Ringo? Oh, yes, we're all *hungry* for victory, fame, whatever! For many of us, this may be our last chance, and I hate anyone who spoils it for the rest. I hate myself when I do things like I've just done! But to tell you the truth, I may do even worse if we don't get some fire into this play!"

Simon Nero interrupted. "Jonathan, you're being unreasonable. Sure, our performances have been a little rough; they always are at this stage. But when the curtain goes up, I'm convinced we'll see that 'fire' you keep talking about."

Ainsley began to speak, this time quietly. An intense look crossed his face as he began, "You all know your lines, and you are all professionals, so you read them expertly. But in *this* play that's not enough. Let me try to explain the heart of it. You know the plot, of course, but you've got to go *deeper* than that!"

Dani was on the outer circle, a spectator rather than a participant. She tried to disassociate herself from the glamor of the world of the theater and from the eloquence of Jonathan Ainsley. Carefully she listened as he leaned forward, his voice hushed, almost a whisper at times. "This play is about human existence. It's about man—not man as he is, but as he can be! As I look at history, I don't see that man has made particularly great advances. We can make a bomb that can destroy half the globe, but we can't control our appetites sufficiently to become what we should be. And what is it that man—all of us—should be? We should be powerful! Animals have instinct, but marvelous as that is, it is a dead-end street. Bees can build a hive, but they can't write a symphony! They have no power to *create*. Only man has that!"

He paused and looked down at his hands. His face was pale, and suddenly Dani knew that no matter how theatrical and overly dramatic he seemed, this part of Jonathan Ainsley was *real!* She leaned forward, forgetting to watch the faces of the cast, caught up in the intensity of the man.

"So . . . so this play is about man. It's a metaphor, as I've said. The plot is simple. A group of people have met in a mansion to settle a power struggle. A huge company is at stake, and those who are gathered long for the power that will be in the hands of whoever controls the firm. All types are there—religious people, artists, and intellectuals. But in the end they all give up whatever has been an ideal to them. They all try in one way or another to seize the power. That's why there's so much violence in the play because the world is exactly like that!"

Ainsley lifted his eyes and looked from face to face, a faint smile on his lips. "Perhaps you have noticed that this cast is not totally different from the characters in the play. Among us too is that struggle for power, for first place, at any cost. Don't be shocked at that. It's the way the world is and the way we must portray it in my play. We must *dramatize* this struggle for power, and we must *demonstrate* that man can be the victor in the bloody struggle!"

Ainsley seemed to have exhausted himself; his shoulders slumped, and his head drooped. "Simon, take over."

Nero moved forward, commanding briskly, "All right, let's take it from the beginning!"

The cast moved into action, and Danielle took her place as prompter. She had read the script several times, and as the play progressed, she found herself wondering about Jonathan Ainsley. He had attacked and humiliated the cast, but they were delivering fine performances. Whether it was because of his words or for some other reason, she couldn't tell.

It was a long play, over two and a half hours, and by the end of it Danielle was convinced they had given a great performance. She said as much to Tom Calvin while she waited for Jonathan to change and take her to the apartment she had sublet on the West Side. She knew the unit wasn't much to look at, but in a city as crowded as this one, it was a real find on such short notice.

Tom stood there, his eyes fixed on her. Then a strange smile touched his lips. "A great performance, Danielle? Which one?"

"Why, the play, Tom."

"The play? Well, that was better than usual. Jonathan knows how to get the most out of a cast. That's his strength. But I thought you might have meant some of the other performances."

"What are you talking about?"

"I've already been a gossip once tonight."

"No, tell me," Danielle insisted.

"Well, aside from the Amber-Jonathan conflict, maybe you've heard that Lyle Jamison was suspected of murdering a woman."

"Why, I find that hard to believe, Tom!"

"And the woman was Simon Nero's wife."

"No!"

"Just take a look at Simon's eyes sometime when he's looking at Lyle. Pure hatred. He loved his wife and is convinced that Lyle did her in. I expect he'll take a shot at Lyle sooner or later." He gave her a sudden mirthless smile. "Or take the case of the luscious Carmen Rio. She's been 'close' to Ainsley, but she's been replaced by another member of the cast. Can you guess who?"

Danielle thought about it. "Lily Aumont."

"Give the lady a cigar!" Calvin smiled. "The only problem Carmen has is deciding whom she hates the most—Jonathan or Lily."

Danielle was quiet for a while before asking, "Any more skeletons, Tom?"

"Well, there's Ringo Jordan, who's got some sort of hatred bottled up inside. I think he's likely to go off at any moment. Or take Mickey Trask. Mickey was a juvenile star but wants to be a director. Jonathan promised him this play but gave it to Simon. So now little Mickey hates Jonathan and Simon. I might also add that Mickey had a little romance going with Lily, but now she's Ainsley's girl. So Mickey is miffed over that. And of course there are the Lockridges. Poor Adrian is an alcoholic, and his wife spends all her time covering up for him. Add to that that they both despise Jonathan, who delights in lording it over the old man. I guess we're just one happy little group, Danielle."

Dani asked quietly, "What about you, Tom?"

"Me?" Calvin's face flushed; then he forced a grin. "My father was one of Jonathan's best friends. When Dad died, I fell apart. Drugs—the whole bit. Then I found an answer, but for some reason Jonathan despises me for it. He gave me this job just to poke fun at me."

"What answer did you find, Tom?"

He stared at her, then blurted out, "Well, I became a Christian. Now you can laugh at me along with Jonathan!"

Dani asked suddenly, "Isn't today Saturday?"

"Saturday?" Her question unsettled him, and he looked at her suspiciously, fearing ridicule. "Yes, it is."

Dani smiled and put her hand on his arm. "Then you can come by my apartment and take me to church with you tomorrow morning."

He stared at her. "You're making fun of me!"

"Not at all." She gave him her address. "Apartment 212," Dani added. "Don't forget!" Ainsley had appeared, and before he got to them, Dani whispered, "I hate to walk in late, so come early."

As she left with Ainsley he asked, "What was Tom moaning about?"

"Oh, we have a date."

"A date? I'd better warn you about these city boys, Danielle. You small-town girls can get in trouble with that type!"

"I don't guess we can get in too much trouble, Jonathan. He's taking me to church."

"Oh?" Ainsley said slowly, then shrugged. "Well, we'll see how long your religion lasts in the Big Apple, Danielle. By the way, what's your impression of the cast?"

"Oh, I don't know, Jonathan." She shrugged as they walked out into the cold night air. "Most of them want to kill you, of course, but aside from that, they're just one big happy family!"

Three

THE PHANTOM STRIKES!

I was never in a play that was ready for opening night, but this is getting ridiculous! We open in four days, and we still haven't had a dress rehearsal!"

Danielle heard Mickey Trask's words as she came onstage from the left wing. Mickey had cornered Lyle Jamison and Ringo Jordan against the right wall of the set. The Lockridges were, as usual, off by themselves, having moved as far away from the others as possible. They were wearing their costumes, and as Danielle passed by, Lady Lockridge said, "Oh, Danielle, my dress seems to pull somewhat under the left arm. Would you check it for me please?"

"Surely, Lady Lockridge." As Danielle moved to her side and began to check the dress, the older woman said, "You've done a wonderful job with our costumes, my dear, and in only a few days."

Danielle smiled. "With modern dress, there's not much to do. I'd be lost if this were a Shakespearean production.

Sir Adrian shook his head firmly. "Don't believe a word of that! You're most efficient, Danielle, the sort of person who makes things work." He smiled as she looked in his direction, adding, "I never saw anyone learn a script so rapidly. Most prompters lose their place so often that the actors have to prompt *them*! But you've got the whole script memorized—every line by every character! I never saw the likes of it."

Danielle flushed under his praise, explaining, "I—I just have a good memory, Sir Adrian." She added quickly, "We'll have to give you more room in this dress, Lady Lockridge. I'll take care of it after rehearsal!"

As she moved away, Victoria said, "If everyone were as thoughtful as that young woman, this would be a pleasant experience." Her eyes narrowed as she watched Simon Nero come down the aisle and mount the stage. "Dear, if that man raises his voice to you one more time, I'll poison him!"

"He's nervous about the play, sweet. It's just nerves."

"That gives him no right to shout at you. And Ainsley has done everything he can to upstage you. He does everything but eat the scenery to attract attention to himself!"

"I know. He's that kind of man. But we've always known what he was, Victoria. We must simply bear it, I suppose." He looked up and frowned. "Oh dear—Ainsley and Nero are in some sort of a dither."

Everyone had watched Nero come from the front of the auditorium and whisper something to Ainsley. The two of them carried on a hurried conference, with Nero waving his arms around angrily. Mickey Trask leaned over and said to Lily Aumont, "Bet I know what's eating Nero. Amber's not here. I'll bet you five bucks she's going to be late again."

Jonathan said something to Nero in a tone so vitriolic that the director's face grew pale. "All right, Jonathan!" Simon said loudly. "But we can't go on like this. She's blackmailing you! Can't you see that?"

Ainsley shook him off, then raised his voice. "We will be a little late starting tonight, everyone. Take a thirty-minute break." He broke his words off shortly, then left the stage and headed for the office, his face rigid and angry.

"What did I tell you?" Trask nodded with satisfaction. "Let's go across the street and get something to drink, Lily."

"I don't think so, Mickey," the young woman answered. "Can you bring me back a hamburger with onions?"

Trask gave her an angry look but just said, "You'd better skip the onions. Lyle may not like your breath in that sizzling love scene in Act Two."

"Get the onions," Lily ordered. Lyle Jamison was standing close by, and she gave him a tiny smile. "He won't mind."

Everybody went their own way, and Danielle was left alone on the stage except for Ringo Jordan, who sat in a chair tilted against the wall, reading a newspaper. As she walked past him to go to the dressing room, he said, "Hey, Danielle, you see this in today's paper?" She paused and looked at the *New York Post,* and a small shock ran through her, though she didn't let it show.

"No, I didn't see it, Ringo." It was a fairly long article in the Entertainment section, with the headline IS THE PHANTOM OF THE OPERA BACK IN BUSINESS? Dani felt angry as she read the article. The story was filled with quotes from Jonathan and laced with graphic descriptions of the two attempts on his life (without mentioning the letters). The reporter had added his own touches, slanting the article so that it appeared that a mysterious killer was at large, stalking the famous actor Jonathan Ainsley.

"May I borrow this, Ringo?" she asked.

"Sure." Jordan nodded. "Doesn't come as too much of a shock, does it? That someone's doing a number on Ainsley, I mean. You're a pretty smart cookie, Danielle. I saw that right off. You think like a quarterback, always watching, seein' what's going on. Now me, I was a linebacker. Didn't have to think much—just had to see who had the ball and deck him."

"It wasn't that easy, Ringo," Dani said with a slight smile.

"Sure, it was. I was a degenerate, just like all the rest. Good training for being an assassin, bein' a linebacker. When you think about it, we all talked like we were soldiers—putting on a blitz and stuff like that. And the name of the game is to kill the guy in front of you." Ringo's eyes narrowed, and he shrugged his massive shoulders. "Guess the guy that's tryin' to hang one on Ainsley is pretty tough. Calls his shots, then lets the hammer down. Course, it could all be something Ainsley just dreamed up."

"I don't think so," Danielle answered.

He studied her, his steady gray eyes expressionless, then nodded. "If you say so, lady. I guess nobody in this play would have a breakdown if Ainsley bought it. You ain't missed that, I guess."

"Nobody likes to see anyone get killed, Ringo."

"You can't be that innocent, kid," Ringo said quickly. "If you are, I hate to think about what will happen to you when you wake up and see the real world. Take the paper—nothing but lies in it."

Danielle left and went to the dressing room, then made her way to the office. Ringo's pessimism made her nervous, and she wanted to talk to Ainsley. She found him in his office, staring out the window at the rain that looked like silver in the reflection of the streetlights. He took one look at her and barked, "What's wrong, Danielle?"

She shoved the paper at him, her voice short as she exclaimed, "This is what's wrong!"

He looked at it briefly, then shrugged. "I'll sue that fool newspaper!"

"You *gave* them this story, didn't you, Jonathan?"

He was not a nervous man, but the angry spark in Danielle's greenish eyes and her aggressive stance as she stood there glaring at him set him back. "Now, Dani, don't get the wrong idea! This reporter is a friend of mine. We were having a few drinks—you know how it is."

"No, I don't know how it is, Jonathan!" she said angrily. "What I know is that we had a very small chance of discovering who's been trying to kill you. Now with everything out in the open, we have none. I'm leaving. Good-bye!"

Ainsley leaped forward and grabbed her as she turned and headed for the door. His face was pale, and uncertainty threaded his voice as he pleaded, "Danielle, you can't leave, not now! Look, I swear I didn't know this was going to be in the papers. The fellow swore he wouldn't use it—the blasted liar!" Anger swept over him, but then he shook his head, and his voice softened. "This is a troublesome development, but I still have no one to help me but you. The police aren't going to help—not without more proof than I have . . ."

Dani's anger slowly drained away, and she felt disgusted with herself. She thought she'd learned to control the temper that had plagued her in adolescence, but here she was acting like a spoiled child. She thought, *You acted like a moron! Losing your temper as if someone had stolen your Popsicle!* Taking a deep breath, she nodded. "All right, Jonathan, all right. I'm sorry I flew off the handle. It's just that—well, I've been thinking about this case night and day and have come up with nothing—zero."

"Don't blame yourself. There's nothing to go on except the notes."

"Not much help there." She noticed that he was still holding her as she looked at him. "You can let go of me now, Jonathan. I won't run away."

He didn't release his grip but instead moved closer. "I don't want to let you go, Danielle."

She smiled briefly. "You never want to let any woman go, do you, Jonathan?" He pulled her forward, but she turned her head away and moved back, eyeing him carefully. "I wondered when you'd make this move."

"You knew I'd try to kiss you, of course?"

"Doesn't take much of a detective to figure that out." She paused, then added, "I feel sorry for you, Jonathan! You don't know any other way to approach a woman. It's sad, really."

Stung, he dropped his hands at once. His vanity had been exposed, and even his smooth actor's façade couldn't hide his resentment. "You'll come around, Danielle," he stated finally, then managed a smile. "You've just never known a man like me."

"No, you've never known a woman like me, Jonathan," she stated instantly. "I'd better get back."

"I'll go with you," he offered. "Perhaps Queen Amber LeRoi will condescend to grace our lowly cast with her presence," he added angrily.

As they walked down the hall toward the lobby, Dani asked, "She hates you very much, doesn't she? Is it possible she sent those letters?"

"Letters, yes," Jonathan answered bitterly, then shrugged. "But the rest of it, no. She hates guns."

"But she could have *hired* someone."

"She could, Danielle," he agreed quietly. "But it's not her way for one very good reason." A bitter smile crossed his face as he opened the door for her. "She's enjoying killing me a little at a time much more than the one brief instant of happiness that would come with shooting me. She knows I hate her, that I think she's the most abominable excuse for an actress ever to step on a stage. I'd love to see her dead so we could get a decent actress to grace this play of mine, and Amber knows that. When we were in love, she learned all my weaknesses. And I learned all of hers."

They were almost at the pit now, and he lowered his voice. "So cross Amber off your list of suspects. She'd be miserable if anything happened to end my suffering, Danielle. She enjoys tormenting me in the same way boys love to pull wings off flies! I wish she'd have a coronary!"

He moved up the steps and walked over to Nero, waiting onstage. "Is she here yet, Simon?"

Nero shook his head, his face gray with strain. "She called and said that she has a headache, that she can't rehearse tonight."

That was too much for Jonathan Ainsley, and he lost control. He cursed and ranted and walked back and forth on the stage, consigning Amber LeRoi to the lowest pits of the Inferno. Danielle was taken aback by the depth of hatred in the heart of the man. He ended by saying, "I wish the little tramp was dead! I'd put a bullet in her brain tonight if I could do it without going to jail!"

The rest of the cast stood silently, and Dani knew they had witnessed that sort of behavior before. A sort of satisfaction gleamed in Lady Lockridge's eyes, but the others seemed fearful. Lily spoke for them all when she came close to Ainsley and said, "Jonathan, how can we practice without her?"

"We can't, of course," Jonathan answered gloomily. "We might as well all go get drunk."

"No need of that, Ainsley." Sir Adrian had a strange smile on his face. When he had everyone's attention, he explained, "We have a fine stand-in for Amber."

"Stand-in?" Jonathan stared at Lockridge as if he'd lost his mind. "What are you babbling about?"

"Danielle can walk us through the play." Lockridge nodded. "She knows Amber's role word perfect, not to mention all the rest of them."

"Oh, I—I couldn't!" Danielle protested instantly, shaking her head.

But Ainsley immediately picked up on the idea. He stared at her, then nodded. "Of course! You *do* know every line of the play. We've all been amazed at your ability to learn so quickly." He suddenly clapped his hands together and shouted, "Well, Nero, you're the director of this play, and we're all here, so start directing!"

Dani found herself caught up in Ainsley's excitement, and the rest of the cast joined in. "You can do it, Danielle!" Lyle Jamison whispered. "Much better than that old witch Amber!" They all urged her to go on, even Ringo Jordan, who grinned with unexpected humor. "Go for it, kid," he said, nudging her with his elbow. "Knock 'em dead!"

She found herself pushed into place on the stage and felt Ainsley's hand on her arm, his face close to hers. "You can do this, Danielle!" he whispered. "You're the sort of woman who can do anything she makes up her mind to do. Now let's see you perform!"

When it was time for Dani's first entrance, she froze, unable to move to save her life! Just as she was about to turn and run, Mickey Trask came up behind her. He whispered, "Break a leg, Danielle!" He shoved her forcefully out of the wings and onto the stage.

She almost fell but came face to face with Ainsley, who caught her, pulled her upright, and ad-libbed with perfect timing, "Well, Marian, we'll have to have that carpet fixed so you won't trip over it again, won't we?"

Danielle looked into his eyes, sparkling with humor, and lost all her gawkish insecurity. She spoke her first line strongly and experienced the near miracle that had always taken place when she'd acted in college. Everything except her role seemed to fade away. In college time after time she had made her entrance on the stage, frightened and uncertain; but as she forced the audience and everything else from her mind, concentrating on her character, she had moved through the drama as if it were the real world. At the end, with a feeling of abrupt shock, the world of pretense closed, and she jolted back into reality.

She moved through the complicated scenes of *Out of the Night* concentrating on her lines when she was onstage and on the lines of others when she was off. She was even able to prompt Sir Adrian once when she was in a scene with him, but she did it so smoothly that an audience would never have noticed it. Sir Adrian, delighted with her wit, gave her a sly wink.

When the curtain came down, Dani felt totally exhausted, but ecstatic members of the cast surrounded her, singing her praises. "You were terrific, Danielle!" Trey Miller grinned and then was shouldered aside as Lyle and Mickey grabbed her with hugs that lifted her from the floor. "Let the witch look to her laurels!" Lyle whispered in sheer delight. Carmen Rio had nothing to say, nor did Lily Aumont, but Ringo gave her what he thought was a gentle squeeze on the arm and murmured, "Hey, I give you odds—the LeRoi dame won't miss no more practices, Danielle! She'll turn green when she hears how well we got along without her."

Finally Jonathan came and took both her hands in his. He studied her with a level gaze, then shook his head. "You don't really know what you did tonight, Danielle."

Dani shook her head quickly. "I just read the lines, Jonathan."

A quick mutter of disagreement ran around the cast, and Ainsley shook his head. "No, no, that's not what you did. You *became* Marian Powers for almost three hours." Wonder filled his eyes, and he said, "Let's get out of here. I know you must be tired."

He turned, and they moved to leave the stage when Carmen said, "Jonathan, this is for you."

Ainsley turned and took the envelope from her. "What's this?" he asked.

Carmen shrugged. "I thought it was yours. It was on the table over there by the couch, and it has your name on it."

Danielle watched as Jonathan ripped open the sealed envelope, and she saw his face grow suddenly stiff with fear and shock. He stood there peering at it, then handed it to her without a word. A tremor shot through his lower lip, and he blinked his eyes more rapidly than usual. Looking down at the paper, she saw that it was another threat, using the same form as the others.

> YOU HAVE CHOSEN TO IGNORE MY WARNINGS. NOW IT IS PUT OUT THE LIGHT, AND THEN PUT OUT THE LIGHT. YOU OWE GOD A DEATH. YOU HAVE TWENTY-FOUR HOURS TO LIVE.

Danielle looked up quickly and said, "Jonathan, it's time to get more help."

"Is it another threat?" Simon Nero asked quickly. "If so, Danielle is right. We have to call the police."

"No!" Jonathan shook his head violently. "We'll handle this ourselves. I'll take every precaution, and all of you, keep alert. If we keep a tight ship, this maniac won't be able to do a thing."

"One thing, Jonathan," Danielle said slowly. "How did the letter get on that table? It wasn't there when we started the rehearsal."

"It must have been!" he contradicted her quickly.

"No, I cleaned everything off," Trey Miller admitted.

"It wasn't there after the end of the first act," Sir Adrian spoke up. "I set my glass down there, just as I always do. There was nothing on that table."

The room was silent. Then Jonathan commented, "So it looks like we have a family problem, doesn't it? Well, to paraphrase *Hamlet*, there's something rotten in the state of Denmark, or more accurately, there's something rotten in the cast of my little play!"

Dani said, "I was too nervous to see anything. But that table is right by the wing. Anyone could have slipped it there during the set changes, couldn't they?"

"It's possible, Danielle," Trey Miller agreed slowly. "There's so much going on, and it's pretty dark. If someone were backstage, it wouldn't have been much of a trick to drop an envelope on a table."

"He'd have been noticed," Jonathan stated flatly. "It had to be someone nobody would notice—and that's the cast and the crew."

"Wait until the papers get ahold of this one!" Ringo grunted.

"It'll make page 1!"

"They're not going to get it," Jonathan insisted angrily. "We've got to keep our mouths shut!"

But despite his urgent words, the next day a newspaper story spread the word that "The Phantom of the Theater" had called his shot and would strike again within twenty-four hours.

At rehearsal that day, Jonathan introduced a tall, thin man with a hatchet chin and a pair of indolent black eyes. "This is Charlie Allgood," he announced angrily. "He's my good friend—and he's also putting the garbage in the papers—this 'Phantom of the Theater' business. I brought him along to see that it's all nonsense. Some actor I turned down for a part is getting his jollies—that's all! It's a nuisance, but we can weather it."

"How did you get your information about what happened last night, Mr. Allgood?" Sir Adrian demanded.

"I got a call last night at midnight. The guy wouldn't give his name, but he told me the whole thing."

"What did he sound like?" Jamison asked.

"Sounded British," Allgood answered.

"Anybody can do an English accent," Jonathan admitted disgustedly. "Well, I'm inviting Charlie to all the rehearsals. Nothing is going to happen, but if it does, I don't want any rumors flying around. Charlie, you let me down by printing what I told you in confidence, but you can make it up by playing fair with us."

"Sure, Jonathan. I'll try not to get in the way, and you'll get nothing but the truth in our paper."

"All right, that's it." Ainsley nodded. He looked around and smiled slightly. "Well, Amber, I see you feel well enough to be on your feet." He paused, then added, "If you don't feel up to it, I'm sure we can muddle along again. I suppose you heard how well Danielle did last night."

Amber LeRoi gave him a killing glance and stared at Danielle. "I can't stand amateurs!" she declared vehemently. "Let's get to work."

Danielle found Amber's obvious animosity juvenile and rather unpleasant. But she put it out of her mind and took her place as the curtain went up.

It was a good performance, so good that she lost track of the speeches. She moved around watching Trey and his helpers, a small Mexican named Julio and a strongly built black man named Earl, as they moved the stages around. She had been fascinated from the first by Miller's genius and with the intricate design of the staging. The play called for a number of settings—an ornate sitting room, a bedroom, a library, an outside patio among them.

Trey Miller had designed a stage in two sections, one behind the other. He had mounted them on silent rubber wheels so they could move either forward or sideways. He had made each stage in two sections, so they could separate exactly down the center. When the stage closest to the footlights needed to be replaced, it was pulled apart and each half moved into the wings. Once it was separated and out of the way, stage number two was drawn forward into place. The two halves of the first stage, being out of sight, could be rearranged or completely changed. When the next setting was required, the other stage was pulled to one side.

Moreover, the stages were so exquisitely and carefully designed that it took only a few seconds to replace stage one with stage two. Sometimes the lights were turned down for a few seconds, and when they came up, the audience would be amazed at how the setting had changed seemingly instantaneously.

Trey and Julio had to work frantically to make the set changes, and Danielle felt that the others were right when they said the set would almost certainly win many awards. "I won't be able to afford Trey after this," Jonathan said ruefully to Dani. "He'll be the most sought-after stage designer in America!"

The change from the ballroom to the bedroom in act three was particularly difficult. Though the tense scene between Jonathan and Lyle lasted only five minutes, it was a key part of the play. Danielle watched as the three men set up the bedroom stage, then, when the lights went down, rolled the ballroom set offstage and quickly slid the other into place. It took no more than thirty seconds, and when the lights came up, Jonathan was leaning back in a recliner, with Lyle standing directly in front of him.

It was, Dani thought, Lyle's best scene, and she watched carefully. He had asked her to do so, inviting her to make suggestions on his performance. She kept her eyes fixed on him and was pleased with what he did. Jonathan had only five lines in the entire scene. He lay back with his face turned up, just as the scene called him to do so, for it was the point in the play in which Lyle's character was to be totally ruined by King, the character played by Jonathan.

"It's my lazy scene," Jonathan had commented to Dani. "All I have to do is lie there looking up at the ceiling and let the fellow go to his own ruin. I do it rather well, having had considerable practice at such things."

Dani was waiting for Lyle's last cue from Jonathan when Jonathan suddenly leaped out of the chair and, to Dani's astonishment, tackled Lyle, knocking him across the room and falling on top of him!

At the same time a tremendous crash shook the stage, and the air seemed full of flying glass.

"Jonathan!" she cried as she ran onto the stage. One glance at the broken glass and twisted brass on the floor revealed that the huge chandelier used for the ballroom scene had somehow fallen. It had landed right in front of Jonathan's chair—precisely on the spot where Lyle Jamison had been standing! "Are you hurt?" Dani gasped, bending over the two men. Others were running toward them, and she saw that Ainsley had blood on his brow.

"I—I guess not," Jonathan admitted faintly. He rolled off Jamison, asking, "Are you all right, Lyle?"

Lyle pulled himself to his feet, and when he looked at the massive, twisted form of the chandelier, he went pale. "That thing would have—" He broke off and said, "I'd like to sit down, I think."

Ringo grabbed Lyle's arm and steered him to a chair. Jonathan took a deep breath. "I don't feel so good myself." Then he forced himself to straighten up and grew angry. "How in heaven's name could this happen?"

"Better ask the set manager," Amber suggested.

All eyes turned to Trey Miller, who had come out from the wings. He quickly insisted, "Why, I don't—"

"This is your responsibility, Miller," Jonathan snapped. "Explain it!"

Miller stood there with his lips suddenly dry. He shook his head. "The cable must have broken." Turning quickly, he checked the ropes to which overhead items were anchored. He looked down at the nylon rope that held the chandelier. Jonathan followed his gaze and picked up the rope. He stared at it, then exclaimed, "It's been cut!"

Trey cried, "How could that have happened?"

"See for yourself."

Jonathan held out the end of the rope, and they all pressed closer. Dani saw clearly that the rope was not frayed but rather sliced through half its width. She wanted to examine the scene more carefully, but she didn't want to do too much and possibly give away her undercover role. On the scuffed floor, the finish had worn off in several spots. A few old programs and an old glass pop bottle lay to her left. But nothing looked out of place. Fingerprints would be useless, for they had all passed by the same spot time after time.

"It's been cut—there's no doubt about that," Jonathan proclaimed. "But who did it?"

Suddenly Charlie Allgood was there, and he suggested laconically, "Jonathan, you know the answer to that."

"What are you talking about, Charlie?" Ainsley demanded.

Allgood pulled a Nikon from his overcoat pocket and began taking a careful shot of the wreckage. After he snapped the shutter, he looked around and added with a shrug, "It's plain as day. It's the Phantom of the Theater, right on schedule!"

"That's—that's absurd!" Jonathan protested angrily. His face was pale, and Dani saw that his hands were trembling.

"I don't know about any Phantom of the Theater," Dani commented soberly, "but that rope *was* cut, and a man was nearly killed. That's attempted murder. The police will have to be informed, Jonathan."

Ainsley bit his lip, then nodded slowly. "I suppose so. That's just what we need—a story like this spread all over the front page."

Amber laughed bitterly, her lips curling upward. "Come on, Jonathan, we all know that right now you're thinking this will be good for the box office. You'd strangle your own mother to sell a few tickets."

Jonathan stared at her, then turned away abruptly. "I'll call the police. We'd all better stay right here—and don't touch anything."

"Just like on TV," Trey Miller voiced bitterly. He glared at the other members of the cast. "I suppose this is a good time for a little racial discrimination. It'd be a good chance to pin this on me."

"It won't be like that, Trey," Danielle said, offended at the mere idea.

"Really? Wait and see!"

Four

TOO MANY SUSPECTS

Jack Sharkey chewed his cigar slowly, stared at Jonathan Ainsley, then nodded. "All right, lemme see if I got this straight. You and Jamison were alone on the stage, right, Ainsley? So that lets you two out."

The burly policeman had come bustling into the Pearl within twenty minutes of Ainsley's call. He was a big man, tall and with massive shoulders. He had a flushed red face, a flattened nose, and a network of tiny scars around a pair of muddy brown eyes. He looked, Danielle thought, like a parody of a third-rate prizefighter who'd taken too many punches. He shuffled his feet when he moved and spoke aggressively with his hoarse voice. He was, Dani thought, the worst type of police officer and at once jettisoned the idea of sharing her hidden knowledge with him. He would be exactly the type who would despise private investigators. He didn't appear to be highly intelligent, but she had to admit he did go at the thing in the only way possible.

"All right," Sharkey grunted, sending a cloud of foul-smelling smoke from his cheap cigar into the air. "I wanna know where everybody was when this thing fell. One at a time—and I want the straight dope, see? I catch any of you lying, and you'll be in the slammer!"

He talks like a detective in a grade-B movie, Dani thought.

Charlie Allgood spoke up first. "I was in the front row, Jack. That lets me out."

Sharkey stared at him and asked suspiciously, "You ain't no drama critic, Charlie. What are you doing here?"

Dani exchanged glances with Jonathan, sharing the same thought. Would Allgood tell the policeman about the threatening letters? But Allgood only answered, "Why, Ainsley's a friend of mine, Jack."

"Yeah? Didn't know you had any," Sharkey snapped. "Well, you was watchin' the whole thing, and you snoopers are supposed to have pretty good eyes. What happened?"

"The play went fine, Jack," Allgood said. "I was caught up in it, and in the scene where the light fell, I was watching closely." He blinked his eyes, thought carefully, then drawled, "Ainsley was in the chair, sort of laid back and lookin' up, and Lyle Jamison was right in front of him. Course, I wasn't expecting anything to happen, so it caught me off guard."

"You must have seen *something*, Charlie!"

"Well, there was one thing, Jack," Allgood remarked vaguely. "Just before the whole thing happened, I heard kind of a funny sound—sort of a tinkling. Right at the same time almost, I saw Jonathan jump up and tackle Jamison."

"That's right, officer." Ainsley nodded. "In that scene I was in the recliner, looking up at the ceiling. In the play I'm supposed to be ignoring Lyle. The tinkling sound Charlie heard was the sound of the glass pendants on the chandelier. I was staring right at the thing—you can't help it when you're in that chair, you know—and it was right overhead. Anyway, the chandelier was perfectly still, just like always, and then it swung this way and that, and that's what Charlie heard. The thing didn't move much, maybe only a foot or two."

"What happened then?" Sharkey demanded.

"Why, the whole thing suddenly gave way," Ainsley explained, and the memory seemed to make him nervous. He pulled a cream-colored silk handkerchief from his pocket and wiped his brow. "I saw it coming down and tried to get out of the way."

"You saved my life, Jonathan," Lyle added emotionally. "I'd be dead meat if you hadn't pushed me."

Ainsley stared at him, then shrugged. "Well, Lyle, it would make me happy to think I was that sort of hero. But I think you all know me a little too well for that." A smile curled the corners of his wide lips upward, and he shrugged. "I was just trying to get away from that blasted thing, and you were in the way."

Sharkey interjected, "Never mind the hero stuff. We can get along—" He stopped and twisted his huge body around quickly. A man had entered the theater and was mounting the steps leading to the stage. He was no more than average height, trim, and well built. He wore an expensive suit. The exposed label on the camel's hair overcoat he held over his arm, Dani saw as he moved closer, was Hart, Schaffner, and Marx. He had a lean, olive-tinted complexion and a pair of sharp black eyes that missed nothing. He was handsome enough to be a leading man, and she was taken off guard when Sharkey called out, "Hey, Jake, what you doin' here? Didn't they tell you I took this call?"

Dani didn't miss the note of irritation in the burly policeman's voice. *Jake dresses too well and seems too good-looking to be a policeman,* Dani decided, but then she saw that the appearance of this man caused Ainsley to react most peculiarly. A sudden worried expression crossed the actor's face. Dani had grown to know the man's moods well and wondered what it was about the dapper new arrival that disturbed him.

"I finished with the Ullman thing quicker than I expected." The man's voice was pleasant. He continued, "Hello, Jonathan."

"Glad you're here, Jake," Ainsley said. There was no sign of worry in his eyes now. On the contrary he seemed genuinely glad to see the man. Moving forward with alacrity, he shook the man's hand, then turned to the others. "This is Lieutenant Jacob Goldman. The Pride of Homicide they call you, don't they?"

"That they do." Goldman nodded, but the smile on his lips didn't get to his eyes. "Fill me in, Jack." He stood quietly, his eyes going from face to face as Sharkey with some reluctance went over the details. When Jack came to Dani, Goldman fastened his dark eyes on her. She felt as if she were being shaken down—not physically, but roughly nonetheless. She forced herself to meet his gaze. After a long time he nodded as if to confirm something and let his eyes move on.

When Sharkey had finished, Goldman turned suddenly to Allgood. "I've been reading your Phantom stuff, Charlie. You think this is more of the same?"

Allgood was a pretty tough fellow, but he flinched under the gaze of Jacob Goldman. "Why, Lieutenant, that stuff was just standard procedure. You don't think I believe the junk I write, do you?"

"But you came here tonight, Charlie. You must have believed some of it."

"Anything Jonathan Ainsley does is good for a story," Allgood answered defensively. "He told me someone took a couple of shots at him, and the stories went over pretty good. So I just dropped by to get some more grist for my mill. To tell the truth, I didn't really believe Jonathan's tales about somebody trying to kill him—until tonight! I saw Jamison nearly buy it. One thing is sure—somebody is trying to kill somebody!"

Goldman took a platinum cigarette case from his inner pocket and removed a thin, brown cigarette. Drawing out a gold lighter, he lit it, then said, "All right." Smoke curled around his lips, and he asked almost idly, "Anyone want to confess?" He smiled at the silence and shrugged his shoulders. "I always think how much time and effort it would save if murderers would do that, but they never do. Sharkey had the right idea. Which one of you could have cut the rope?"

"Not me, Lieutenant," Amber LeRoi proclaimed quickly. "I was in the dressing room. Tom was with me all the time."

"That's right," Tom Calvin chimed in. "She was trying to get me to convince Jonathan to make her name larger on the marquee. We heard the crash and rushed out to see what had happened."

Lily decided it was time to exonerate herself as well. "I was in my dressing room with Carmen—" She paused, and Goldman picked up on her doubtful expression. "Think of something, Lily?"

"Well, only that I had left the necklace I wear in the next scene in the prop room. I asked Carmen to get it for me."

Carmen Rio glared at the blonde girl, anger igniting her dark eyes, but she explained, "The prop room is just outside the door to your dressing room, Lily. The rope that held the chandelier is all the way across to the right, just outside the men's dressing room."

"What about the timing?" Goldman asked. "Lily, how long was Carmen gone?"

Lily gave a frightened glance at the angry Carmen and whispered, "I hate to say these things, Carmen! She *never* came back, Lieutenant. She left my dressing room and was gone for a while, and then I heard the crash and ran out to see what had happened."

"I couldn't find the necklace," Carmen objected tartly. "It wasn't where you said it was."

"Jack, take Lily with you and check that out," Goldman commanded. After the two left, he continued, "What about the rest of you? Trask—that your name? Where were you?"

Mickey Trask looked like a young boy—a guilty young boy—at the moment. He licked his lips and gave Jonathan a worried look. "I—I ducked out for a quick one, Lieutenant. There's a bar next door, and I didn't have to be onstage for the next four scenes—over half an hour."

"Can somebody vouch for that at the bar?" Goldman demanded.

"Well, not really. The place was packed, and Tony keeps a special bottle for me under the bar. He was busy, so I just reached under the counter and got my own drink."

"Somebody must have seen you."

"I—I really don't think anybody noticed me," Mickey said uneasily. "There was a big party there—some kind of club celebration. I didn't see anyone who knows me."

Goldman stared at him until Trask grew angry. "Well, it's the truth! I may drink a bit, but I'm no killer! And if I were, why would I want to kill Lyle? He's a friend of mine."

"But Jonathan isn't, is he, Mickey?" Amber LeRoi's voice wasn't loud, but everyone turned to look at her. "You've hated Jonathan ever since he didn't give you the job of directing this play. And that chandelier *could* have been aimed at him, couldn't it, dear?"

Mickey moved toward Amber, his eyes blazing with anger. "You harlot!" he cried. "If anyone would want to kill Ainsley, it'd be you! He dumped you, didn't he?"

Amber at once began cursing and screaming. Only the cool, sharp voice of Goldman quieted them both. He turned and said to Sharkey, who had just returned with Lily, "What about the necklace?"

"It was right where it was supposed to be," Sharkey answered, his eyes on Carmen.

"But it *wasn't!*" Carmen cried. "I looked everywhere for it! I—"

Goldman's dark eyes zeroed in on her, and she suddenly broke off. He said, "All right, you're a suspect. What about you, Ringo?"

Jordan stared at the dapper officer defiantly. "No matter what I say, you'll start talking about my record, won't you, Goldman?"

"You're bringing it up, not me." Goldman shrugged.

"What record?" Simon Nero demanded.

"You didn't know Ringo done time?" Sharkey grinned. He puffed on his cigar and took pleasure in stating, "Attempted murder, wasn't it, Ringo?"

"No, it was manslaughter," Goldman broke in. "But never mind that. Where were you when the chandelier fell, Ringo?"

"Stage left, waiting to go on."

"Anybody with you?"

"No."

Sharkey moved over and nudged Jordan with an elbow. "Hey, the inmates up at the pen will be glad to see you again, Ringo. I'll bet—"

He never finished his statement, for Jordan suddenly struck him across the chest with an iron forearm, the sort of blow that had flattened 230-pound linemen. It knocked the cigar from the policeman's hand, sending sparks flying, and Sharkey took two steps backwards, almost falling. He caught himself, and his face turned beet red. Falling into a crouch, he moved forward, his massive right fist cocked and ready. "Why, you dirty con! I'll tear your dumb head off!"

"Sharkey, cut that out!" Goldman was a head shorter than either Sharkey or Jordan, and his trim figure looked frail beside their solid bulk, but he stepped between the two men, his black eyes flashing. "Throw one punch, Jack, and you'll be back pounding a beat! And you'll be back in the pen for violation of parole, Ringo!" He turned away from them in disgust. "Two kids playing at being tough!"

"Officer, I think you might take us off your list of suspects. I'm Adrian Lockridge, and this is my wife, Victoria."

"Of course, Sir Adrian." Goldman nodded. "It's a pleasure to meet you, though not under such circumstances. Can you give me, just for the record, an account of your role in this business?"

Lockridge smiled. "I'm afraid we must exonerate each other, Lieutenant. Victoria and I were in our dressing room. I was trying to help with her dress but was not doing too well. It was a little tight under the arm."

"Did you hear the crash, Sir Adrian?"

"Oh, yes. It was quite loud actually. When we got to the stage, Jonathan and Lyle were already on their feet. But the devil of it is that if you don't believe us, you could decide we might have cut the rope. It was, I believe, one of those just to the left of our dressing room."

"And do you have a motive, Sir Adrian?"

"Of course!" Lockridge's voice was light, but a serious fire brightened his fine eyes. "As anyone here can tell you—and no doubt will—there is little love between Jonathan and myself. You see, he is convinced that he is the best actor in the world, and I am quite as convinced that he is mistaken."

"He thinks *he* is." Ainsley grinned. "But the real reason he hates me, Jake, is that I love acting better than I love a bottle, which he doesn't!"

Victoria Lockridge's cold eyes suddenly turned venomous. "You—you *creature!* Stand under another chandelier, and I will cut the rope with great joy!"

"Now, now, Victoria—" Sir Adrian interjected hurriedly, casting a worried look in Goldman's direction. "You don't mean that!"

"Yes, I do," she enunciated clearly. "He's a disgrace to our profession."

Goldman studied her, then said suddenly, "And you—Danielle Morgan, is it?—where were you when it happened?"

"Where I always am at that point in the play, Lieutenant Goldman," Dani explained at once. "Perched on my stool, stage left. No one was with me, and it would have been very simple for me to walk no more than twenty feet and cut the rope," she added.

Suddenly Goldman smiled at her. "I see. And your motive?"

"I can't think of one."

"Certainly not!" Lady Lockridge snapped. "She's the *one* person in the entire cast who could have no motive. But give you time enough, Jonathan, and you'll corrupt this poor child just as you have corrupted Amber and Carmen and just as you are trying to corrupt Lily."

Despite his perpetual poise, Ainsley seemed taken aback. He opened his mouth to answer in kind, but Goldman forestalled him. "All right, all right, you can have your backstage quarrels on your own time. What about you?" He gestured toward Trey Miller.

"I thought it would come to me, copper," Trey said, his back rigid with indignation. "Can't wait to pin it on a black man, can you?"

His attitude seemed to interest Goldman, who lit another cigarette, then stared at it. "I'm going to quit these things!" Then he gave Miller a straight look. "I can't stand people who think they're innocent just *because* of their race," he said skeptically. "If you're guilty, Miller, I'll do my best to nail you, and I don't care in the slightest who you are or where you came from. You got that straight?"

Dani was startled at the hardness that had suddenly surfaced in Goldman. He wasn't tough in appearance—quite the contrary; but despite that smooth exterior he had unleashed a steel will that made Trey Miller step back. "I'm Jewish," he added softly, "and my people have certainly been mistreated down through the centuries, but I can't stand those among my own nation who think everyone in the world is out to get them. So let's just keep this thing on the basis of evidence, not race."

"All right, Lieutenant." A humbled Trey nodded. "That suits me. But it's not just that I'm—I mean—" When he broke off, perspiration drenched his forehead. "Well, the props are my job, and that includes the ropes that hold up the equipment. I designed the whole thing, and it's my job to see that nothing goes wrong. So when it happened, the first thing that popped into my mind was that I was going to be blamed for it."

"Anybody can cut a rope," Goldman pointed out. "Two questions. Could you have cut the rope without being seen, and do you have any motive for cutting it?"

"I could have cut it, sure." Trey nodded. "It's dark back there, and the boys and me—well, we keep so busy that we could be anywhere."

"Who are 'the boys'?"

"Julio and Earl. They help set the scenes." He motioned to the two young men, who were watching from as far away as they could get. "But I'd sent them up to the balcony to take some lighting equipment to Pinkie, our sound-and-light man. He'll tell you that they were up there with him when the chandelier fell."

"That lets all three of them out," Goldman agreed quietly. "But what about my second question?"

Trey ducked his head, suddenly unable to meet the policeman's eyes. "Well, I wouldn't kill anybody, but I guess you'll find out pretty soon that Mr. Ainsley and I have had our ups and downs."

"That doesn't mean anything, Jake!" Jonathan added. "Trey and I have fought like cats and dogs over the setting, but that always happens. I'm a blasted perfectionist, and that means I'm impossible to work with. I know that as well as anybody. Pay no attention to what Trey says about our differences."

Trey interrupted sharply, "Don't lie to the man, Ainsley! You know that's not what I meant!" He turned his angry eyes from Jonathan to Goldman. "He stole my sets from the last play. Took all the credit and gave me nothing!"

"Why, you blasted ingrate!" Ainsley's face turned purple as he sputtered in his attempt to explain. "I took him away from Harlem, taught him everything he knows. He did some work on my last play, but it was *my* ideas that made that set, not his! From now on he'll never work on another set of mine!"

"Good enough for me! I quit!"

Simon Nero cried out, "Now just a minute, both of you. Don't start on this again—not now!" He told Goldman, "They fight like this all the time, Lieutenant, but it means nothing! If you were in the theater, you'd know this is part of the profession—it goes with the territory."

"Oh?" Goldman asked dryly. "And what about you, Mr. Nero?"

Nero looked at him blankly. "Me?"

"Yes, you. Where were you when the fall happened?"

"Why, I was out front." He seemed suddenly uncertain and added with difficulty, "I—I wanted to see what the play looked like from the rear of the theater."

"I didn't see you, Nero," Charlie Allgood objected.

"Simon, you were beside us before anyone else!" Ainsley said in astonishment. "You and Dani. You couldn't possibly have gotten there so fast from the back of the theater."

"You're right!" Lyle Jamison had come to stand right in front of Simon Nero. His eyes were fierce, and sternness edged his voice as he added, "He's said more than once, in public, that he's going to kill me."

Nero glared at him. "And I may do it, but I'm not stupid enough to do it so that I'll go to Rikers Island for it! No one's putting me in jail!"

"So you *have* made threats against Mr. Jamison." Goldman

thought about that for a moment. "And you did lie when you said you weren't backstage when the rope was cut."

Nero looked around with a furtive expression. "I'm not saying a word. You can talk to my lawyer!"

"Want me to take him in, Goldman?" Sharkey asked eagerly. "He looks like a good bet to me!"

Goldman shook his head. "No." He walked over and picked up his overcoat. "Come along, Jonathan. We'll have a little talk."

"All right, Jake," Jonathan said. "But what about the play? I mean, opening night is the fourteenth. This business, dreadful as it is—it won't change that, will it?"

Goldman stared at him. "The show must go on, eh?"

Ainsley flushed but then held his head high. "That may sound like foolishness to you, Jake, but the theater is my world." He looked around and added, "I think all of us want to go on, even with all this."

Goldman cocked his head and stared at him as if he were some exotic species. Then he smiled and commented, "It's good to know some people in this world take their work seriously. But you know I can't order any protection for you. We just don't have the manpower."

"We'll take the risk," Ainsley stated firmly and left the theater talking to Goldman. Sharkey followed them, leaving a cloud of foul smoke in his wake.

Tom Calvin came to stand beside Dani, remarking, "He'd have the play go on even if every one of us were murdered." Then he asked, "Are we still on for church again tomorrow?"

"Of course, Tom." Dani had enjoyed the service she had attended with him the previous week. It had been a little formal for her taste, but the minister had given a very good sermon. "Tom, what do you think? You've been around all these people. It seems unbelievable to me that anyone would try to kill Lyle."

"Well, Nero is crazy enough to pull it off. He loved his wife more than anything. After she was murdered, he had a nervous breakdown. I think he's still mentally unstable."

"But what about the attempts on Jonathan's life?"

"I don't know what to make of that. Doesn't seem to make any sense. Jonathan's the most likely victim. Maybe the chandelier was meant to hit *him.*"

As Danielle turned to leave, she stated, "There's no doubt the house will be full Monday night. Charlie Allgood's story will take care of that."

"Phantom of the Theater!" Tom said in exasperation. "What nonsense!"

"Maybe, but that chandelier isn't nonsense. None of us is safe. Watch out for yourself, Tom. I'd hate for anything to happen to you."

He flushed and took her hand. Turning Dani around, he spoke quietly. "It's been good having you here. I really felt alone before you came." Then he sobered and cautioned, "Don't be surprised if I fall in love with you, Danielle."

"Don't do that, Tom," she urged. To lighten the moment, she added, "After all, I might not be what I seem to be."

He stared at her and admitted, "None of us is, Danielle, none of us is!"

Five

OPENING NIGHT AT THE PEARL

To Dani, Sunday was a welcome island in the midst of a turbulent sea. She had stayed up until two o'clock Saturday night trying to make sense out of the case. Finally in desperation she called Ben Savage, and it was comforting to hear him say, "What's up, boss? You showing the Big Apple police how it's done?"

"Oh, Ben . . ." she sighed. "I can't figure out what's happening. It's so crazy, and it's impossible trying to make anything fit!" She talked for an hour, telling him every detail. "I can't make anything of it, Ben. It's like—it's like trying to put a jigsaw puzzle together in the dark!"

He laughed softly at her. "I know you, boss. You've just got the acting bug and are looking for an excuse to stay in New York and become an aspiring actress. Say, I've got an idea!"

"You have? What?"

"My dad's got a barn—let's put on a show!"

Dani laughed loudly, her tension easing. "You clown!"

"What's wrong? That always worked in the old Judy Garland movies!"

Dani shook her head, but she felt a little better. "Tell me what's happening at home." She listened as he brought her up to date on the cases the agency was working on.

Finally he said, "Hey, you want me to come give you a hand? Your dad's putting in half a day at the office now. We got a new guy too. Name's Roy Rogers. He came right out and admitted it! He's done some work for the feds, and it looks like he'll work out."

"Oh, Ben, I don't think so. This little world of the stage is really tiny. It's like a ship out in the ocean. We're the crew, and Jonathan is the captain, sitting alone and steering our little vessel. A stranger would be spotted right off."

"Okay, but call if you need me." He paused, then added, "Don't get sore now, but I know how you hate to ask for help. You think it's some kind of weakness. That's because you're afraid to be afraid. You're trying to make it in a man's world, and you think you have to be tougher than any man, so you hunker down and get beat up because you're afraid someone might think you're weak. I bought a book last week—*Feminine Psychology Made Simple*. That's how I know all this stuff about you. Now, do you want me to come or not?"

She smiled into the phone and said, "No. Buy a better book. I'll call you again later. And don't let Dad work too hard." After she hung up, she lay there thinking of Ben. The two had grated on each other from the first. She thought of the fights they'd had, most of them of her making. *That book wasn't all wrong*, she thought ruefully. *It is hard for me to ask for help, especially from Ben!* She drifted off to sleep but slept poorly.

The next morning she dragged herself out of bed late, skipped breakfast, and was barely ready when Tom came to get her. As they drove to church, he asked, "You look tired. Didn't sleep much?"

"No. I kept thinking of what it would have been like if that chandelier had fallen on someone. And I keep wondering if something like that will happen again."

"Yeah, me too. All of us are. It's strange, Danielle—most of us don't like Jonathan. But if something happened to him, the play couldn't go on. If someone in the cast or crew is trying to get at Jonathan, doesn't that mean he'll be cutting off his own nose?"

Dani said slowly, "When people hate enough, they don't use much reason, Tom."

He said no more about the situation, and they got to the church just as the service was beginning. The singing was slightly heavy and ponderous, but the sermon was not. The pastor, Reverend Edwards, was a tall, fair-haired man with a clear voice and a set of eyes that missed nothing. He preached on prayer from James 5:16: "The effectual fervent prayer of a righteous man availeth much." He accused Christians of cutting themselves off from the best things simply because they don't ask for them. "What is the right thing to pray for?" he demanded. "Whatever is needed! Not *wanted*, you understand, but that which is needed. If you need food, that is what you should pray for. If you need health, that is a proper need. If you women need a husband, ask for one."

"There you go—just ask for *me*," Tom whispered, nudging Dani with his elbow. "That's sound theology!"

Dani shushed him as the pastor continued.

"It's right to pray for rain, and it's right to pray for no rain. Verse 17 says plainly, 'Elijah was a man subject to like passions as we are, and he prayed earnestly that it might not rain.' And you know what happened." Reverend Edwards nodded firmly. "There was no rain for three and a half years!"

After the service, Tom took her out to lunch. They ate lobsters, and Tom asked as he was cracking a huge claw, "Do you believe what the minister was saying, Danielle, about asking for what we need?"

Danielle squeezed a triangle of lemon over a morsel of firm, white lobster meat, put the food in her mouth, and chewed it thoughtfully. "Yes, I do. The trouble is, of course, it seems not to work very well."

"That's exactly what troubles me." Tom nodded. "It didn't even work with Jesus, did it? I mean, He prayed for the cup to pass from Him, and it didn't. If it didn't work with Jesus, how can we hope to do any better?"

They talked about prayer for the rest of the meal, not coming to any conclusions. As they were having a strawberry ice for dessert, Tom said, "Danielle, this is fun, isn't it? I mean, I have to go to stupid cocktail parties and watch people drink until their brains are yogurt. They think they're saying clever things, but they aren't. I get sick of the world of show business!"

"Why don't you get out of it, Tom?" Dani asked. "You're a business manager. There are good jobs elsewhere."

"Well, I guess I'm afraid I can't cut it, to be truthful," Calvin explained moodily. "I hate my job with Jonathan, but it's safe."

"But it's not enough, is it?" Dani queried quietly. "There has to be more than that to life, especially for a Christian. God's not going to let you down."

"No, He won't," he answered with some hesitation. He looked at her with an eager light in his eyes. "If I had a girl like you, I could manage my life a lot better! What about it, Danielle?"

"What about what, Tom?" Dani asked. "We're friends, and I'd like to help you, but you don't need a crutch. And that's really what you want me for, isn't it?" She laughed at the expression on his face. "I know what it's like to want a crutch, Tom. I spend a lot of my time steeling myself to keep from asking for one. Come on, I've got to get back home and get some chores done."

She made him take her back to the apartment, telling him on their arrival, "No, you can't come in. I have some letter writing to finish, cleaning to do, and all kinds of other unpleasant but necessary tasks. I'll see you tomorrow. And I think both of us ought to pray for Jonathan—for all of us. I think God has the two of us involved with this play for a purpose."

Tom promised he would be praying, and as she went about her work, she thought about him and their conversation. That night she thought as she drifted off to sleep, *He's got to stand on his own two feet.*

The next day was a whirlwind. The entire cast gathered at one o'clock and had a final practice—and it was the worst rehearsal Dani had seen. She had to prompt almost everyone several times, even Jonathan who had a reputation for being the best study in drama!

After the final curtain Nero exclaimed shakily, "Well, the worst thing they can do is throw rotten eggs at us." He shook his head in despair, his confidence gone. "Jonathan, we can't go through with this! They'll laugh us off the stage."

"We'll do the play, Simon. And if they all get up and walk out, we'll do it to the empty seats!" Jonathan shot back. "Let's take a break. Everyone be back at six o'clock."

Dani started to leave, but he stopped her. "Danielle, I want to talk to you."

Lily had started to come to his side, but hearing his words to Dani, she turned away, running blindly into Carmen, who whispered, "Ah, poor little thing! Now you know how it is, Lily. Maybe you and I should form a club, along with Amber, of course. We could call ourselves 'the Ex-lovers of Jonathan Ainsley'!" Lily struck out at her, but Carmen avoided the blow and laughed as the girl ran off the stage.

"That's the way to give it to her, Carmen." Mickey Trask grinned, a tough light in his eyes. He shook his head, adding, "She's got it coming." He moved closer and put his arm around Carmen, saying, "You're more my type anyway. I never should have taken up with her."

"She should have been more careful with her accusations," Carmen answered. "She lied about that necklace just to make me look guilty."

Trask watched her leave, then turned to Ringo, who was standing in the middle of the stage, staring up at the ceiling. "Trey put a metal cable on this chandelier," the big man told him. "It won't fall on anyone." There was a gloomy light in his eyes, and he shrugged fatalistically. "I figure that if your number is up, then it's up. There was a guy in prison, and word got out that he was going to get rubbed out. He had dough, so he hired six of the toughest cons in the joint to protect him. But he got it anyway. One of the six did it." He moved away, and Mickey stood staring after him for a moment, then left and went directly to the bar, where he stayed until six o'clock.

Dani followed Jonathan out of the theater, and they got into his car, a black BMW. "I just want to get away from all this for an hour," he said. "Let's go for a drive."

He pulled onto Broadway, and as they moved through the theater district, he seemed preoccupied. He asked her about her own life, and she told him how she'd become an accountant, then had done a year's work with a firm while she earned her CPA. She told him how she'd gotten involved in working with the federal court through accounting, then had gone to work for the assistant district attorney in Boston.

She faltered, and he shot a glance at her. "What then?"

"Well, I met a man. He was planning to be a missionary. I fell in love with him, and when he died . . . well, I decided to do what he couldn't do. So I quit my work and went to school to study for the mission field."

"A lady preacher." He nodded. "I read that in the story about Maxwell Stone. Pretty big jump from being a missionary to a private eye."

Dani sighed. "It is that, Jonathan. It was my father's agency. He had a heart attack, so I went home to help, and I'm still there."

"No more missionary zeal?"

"Someday maybe. Or maybe I was just feeling guilty. It was my fault that my fiancé died in an accident." She shook her head and exclaimed, "You must be bored stiff hearing my life story! I'm nothing special. *You're* the celebrity. Let's hear your story."

He smiled, and she noted with satisfaction that he had loosened up. "A hit at twenty-two, a bum at twenty-eight," he said, trying for a light note but failing.

"Oh, don't be silly! You're no bum, Jonathan!"

"No? What have I done since *Climax*? Nothing that really matters. But this play is *good*, Danielle! Oh, I know you don't agree with the philosophy I've put into it, but you don't have to agree with Lady Macbeth to admire the drama of her life."

"Certainly not, and the play *is* great," Dani agreed. "It'll put you back on top of the theater world again!"

He laughed and moved one hand from the wheel, taking hers. "You're good for me, Danielle! I'm going to load you down with jewels!"

She let him hold her hand lightly but asked mischievously, "'Why, Mr. Rochester, you wouldn't make a plaything of me, would you?'" She laughed at his expression, then patted his hand. "I've seen you do that scene from *Jane Eyre* at least fifty times, Jonathan!"

"Well, you *are* a lot like Jane Eyre," he answered, smiling broadly. "Headstrong and determined to do nothing wrong! And I love you for it."

"Never mind all that," she said quickly. "Are you feeling better?"

"You know what a man needs, Danielle!"

"Never mind *that* either!"

They drove past the towering skyscrapers for an hour, stopped for a sandwich, then drove back to the theater. It was a little before 6 when he led her back onto the stage, and everyone was there. Dani never forgot how he talked to them, for he was masterful. It should have been Simon Nero's job as director, but he was incapable of it. Ainsley moved around the room, talking about the theater as only he could talk—the traditions, the struggles, the agony, the heartache of their profession. He said something personal to each actor. Slowly the tension began to dissipate, and by the time he ended, Dani knew that he had performed a miracle.

"Some of you hate me," he concluded in a quiet voice. "No doubt I deserve it. But for the next few hours I'm not important, and you're not important, for we are part of a small body. Some members such as Trey are small and not seen by the public. Others are more visible. But each member is a part of that body, and while the play is in motion, no single member is unimportant! I get the headlines, but where would I be if I went out there alone? Or if Pinkie walked away from the lights? You may not believe this, but it's true—when the play is taking place, I never think of myself as an individual but only as a part of the play, just as you are all part of it."

Silence had gripped his listeners, and he continued, "We all know there's danger. A maniac is loose, and who knows what he's up to. I can't help that. I can't go hide in a hole, and I don't think any of you can! So the play must go on!"

"Amen!" Sir Adrian's mellow voice broke the silence, and Lyle eagerly broke in, "Let's do it!" A murmur of agreement ran through the group, and they all went to their places.

"Ten minutes to go," Simon told Ainsley. "You really pulled them together, Jonathan. Magnificent!"

Dani was standing in her usual position, and she looked past both men to see Tom coming through the curtain.

"Special delivery for you, Jonathan," he explained, handing the actor an envelope. "Trey signed for it. Probably just good wishes from an admirer."

"Oh, all right," Jonathan said. "But you could have saved it until after the performance." He tore the envelope open and glanced at it, and Dani saw his features freeze and the color drain from his face. He slumped, and both Nero and Calvin grabbed his arms.

Dani took the paper from his hand and gave it one quick look. "Another threat, in glued-on letters just like the last ones," she said to the other two. She read it aloud: "'O villain, villain, smiling, damned villain'—that's from *Hamlet*! Then it says 'Death, a necessary end, will come when it will come.'"

"From *Julius Caesar*," Nero whispered. "What else?"

Dani said, "Only a line from *Macbeth*—'She should have died hereafter.' It looks like the other ones, doesn't it, Jonathan?"

But Ainsley was staring into space, his eyes wide with shock.

"Jonathan, come out of it!" Tom ordered hastily. "The curtain's going up any minute!"

"He can't go on the stage in that condition!" Nero worried. "Why, he can't even stand! I'll have to postpone the play."

"No . . . Wait!" Jonathan pulled free from the two men. He took a deep breath, then another. Finally he said, "I'll be all right. It—it just caught me off guard."

"Are you sure?" Dani asked. "You're trembling all over."

"I tell you I'm all right!" Ainsley shook his shoulders, and at that moment the curtain began to rise. "Call the police," he directed urgently. "This is serious!"

"It always was, Jonathan," Dani commented quietly.

Ainsley walked onto the stage, and a thunderous ovation filled the theater. "Simon, call the police," Dani said, and the director scurried off. Dani and Tom stood there, muscles tense, as the first scene unfolded. "You'd never know he was so helpless five minutes ago, would you?" she whispered. "The man is an actor, no matter what else he is!"

The first act seemed to fly by. Just as the second act started, Dani heard her name called and turned to find Lieutenant Goldman standing beside her. "I picked up the call," he explained. "Nero told me what happened."

"I'm glad you're here," Danielle admitted fervently. "I think you should move around a lot—let all of us see you."

He gave her a quick grin. "The sight of the police might discourage the killer? Not a bad idea." He watched the actors on stage, then asked, "Anyone in particular you think I ought to watch?"

Dani gave him a startled glance. She was exactly his height, and their faces were close. "No, Lieutenant. Why ask me?"

He held her eyes, then explained, "You're new to the troupe, and you're the smartest one here." He grinned at her look of surprise, then added, "I'm pretty smart myself, Danielle. It takes one to know one. Maybe sometime we can have dinner. I'd like to pump you—as a trained officer of the law."

He was an unusually attractive man, and Dani found herself drawn to him. At the same time, she knew there were several reasons why she could not afford to get involved, not the least of which was the fact that when he found out she was a private investigator, he would not be happy, to put it mildly.

"Sometime," she put him off.

"Nero said Jonathan took the threat very badly."

"Well, yes, he did. It hit him much harder than the others. At least he was much more shocked at this one than when he got the last one."

"You were with him at the time?"

"For the last one, not the others. He was alone when he got them."

Goldman stared at the stage where Jonathan and Amber were going through a scene. "Wonder why it shook him so much? Jonathan is pretty tough for an actor."

Dani didn't answer, for she couldn't explain the raw shock that had washed across Jonathan's face when he had first seen the letter. "I suppose it caught him at a bad time, just seconds before he was to step onto the stage," she suggested.

Goldman thought about that, then nodded and left. Dani saw him several times as the play progressed, always moving about, watching the cast and crew.

"What's that cop doing?" Ringo muttered as he came off the stage after a scene. "He's underfoot everywhere I turn. And that ugly one, Sharkey, is on the other side of the stage. What's going on?" He listened carefully as Dani explained, then whistled. "That's something! But with those two guys watching every move we make, nobody would be nuts enough to pull something."

"I pray not," Dani said shortly. "But keep your eyes open, Ringo."

"Yeah, you too, kid. And thanks."

"What for, Ringo?"

"Why, you wouldn't tell me to keep my eyes open if you thought I was the killer!" He touched her shoulder lightly with his huge fist, smiled, and added, "That means something!" Then he left, disappearing into the darkened area toward the rear.

The second act ended, and the third was half finished when Amber came from her dressing room. She was wearing a snow-white evening gown that made her look exceptionally beautiful. "Nothing yet?" she asked Dani nervously.

"Nothing will happen, Amber," Dani encouraged her, noting

the way the woman wrung her hands. "The play will be over in fifteen minutes. You're doing a great job."

Amber LeRoi licked her lips, then asked, "Really, Danielle? I hope so!" She stood there silently, watching Lyle and Lily for a long time. She turned to face Dani again. "I guess you think I'm the worst baggage God ever made, don't you? Well, you're right, I guess."

The words caught Dani off guard, for the woman had never shown any softness; she had barely been polite. But now there was some sort of brokenness in her. Perhaps it was simply the fear touching all of them. Her eyes were bitter, and she spoke sadly. "I've never done anything but show business. It's a miserable life, Danielle. Men after you all the time, always facing the choice, Do I give in to climb the ladder to the top? I—I gave in." She looked straight at Danielle and said, "This might sound crazy, but I wish I could have been like you. My dad was a Christian. I remember that about him most of all. He'd take me to Sunday school; then we'd talk about the lesson on the way home."

Dani said quietly, "I'm glad for that, Amber."

"Yeah, he was one sweet guy. It nearly killed him when I went wrong." She ducked her head, then dabbed at her eyes. "I don't know what's got me thinking about him. I always cry when I do."

"We all cry over things like that, Amber. Things we wish we'd done or hadn't done."

Amber stared at her. "Not *you*. I've watched you. I'm not too smart, but one thing I'm good at, and that's spotting phonies. Which is what I picked you for. But you're the real goods—just like my old man." She looked out at the stage and whispered, "Here I am, wishing I was what I'm not. It's too late for me."

"It's never too late, Amber," Dani said gently. She heard the lines leading up to Amber's entrance and added, "Jesus loves you, just as He loves me. Just give yourself to Him, and you'll find what you've really been looking for all along."

Amber LeRoi was diamond hard; yet when she looked at Danielle at that instant, something of the little girl she'd been appeared in her eyes. Her lips parted, and Dani told her quickly, "Ask Him into your life today." Amber's cue came, and Dani whispered, "I believe God is reaching out to you! We'll talk later."

Amber nodded slowly, her eyes fixed on Dani's. She paused and said, "All right," then turned and walked onto the stage.

As Amber spoke her first lines, Jonathan came to stand beside Dani, awaiting his cue. "I don't like this scene," he muttered. "Where's Trey?"

"Right here." Trey appeared suddenly at his side.

"Give me the gun," Jonathan ordered.

"Here it is. Don't point it at her eyes," Trey instructed. "These blanks throw off black powder that can damage the eyes."

"You tell me that every time," Jonathan whined. Trey left, and the actor put the revolver in his pocket. "I'll be glad when this is over," he muttered.

"It's going well. The audience loves it."

"Do they?" He seemed nervous and moody, and when his cue came, he strolled out onto the stage in a jerky walk, not at all with his usual stride.

Goldman suddenly appeared and asked, "Well, it's almost over, isn't it?"

"Yes. This is the next to the last scene. Did you like the play?"

"Not much. I don't believe what it says."

Dani stared at him in surprise. "I don't either."

"Old hat, that biological determinism." Suddenly Goldman tensed. "What's this?"

Dani turned to watch the stage. "Haven't you guessed the ending? I hate to spoil it for you, but—well, just watch."

Onstage, after a heated discussion, Jonathan pulled the gun from his pocket. He said his line well. "You've become unnecessary to me, my dear. I'm afraid I'm going to have to rid myself of you."

"You can't!" Amber whispered.

Jonathan spoke again, but Goldman's voice in her ear caused

Dani to miss the lines. "Nobody said anything about a gun," he rapped out.

Danielle started to speak, but just at that moment Amber raised her eyes and looked full at her. Her back was half turned to the audience, and she suddenly smiled and lifted her hand. It was a secret smile, just for Dani.

At that moment Jonathan raised the gun and spoke his line. "Good-bye, my dear." Then he pulled the trigger.

The gun's explosion filled the stage with noise, and Amber was driven backward as if a giant fist had struck her.

That's all wrong, Dani's numbed mind objected. Every other time, in practice, Amber had staggered, then collapsed gracefully to the floor.

Goldman yelled, "Get that curtain down!" and swept across the stage even before he finished his words. The curtain fell as he reached the crumpled form of Amber LeRoi. Shaking off her shock, Danielle followed closely. Goldman knelt at the woman's side, and as Dani looked over his shoulder, she saw a brilliant crimson stain flowing across Amber's chest. She had forgotten that blood was such a violent red, and the sight of the stain against the pure white dress brought on shock—weak knees, nausea, labored breathing.

Dani turned away, stumbling as she left the stage. Others rushed to where Goldman bent over Amber, and the air was filled with voices crying out, but she saw only Jonathan Ainsley.

He stood there, holding the gun in his hand, and his eyes were so wide that she could see the whites on all sides. Goldman suddenly appeared, snatching the gun from his hand with a handkerchief. She heard Lady Lockridge say, "Well, you always said you'd like to kill her, but I didn't think you'd do it!"

Dani stopped suddenly, then forced herself to go and kneel beside Amber. As she leaned down and put her hand on the dead woman's hair, all she could think of was the last thing she'd said to the actress: "We'll talk later."

There would be no later for Amber LeRoi—no further opportunity for conversation or repentance at all. Dani Ross knew that she would never forgive herself for letting so many chances go by to speak to that woman about Jesus Christ! One hope came to her: *She smiled at me and she heard the Gospel moments before her death. Perhaps she cried out to Jesus!* Dani hoped that somehow in the last few minutes of her life Amber LeRoi had responded and had found the Christ whom her father had pointed her to so many years ago.

Six

ALL THE KING'S HORSES

Jake Goldman's office was completely out of keeping with the "decor" of the Homicide Department of the New York Police Department. Every other member of the squad had an office battered and scarred by a thousand days and nights of encounters with the denizens of the underworld—desks ringed by a thousand cups of coffee and branded by a thousand cigarettes and cigars, walls punctuated by oily spots from a thousand greasy heads, tile floors bearing the hieroglyphics of a thousand pairs of guilty feet. The odor of crime was composed of sweat, fear, guilt, stale coffee, rancid bodies, and whiskey breath; every office in the section, except Goldman's, reeked with it.

Sharkey hated Goldman's office as much as he despised everything else about the dapper lieutenant; he always had and always would. He sat down in the pale blue chair and felt tempted to dump his cigar ashes on the mauve carpet. But Goldman's look convinced him to gingerly deposit them in an immaculate crystal ashtray. The odor of Goldman's office was money, not crime, and as Sharkey looked at the solid-walnut bookcases on the left wall, the rosewood desk with matching chairs, the austere brass lamp that cast its light over a modest painting of a small boat riding green ocean waves, he wondered sourly why Goldman didn't leave the department. The picture, he had been told, cost more than Sharkey's annual salary. The sight of it always enraged him.

But he said nothing of this to Goldman. The dapper officer who sat staring at the wall knew how he felt. *He knows how everybody feels!* Sharkey thought with a twinge of envy. He took his mind off the picture, interrupting the lieutenant's thoughts with, "Well, it looks like an easy one." Goldman's eyes flickered toward him, and Sharkey added nervously, "It's got to be Miller!"

Knowing the other man's prejudices, Goldman said idly, "Ainsley pulled the trigger last night, Jack."

"So what? Anybody can see he's a basket case. Nero had to get his private doc up here to give him a shot."

"He's an actor. That means, Jack, you can't believe a thing about what he looks like."

Sharkey shook his head and puffed on the cigar. "Naw, he's really had it, Jake. I seen enough guys put on an act to know the real thing. His eyes were like a dead man's. Anyway, Ainsley's not crazy, which he'd have to be to kill that broad before 2,000 witnesses!" When Goldman turned to look at the picture, Sharkey got angry again. "Anyway, the LeRoi woman was where he went to get the dough to put on the play, right? He wouldn't kill the goose with the golden egg!"

"Get Miller in here. Let's hear his story."

"Jake, why don't you let me help him tell the truth—down in the interrogation room? I could open him up . . ." Sharkey got the full effect of Goldman's piercing eyes, then rose abruptly. "All right, all right, I'll bring him in!"

Sharkey lumbered out of the office and came back with Trey Miller. "Sit down there," he ordered, then stationed himself with his back to the door.

Goldman swiveled his chair around and commented, "Trey, you're in a bad spot. I might have to book you for attempted murder."

Goldman's words brought Miller out of his chair. "What! You can't do that, Goldman!" He brought his fist down on the desk, shouting, "I knew it would be this way! Why don't you arrest some of the white suspects?"

"Because none of them handed a .38 with live ammunition to

Ainsley," Goldman pointed out. "If I arrest you, you'll be able to get out on bond. I can help you if you tell me the truth, Trey. Do you want my help or not?"

Miller stared at Goldman, brought up short by the abrupt manner of the policeman. He had been informed by several black leaders that Jake Goldman was one policeman who *could* be counted on to give a black man a fair shake.

Trey swallowed, then nodded and sat down. "I want your help," he agreed humbly.

"All right. Let me say right upfront that I don't think you did it, Trey. You're not stupid, and I can't think of anything more stupid than if you were to kill Amber LeRoi in such a way. You had a motive for hating Ainsley, but as far as I can discover, you and the woman weren't enemies. Now, how did live ammunition get into that gun?"

Miller's face contorted with doubt. "Lieutenant, I only know two things. One, I didn't put it there! Man, I'm on top of the world! My sets just might win every award this year, and I've got producers lined up begging me to work for them! Why would I throw all that out the window to kill Amber? We weren't friendly, but she never did me any harm."

"What's the second thing, Trey?"

"The second thing, Lieutenant Goldman, is that anybody in the cast or in the crew could have put real bullets in that .38." Miller shook his head mournfully, then plunged ahead. "I buy the blanks from Blake's Gun Shop over on Ninth Avenue. The owner is a friend of mine, Orson Green. When I got this job and found out it meant using blanks for a scene, I went to him and told him to fix me up. He made up a hundred blanks. You can check that out."

"That wasn't no blank that wasted LeRoi," Sharkey interposed.

"I don't even have a gun, and I never bought any ammunition in my life!" Miller snapped. "But in a way I guess I'm to blame. I kept the gun and the blanks in the prop room. That's stage left, just outside Amber's dressing room."

"Was it kept locked?" Goldman asked.

"Not the room itself, but I kept the gun and the shells in a wall cabinet. It has a combination lock."

"How many people know the combination?"

"Just me, but I only locked it when we left for the day. And last night I opened it before the play started—and I didn't lock it again."

"Pretty careless, ain't you?" Sharkey accused.

"Careless with blanks? I guess so."

"When did you load the gun, Trey?"

"Before the performance. I'm plenty busy after the curtain goes up, so I loaded it ahead of time and put it in the cabinet."

"How do you know it was blanks you put into the gun?"

"Well, Orson showed me how he made the blanks," Miller explained. "He took the lead out of one of the real shells and just put some sort of packing in its place—to hold the powder in, I think he said. Then he made me hold it in one hand and a real shell in my other hand. The real one had the lead sticking out in front, and it must have weighed four times as much! So that's how I knew. I looked at it, like I always do, and saw that it didn't have any lead in it."

"But you put it back in the cabinet, not in your pocket?"

"That's right. As a matter of fact, Lieutenant, Mickey was getting his umbrella out of the prop room. He saw me take the gun. Even said, 'Don't blow my brains out with that thing!' He can tell you. But *anybody* could have come in and put real bullets in the gun."

Goldman sat quietly in his chair, studying the other man's face. Finally he said, "Miller, I don't think I'll have to charge you, but don't leave the area. If you were to disappear and I needed to ask you some more questions, that would make you look guilty. That's all for now."

Miller got up and turned to leave, but Ainsley entered. Trey glared at him with hatred. "I'm through with you and your play. Get yourself another man!" Then he left the office without waiting for a reply. When he passed down the hall, he paused at the door marked WAITING ROOM and went inside.

The cast and crew of the play were all there, with the exception of Lady Lockridge. They all looked up at him, and Mickey asked at once, "How'd it go, Trey?"

"How do you think?" Miller answered, shaking his head. "They just might charge me with the murder."

Most of the cast showed some shock, and Ringo growled, "They won't be able to hang it on you, Trey!"

"I know that, but I'm through. I've had it with this play and with Ainsley." He hesitated; then his voice and his face softened. "I just wanted to say, you guys are all right. I wish you all the best, but I'm out of here!" He turned and left, closing the door violently, as if shutting out part of his life.

Dani was sitting beside Sir Adrian. The room was L-shaped, and the two of them had taken chairs in the short, lower section. Though they could hear the subdued mumble of voices from the others, they had some privacy.

"Do you think they'll arrest him and find him guilty?" Sir Adrian asked anxiously. He looked older under the harsh fluorescent lights, and his hands were unsteady. He seemed tired, almost ill, at close range. He had left twice—to go to the rest room, he said—but had come back smelling like the powerful licorice breath mints he used so often. Dani pitied him for the way he tried to cover up his drinking.

"Oh, no," she said quickly in answer to his question. "And even if they arrest him, they'll never get him into court."

"Really? How can you be so sure of that, Danielle?"

"Trey denies putting the live ammunition into the gun. As he says, any one of us could have done it. They don't have any hard evidence. So if the district attorney had little enough sense to book him for murder, Trey would be defended by the NAACP and the ACLU and every other civil rights outfit. And the D.A. doesn't want to get the black community upset because he's going to run for governor next election. The department probably feels it has to charge somebody, but if it's Trey, he won't ever see the inside of a jail, Sir Adrian."

He stared at her in amazement. "My dear Danielle, how do you know all these things?"

Dani suddenly realized she had stepped out of character. "Oh." She quickly made up an excuse. "Tom Calvin's been talking to the lawyers. He told me about it." She felt guilty about the quick lie but evaded more questions by turning to another concern. "I can't stop thinking about Amber, Sir Adrian. I—I can't believe she's dead!"

"It was very tragic—an awful thing!"

"I'm hoping it will turn out to have been an accident," Dani almost whispered. "I've been blaming myself for being so distant with her. You see, Sir Adrian, I believe that we all have to meet God. And as a Christian I didn't show enough concern for Amber. I didn't reach out to her like I could have."

Lockridge stared at the floor, his features strained because of the sleepless night. "I doubt she would have listened to you, Danielle," he said, trying to comfort her. "She was a very hard woman." He shook his head. "I shouldn't speak that way of the dead, but I knew Amber better than most."

"You'd performed with her?"

The question caused Lockridge to lift his eyes to meet Danielle's, and she saw a flash of blind anger in him. It was a sudden glimpse into the depths of the kindly man, a side of him she would not have dreamed existed. "You're mocking me! I didn't think you could ever be cruel, Danielle!" When he saw the confusion that swept across her face, he immediately reached over and touched her hand. "Forgive me, my dear! I—I'm not myself." He licked his lips, slumped back in his chair, and with his eyes closed confessed, "I forget you're not in the theater. If you were, you'd know all about my foolish ways."

Dani had a sudden thought. "You and Amber were . . . ?"

"Yes! I made a fool of myself over her." His voice sounded weary, but he seemed unable to stop. "It was years ago, Danielle. I was a star, and she was a beautiful young girl. I don't want to go into the sordid details. It almost killed Victoria. That was the worst part of it." His head rolled from side to side, and he whispered, "We've been married twenty-five years, and I've been faithful to her always except for that one time."

"I'm so sorry," Dani consoled gently. "But I've learned that God can take away guilt. Do you know that, Sir Adrian?"

He opened his eyes and stared at her. "God may forget it, but I never can!" He spoke bitterly. "She blackmailed me, Danielle. I didn't care what the world thought of me, but I cared desperately what Victoria would think. So I paid and paid, but in the end she told Victoria anyway. So Victoria left me—for a year. I almost died, and so did she. You see, Danielle, we have one of those great loves, the kind you read about. I love her more today than I did when we first met, and she feels the same about me."

"I think your love for one another is wonderful, Sir Adrian!" Dani whispered. "Thank you for telling me everything."

"You're an easy person to talk to, my dear. You really should be a psychologist or perhaps a minister. And I'll remember what you've said about God being able to forgive and take away bad memories." He grew even more serious. "God knows we need it, Victoria and I!"

At that moment the outer door opened, and both of them got up in time to see Ainsley and Goldman enter. Ainsley's face was tense, but he managed a smile. "I'm being charged with the murder, though I'll be able to get out on bond right away. Amber's funeral will be at two o'clock tomorrow at Stevens Funeral Home. I know you'll all be there. Now Lieutenant Goldman has something to say to you."

"I'm going to ask four of you to stay. The rest can come back and give your statements tomorrow. Miss Morgan, Mr. Nero, Mr. Trask, and Miss Rio, you will remain. The rest of you can go. Miss Morgan, come with me please."

Dani followed Goldman into his office, and her eyes widened as she took in the expensive furniture. He saw her reaction and countered, "Didn't Sharkey warn you that I'm not your average policeman? Everything here is legal, so don't worry about this being a shakedown."

Dani sat down and looked at the painting, then back at the officer. "You must be loaded to have a genuine Turner. I didn't know police work paid so well."

"It doesn't." Goldman offered her a cigarette from his case, and when she refused, he explained, "I play the stock market. But making money bores me. I'm a policeman because I enjoy the work."

"Most people like having power."

"Do you, Danielle?"

She gave him a startled look. "I suppose I do, though I know I shouldn't. Who was it that said, 'Power tends to corrupt and absolute power corrupts absolutely'?"

He grinned at her. "You know who said that. You're still trying to play dumb. But I'm on to you, Danielle. The only way you could fool me is to pretend to be smart. That would confuse me because I know you're a smart girl trying to play dumb, though I'm not sure why." He studied her before asking, "What's the reason? Want to tell me?"

Dani did want to tell him and almost blurted it out. But she had to talk with Ainsley first, so she just smiled and tried to throw him on the defensive. "You just like to make things complicated, Lieutenant. All public officials are like that."

He leaned back in his chair and, ignoring her ploy, asked suddenly, "Call me Jake. Will you go out with me?"

The question caught her off guard. Her cheeks flushed, and she said too quickly, "No, I won't."

"Is it because I'm Jewish?"

"No! Of course not!" She didn't know how to explain that it had nothing to do with his background, but everything to do with her faith in Christ.

"Why such a dramatic no? Is it because you're a Christian?" He laughed then. "*How does he know that?* you're thinking. I have my methods, Watson."

"Tom Calvin told you."

"Yes, he did." He leaned forward and put his chin in his hands.

His dark eyes were fixed on her, and she couldn't read what was in them.

"You're a peculiar sort of policeman," she responded. "Do you ever catch any criminals, or is this just a way of getting dates?"

"I catch lots of criminals." He smiled back. "And you're the only suspect I ever wanted to take to dinner."

"I'm not a suspect," she jeered. The only way to handle Jacob Goldman was to match his wit. "You may be a spoiled, rich cop, but you're too smart to think I had anything to do with killing Amber LeRoi. Why, you can't even make the charges stick on Trey or Jonathan. You just have to do something to satisfy the captain and the police commissioner, at least until you get something real to go on." She laughed outright at his expression, which for once was filled with surprise. "See, I really am as smart as you are, Jake!"

He grinned at her before retaliating, "That proves I was right about who, or what, you really are, doesn't it? Now, what about this killing? Who did it?" He leaned back and went over the facts, admitting at last that it would be idiotic for either Jonathan or Trey to kill Amber LeRoi. "But we've got a *corpus delicti*, Danielle, and somebody's got to go down for it. That's what the D.A. says, and around here that's as binding as if it's handed down from Mount Sinai. I thought perhaps you could give me some help."

"I would if I could," Dani answered soberly. "I can't stop thinking about Amber. She had enemies, but I think she might have changed."

"Changed how? And who are these enemies she had?"

"Oh, I don't have anything but a feeling to go on. I talked to her just before she went onto the stage. She seemed vulnerable. I think she was tired of the way she was living."

"What enemies?" Goldman pressed.

"She wasn't such a nice person, Jake. I'm sure you can get the details from the cast. I don't really know much. I really don't have any more information for you. Can I leave now?"

"Sure, Danielle." He got up to open the door for her. "I'll see you at the funeral tomorrow." He added quickly, "Yeah, I'll be there. I want to watch the faces. We homicide cops are just a bunch of vultures."

She shook her head. "I don't think that's true, Jake. It's certainly not true of you." Dani paused before adding, "A lot of smart people don't seem to have much of a heart, Jake, but you and I do." She walked away, knowing that he was watching her with a look of admiration in his dark eyes.

He shook his shoulders and barked, "Sharkey, get Nero in here!"

♦ ♦ ♦

A pale iron-gray sky covered the mourners' grief. As six hefty men carried the casket from the sleek ebony hearse, the cast of *Out of the Night* stood awkwardly around the gaping hole in the earth. The rich green of the carpet surrounding the cavity was as obvious as the layer of rouge on the cheeks of a withered crone, aged in death.

The funeral had been ornate, but most of the crowd of show business people that had filled the small chapel had not come to the cemetery. However, the number of poorly or thinly dressed fans who came to stand in the fine sleet that stung their cheeks impressed Dani.

The minister took his place, read a psalm, then offered a brief prayer. When he was finished, the crowd turned and moved hastily away, threading their ways cautiously through ancient, mossy stones that seemed to reach upward with harsh fingers.

Once they got to the cars, Jonathan invited, "Ride back with Nero and me, Danielle."

She got in, sitting between the two men. None of them said a word all the way back to the funeral home. As she got out of the black limo, Jonathan said, "My car's over here. I'll take you home."

She nodded and got in the front seat. Nero slid in the back. As

Jonathan drove through the city, he spoke of his student days and of the hardships of getting into the world of drama. Dani listened with part of her mind, while the rest of it struggled to shake off the gloom that had fallen on her at the cemetery.

Caught up in her own thoughts, she was surprised to see that Jonathan had stopped in front of her apartment. Dani got out. "Thanks for the ride, Jonathan," she said. He surprised her by asking, "May I come in? We need to talk."

"Well, it's not a fancy place, you know."

"Doesn't matter."

After Nero hailed a cab, Jonathan followed her inside. Dani was glad she had cleaned the small rooms before leaving. She took him inside and motioned to the couch. "Sit down," she offered. "I'll fix coffee."

"Not for me," Jonathan said. He walked to the window and stared out. Dani stood there awkwardly, wondering what he wanted to say.

"What is it, Jonathan?" she asked finally.

He turned, and she noticed his bloodshot eyes. "I'm going to go on with the play, Danielle. And I want you to help."

"I don't see how you can do it," Dani objected. "It's pretty obvious that someone in the cast is homicidal. I'm not sure the police will even let you perform."

"I've been through all that, with our lawyers and with the police," Ainsley explained quickly. "The police don't like it, but legally there's no way they can close us down."

Dani shrugged. "That may be so, but Trey Miller won't work for you anymore, and that set can't be operated by just anybody. Besides, you don't have a leading lady. How long will it take to hire an adequate replacement? At least two weeks, right? And I'm not sure the rest of the cast will stay on board. Some of them are too shook-up to continue, Jonathan, and I don't blame them."

Jonathan nodded. "I know, Danielle. Do you think I haven't told myself all that and more a thousand times? Humpty Dumpty's broken, and all the king's horses and men can't put him together again!"

He fixed a sudden, penetrating stare on her and quietly stated, "I want *you* to stay, Danielle."

"I'm tempted to say no, but . . . If I stay, it has to be on one condition—Goldman has to be told that I'm a private investigator," Dani stipulated. "Policemen are funny about things like that. He could get my license revoked."

"Jake will be all right," Jonathan assured her. "He's a friend of mine. Besides, I think he already suspects you're more than a prompter. He's pretty sharp."

Dani studied him. "He suspects, but he needs to be told straight out. And I still don't think I should stay or that the play should go on. You need police protection, and I can't watch you all the time."

"Neither can they," Jonathan pointed out. He moved closer and said, "Danielle, I want you to stay, but not as a prompter." He saw her think that over and interjected, "We can get someone to do the sets, but I want you to take over Amber's role."

Nonplussed, Dani stared at him. After a short, humorless laugh, she shook her head. "That's out of the question."

"Why is it?" Jonathan asked.

"Well, the obvious reason—and I'm surprised you haven't seen it—is that I'm not a good enough actress."

"Yes, you are." He nodded at her and added emphatically, "You sure know the lines. And the night you took Amber's place in rehearsal, I saw that you have the acting ability."

Jonathan saw Danielle's expression and began to speak more persuasively. "Danielle, listen to me, please! You have so much in your life! You have your career, your family. You have God. All I have is the theater. And if I don't succeed with this play, I'm finished. I know you can do this part!" His voice had begun to rise, and she saw that he was having difficulty controlling himself.

He dropped his head, struggled for a few seconds, then lifted his eyes to hers. "You're a strong-willed woman, Danielle. I know you won't do this thing unless you think it's right. I—I'm not accustomed to dealing with people who think like that. Instead of what's right, it's always, What's in it for me? So all I can do is beg—something I've not done much of," he added ruefully. "Will you help me, Danielle, please?"

Everything told Dani to say no, but instead she walked to the window to give herself a moment for thought. As she stared out into the cold, gray sky, her mind swarmed with thoughts so varied and jumbled that she could barely think. Finally she began to pray. *I don't know what to do, Lord,* she entreated humbly. *Show me the way.*

Jonathan stood there silently, his face tense and pale.

Finally Dani took a deep breath and turned to face him. "All right, I'll do it," she agreed evenly.

"Thank God!" Jonathan's face and voice both expressed relief.

"And I can help you with two of your other problems too," she said. A smile touched her lips. "You need two men—one to be a bodyguard, the other to run the sets. And I have a recommendation."

"Who are they?" Jonathan demanded.

"Their name is Ben Savage." Dani spoke emphatically and laughed at the expression on the actor's face. "You haven't forgotten your last meeting with him, have you, Jonathan?"

"No!" Ainsley said ruefully. "I can see the bodyguard role well enough, but can he run the sets? They're pretty complicated."

"Ben's got that sort of mind. He rebuilt an old biplane from scratch, and he's always coming up with nutty inventions that actually work. Give him two days and a couple of rehearsals and he'll do it as well as Trey. But I want him to come undercover. Don't tell anyone he works for me."

"That would undoubtedly be best," Jonathan agreed. "Call him right now."

She nodded. "All right. I'll have him here tomorrow. Now let me get busy."

As soon as Ainsley left, she picked up the phone and dialed

the number of the agency. She expected Angie to answer, but Ben picked up the phone. "Ross Investigations," he said.

Suddenly Dani wasn't sure what to say to him. The little speech she had made up suddenly deserted her. She said slowly, "Ben? I need you!"

After a slight pause, he spoke in a peculiar tone that she had never heard from him before. "All right, boss. Just tell me how and when."

Seven

THE NEW MAN

The interior of the Pearl Theater felt oppressive to Dani as she stood with her back to the apartment that made up the first set. She tried to shake off the almost palpable gloom that had risen in her from the moment she'd walked onto the stage but could not do so. *It's too soon after Amber's funeral—only two days*, she told herself as Simon continued to recite his speech about the performance. Glancing at the spot on the stage where Amber's body had lain, Dani involuntarily checked for dry bloodstains. None were there, of course, but the memory of the dead woman remained clearly etched in her mind. *I still feel guilty for not having said more to Amber about the Lord*, she reflected.

The rest of the cast seemed in little better shape. Summoned to appear at the Pearl for a walk-through rehearsal, most of them, Dani saw, were still edgy and in bad spirits. None of the usual rough joking was in evidence, and by the dim lights their faces looked tired and fearful. She tried to make herself pay more attention to Nero as he tried to stir them out of their dullness.

"I know it's hard," he was saying in his quick manner of speech. "But it would be hard even if we waited a month, wouldn't it?" He glanced around and saw that none of them was really listening. In despair he finally gave up. "Well, Jonathan, I don't know what I can do. Everyone acts like a zombie!"

Jonathan nodded. "Can't blame them for that, Simon. I feel pretty sick myself." A cynical twist of his lips signaled his thoughts, and he said, "It's like that old Ronald Reagan movie, isn't it? You know, when he died saying to Pat O'Brien, 'Someday when the team is losing, tell them to win one for the Gipper.'" He seemed to ponder that for a moment. "Well, Amber was no saint, but she was one of us. And acting was her life. I know better than to say, 'Let's win this one for Amber, gang!' and expect you to rouse up like a football team. I guess we've gotten too subtle and smooth and sophisticated for any sort of emotional appeal like that. But in a way I suppose that's what I'm saying." He shook his shoulders, and his words came out clipped and short. "I guess Amber didn't care about much in this world, but this was her last performance. I believe I'd like to see us make it work for her—and for all of us."

He lifted his head, looked around, and said, "Well, let's go through the rehearsal. I know you're all fatigued and disheartened, but let's do it anyway."

Dani quietly broke in. "I have to say this, Jonathan." She turned to face the cast. "All of you must think I'm crazy to even think about doing this role. But believe me, none of you thinks that as much as I do!" She attempted to smile but failed, then fell silent.

Lyle Jamison roused himself. "Hey, don't talk like that! You can do it, Danielle!" He came over to stand beside her, put his hand on her shoulder, and looked around at the others. "Come on, let's do this play!"

"Yeah!" Mickey Trask echoed, a smile on his smooth face. "Let's win this one for Danielle, you guys!"

The mood grew lighter, and Nero said quickly, "That's it! Now, from the top!"

In this strange rehearsal, they used no props and made no set changes. Jonathan had promised that a new set man would be on the job soon, and they performed the entire play right in the center of stage one. The lack of scenery and props made the entire play seem surrealistic to Dani, and for the entire two and a half hours she was horrified to find out that she could do nothing right!

She had always been a gifted actress, a quick study, and able to fall into the mood of a character. This had been her strength in college drama, and more than once she had been pressed into service when an actress had to be replaced. She had taken pride in her ability to take over a tough role and do a competent job.

But tonight she could not put herself into the attitude of the character she would portray in the drama—Marian Powers. She knew the script, had studied it for long hours, and had seen Amber's interpretation. Yet all she could do was say the lines automatically. She felt *exactly* like a zombie!

As she fumbled through the role, Simon had a brief word with Jonathan. They were standing in the wings, waiting for the actor's next entrance, and the director nervously objected, "It's not going to work, Jonathan!"

Ainsley shook his head stubbornly. "I think it will. Give it time, Simon. She did the role much better when she was just walking through it, filling in for Amber. Now the pressure is on, and she just needs a little time to settle into the role. I'll talk to her later, try to get her to calm down."

Finally the last line was said, and Simon called out, "All right, that's it. Everybody be here at noon. We'll keep going through the whole thing until it feels right."

Humiliated by her performance, Dani ducked her head as the others tried to encourage her. It was a relief when Jonathan said, "Come on, Dani, I'll take you home."

She almost fled the Pearl, slumping down in the leather seat beside Jonathan. Neither of them said much on the way to her place, and when he got out to open her door, he said, "Let's talk a little, Danielle."

"Not tonight, Jonathan!" she exclaimed. But he took her arm and, ignoring her protests, accompanied her up the steps. Inside her apartment, Dani pulled her coat off and hurled it at the couch. "All right, let's face up to it," she told him bitterly, her lips twisted. "You had a big idea that just isn't going to work."

He tried the light touch. "It's not unusual for even a professional actress to have trouble getting into a role, Danielle. And you're not only new to the role, you're emotionally upset. Amber's terrible death would make it hard for anyone to concentrate on the play."

He kept talking, but he could see it was doing little good. Dani's lips remained stubbornly pulled together, and she was obviously only partly listening. She walked the floor nervously, then finally interrupted him. "Jonathan, go home. I don't want to listen to you any longer."

"All right," he agreed. He knew she was close to quitting completely. "I'll call you early. Let's have breakfast together."

Dani just wanted to be alone, and as soon as he left, she soaked in a tub of water as hot as she could stand it. Lying in the steaming water, she tried to forget her miserable performance but couldn't. As she was drying off, the doorbell rang. Thinking it was Jonathan again, she refused to answer it, but the bell continued to shrill persistently. Throwing on a woolly blue robe, she opened the door slightly. "Go away."

A male voice answered, "Come on, boss, let me in."

"Ben!" she exclaimed. She opened the door and stood back as he sauntered in. He gave her a grin, then plopped down on the couch. "Well, the first team is here. You look pretty good, boss. I don't think I ever saw that robe before."

Dani felt so glad to see Ben that she wanted to hug him, but at the same time she was furious with herself for feeling that way. She prided herself on being independent, though at that moment she felt like a little girl who'd scraped her knee and needed a pair of strong arms to run to and a soothing voice to tell her that everything would be all right. But instead of seeking comfort, she drew herself up straight and glared at him.

Savage looked back innocently. His squarish face, more Slavic than anything else, featured deep-set hazel eyes below a bony ridge. He had a short nose that had been broken; his mouth was wide with a thin upper lip resting on a full lower one. A scar on his forehead traced its way into a dense black eyebrow. He was usually poker-faced, but as he stared up at Dani, a glint of humor lit his eyes. It further angered her to know that no matter how she tried to hide her moods, he was somehow able to read them.

"Did you have to come here in the middle of the night?" she demanded sarcastically.

Ben studied her thoughtfully, one black eyebrow lifted quizzically. "I take it you're not happy with your work."

Dani glared at him but was in no mood for word games. "This case is a washout," she finally admitted. "In the first place, we have as much chance of turning up the killer as we have of—of finding Noah's Ark."

"If you'll make me a cup of coffee, I'll let you tell me all about it."

"Oh, all right. I'm not going to sleep a wink anyway!" She moved to the tiny kitchen, and he perched on one of the dinette chairs while she brewed the coffee. By the time she had finished running through the whole story, he'd drained three cups of coffee. She finally put her elbows on the table, rested her chin in her hands, and muttered, "It's no good, Ben. Not enough clues."

He studied her, his face at rest, but his mind casting in all directions. Suddenly he asked, "How are you doing with the acting bit? That going all right?"

Dani glanced at him, stung, and responded stiffly, "No. I'm rotten! I can't act, not professionally!"

Savage looked down at the dregs in his cup, drained the coffee off, then put it down. "Sure you can, Dani. You've been acting ever since I first met you."

"Don't start on me, Ben!" she snapped angrily. "I know you think I've lost my 'identity' as a woman, but after tonight's rehearsal I'm in no mood for your cut-rate psychological treatment! I'm quitting, and that's that!"

Savage seemed unimpressed by her anger. He grinned at her and asked, "Do you know you're beautiful when you're angry?"

She jumped up, shouting, "Get out of here!"

Savage rose and nodded. "You won't quit, boss. You know why? Because you know I wouldn't quit, and you can't let a man be tougher than a woman." He moved toward the door, then turned to add, "And you can do the acting all right. You just needed me to drop by and give you a little encouragement."

Dani glared at him, her fists clenched. She was so angry she almost wanted to strike him, but Ben merely grinned again and added, "Now, can we make a few plans? Like what time do I show up tomorrow? Who do I watch the closest? You know, detective stuff."

Suddenly struck by the ridiculous picture they made—Ben languid and grinning, she stiff and white-lipped—Dani felt the tension drain from her. She shook her head, smiling ruefully. "Good old Doctor Savage," she said. "I thought the treatment for hysterical women was to slap them across the face."

"That's what I was planning next," he admitted. "Now, what's the master plan, boss?"

They sat down again, and when he left half an hour later, Dani went to bed immediately. The darkness of the room closed in on her, and when she thought briefly of the rehearsal the next day, it was without strain. Her last thought was of Ben. *I hate it when he's right and I'm wrong!* Her lips curved up into a smile as she drifted off.

♦ ♦ ♦

Julio Garcia was small and fast. He could move around the complicated world of ropes, pulleys, props, and staging gear quicker than a cat. His hands were nimble, and he had taken over the sophisticated aspects of the settings. Usually his light-olive face bore a smile, but as he sat slumped in one of the upholstered chairs behind the curtain, discontentment drew his mouth into a scowl. "I bet we don't have no jobs when the new dude comes."

"You got that right!" Earl Layne snapped back. He was six feet tall and very muscular. His skin was so dark that he gave the impression of a black panther, which he had been for a time. Unlike Julio, he was short-tempered and touchy. He had been thinking along the same lines as his partner. "Me and you know how to move the sets, and it wouldn't be so easy to break in two new guys. But they'll want white guys. I knew this was too good to last."

The pair sat there waiting, for Nero had told them that the new set manager would be there at 8. At the sound of approaching footsteps, they looked up to see Simon Nero coming down the aisle. Both men stared at the man with him, and Julio muttered, "He's white. Be nice if he's got a heart for us minority groups, but you know how it is . . . !"

"This is Ben Davis," Simon said. "Ben, meet Julio Garcia and Earl Layne."

Layne and Garcia nodded but made no other movement. So Ben stepped forward and put his hand out. "Glad to know you, Julio." He shook the hand of the smaller man, then turned to the other. "Earl," he said. His hand was suddenly engulfed by the massive hand of Earl Layne, and the black man used all his strength. Savage felt the pain in his hand but instantly returned the grip full force and stood there smiling at the other man with no sign of strain on his face. Layne's eyes opened in shock. He threw every ounce of power he could into his grip, trying to crush the hand of the smaller man, but nothing happened.

"I appreciate having two experienced men to help me out," Savage said, his hand suddenly tightening over the larger hand of the other man. Layne felt as if a band of white-hot iron had been forced around his own hand. He felt his bones giving way, and his nostrils flared as he fought back silently.

But as soon as Ben felt Earl's hand collapse, he instantly reduced the pressure of his grip. "I hope I can count on you to be patient with me, Earl, and you too, Julio."

Julio said, "Sure, Mr. Davis." Earl took his hand back, his face marked with disbelief. He stared down at his fingers as if they had betrayed him, then nodded slowly. "You're the man, Mr. Davis," he agreed woodenly.

"Just make it Ben, will you, guys?" Then he asked, "How much time have I got?"

"The cast is coming in at noon. But you won't be able to learn the sets by then. You'll probably have to work some overtime tonight."

Ben looked at the two men, who were watching him carefully. "Can I get you to stay a little late tonight? I'm sort of a slow learner."

Julio looked at Earl with a question in his eyes, and Earl nodded at once. "Sure, we can do that, *Ben.*"

Nero shrugged and left at once.

"I've read the script, but it doesn't help much," Ben admitted. "The only way I've ever learned much was by doing. So if you'll go over the whole play, very slowly, I'll try to keep up."

Earl nodded, and his eyes went to Ben's hand. "Sure, Ben. It ain't so hard." After seeming to struggle with his thoughts, he finally added cautiously, "Me and Julio thought maybe you would want to bring in your own guys."

Ben's hazel eyes glinted, and a smile touched the corners of his lips. "And you figured they'd be white guys, right?"

Julio looked at him nervously, but Earl just grinned, his teeth gleaming against his smooth ebony face. "I heard that kind of thing happens. But you're a minority yourself." He held his thick hand up and commented, "Matter of fact, you're a minority of *one*. Didn't never meet a dude with a better grip than mine."

Ben shrugged. "There won't be a boss here. Just show me the best way the three of us can get this job done together."

"Yeah, well, we'll take it slow, Ben." Earl nodded.

The three of them spent all morning going over the play scene by scene. Once, when Ben stepped outside, Julio grinned and said, "I told you this dude would be all right, didn't I?"

The three of them left at 11 to get a sandwich. When they returned, they found the cast milling around the stage. Nero looked up. "All right, everybody, this is Ben Davis. He'll be taking Miller's place. It's a big job, so let's be patient. Do you think you'll be able to go through the play tomorrow, Ben?"

"Earl and Julio have been pretty good teachers this morning. Far as I'm concerned, we can try it now," Ben suggested.

A wave of surprise swept over Nero's face, but he nodded. "Sure, why not?"

Jonathan was standing close enough to whisper to Dani, "I'm not sure he can do it, but who knows? He's a stubborn fellow, isn't he?"

"He says I'm stubborn and he's firm."

Nero got them into their places, and once the play began, Dani realized that her nervousness was mostly gone. Like the rest of the cast, her mind was on the setting, which called for close timing to make the drama work. She found herself thinking more about Ben and his two helpers than she did about her own work. As a result, by the time the play was well on its way, Jonathan whispered to her when they met in the wings, "I knew you could do it, Danielle!"

When the final curtain fell, the cast gave a sudden cheer, and Dani found herself surrounded. "You were great! Magnificent!" Simon exclaimed.

Dani quickly deflected all their praise. "I think it's our set man who deserves an ovation." She looked around and saw Ben talking with Earl and Julio to the left of the stage.

"Right!" Nero said. "Hey, Ben, you did a wonderful job! Just great!"

Ben looked up, shrugged, and responded, "You don't need me. These two guys did the work. I just got in the way most of the time."

Dani didn't miss the appreciative expressions on the faces of the two stagehands, but they said nothing. The way Savage got along with people was a quality she envied.

"Let's break for dinner," Jonathan announced. "We'll go through the play again tonight, then twice tomorrow. I think if we try hard, we can be ready for opening night next Monday."

"Yeah, if nobody gets killed," Ringo Jordan said scowling. He wheeled suddenly and moved across the stage, disappearing behind the wings.

"Nothing's going to happen," Jonathan interjected quickly. "We'll have a guard here at all times." He spoke forcefully, but Dani sensed that he was covering up his own apprehension. She knew because she felt the same way.

♦ ♦ ♦

The next day was Wednesday. Ben had stayed at the Pearl until nearly 3 A.M. Earl and Julio had drilled him over and over on the mechanics of staging the play, and by the time the cast had finished the afternoon rehearsal, he felt that he could function adequately. The next two days went by swiftly. On Friday Jonathan had Nero issue the notice that the play would debut on Monday evening.

"It's a sellout," Tom Calvin told Dani the next day. "And not just for Monday, but for two weeks."

"How many are just coming to see somebody get killed?" Lyle asked sourly. He was in a bad mood, for Nero had been constantly critical of him for two days, picking at every fault in his performance. The strain showed, and Lyle's good looks were marred by the fatigue on his face.

"Quite a few, I would imagine," Tom answered. "The same way people stop to stare at a highway accident."

The three of them were sitting around a small table, drinking tea, waiting for Nero to signal the beginning of another rehearsal. Calvin said, "You're doing very well, Danielle!"

Lyle nodded, rousing from his bad mood long enough to give her a tired smile. "You sure are. Better than Amber in some ways."

The mention of the deceased woman threw a damper on the conversation. Finally Dani spoke. "I see we have our bodyguard with us." She referred to the uniformed policeman who stood talking with Ben Savage. He was middle-aged, with the beginnings of a paunch and a pair of disenchanted brown eyes. Dani added thoughtfully, "He's not exactly what I had in mind, but then again, no one man is going to be able to watch everyone."

"I don't think the killer will try again," Calvin opined. "Not just because a policeman's standing around all the time but because we're all keeping our eyes open."

Lyle muttered, "Well, if he *does* go after someone else, I've got a candidate for him! If Nero opens his mouth to me one more time, I'm going to knock his brains out!"

There was such a savage look on his face that both Calvin and Dani were taken aback. Jamison was so even-tempered that they hadn't suspected he had a violent streak. He gave them an odd look, then rose and walked away.

"What do you make of that?" Calvin asked in surprise.

"I don't think Lyle meant it," Dani said thoughtfully. "But he shouldn't say such things."

"It's still hard for me to believe that one of us is a killer. Not *you*, of course, Danielle," Tom added quickly. "Murder is something that only happens on the street—or at least I thought so until all this happened." He gave his shoulders a quick shake and asked, "Will you go to church with me again Sunday?"

"Yes." Dani nodded. "I like the minister. He's not very exciting, but he always gives me something to take home."

"All right, let's do it!" Nero called loudly, and Dani moved to her position.

The performance was excellent that night—by far the best they'd done since Dani's first rehearsal. It was one of those almost magic moments when the actors all found themselves doing more than reading lines. Dani had only known such a thing twice in her brief college stage career—when a play becomes almost alive as it unfolds itself. She forgot herself and her problems and for a brief time almost became the woman she portrayed. Others felt the same, and by the time the performance was over, they all felt a heightened sense of exhilaration.

Afterwards Jonathan looked around at the cast. "Well, folks, that's what it's all about, isn't it?"

"If we do half that well Monday night, we'll have a hit." Lily smiled.

"We will do even better!" Jonathan exclaimed. His eyes were afire, and he laughed. "I almost feel drunk! Ah, the power of the theater! Who needs alcohol when we have the theater?"

"Me!" Mickey Trask piped up. "Who'll go with me for a quick one at Leo's?"

The crowd broke up, and Dani went at once to her dressing

room. She was just about to change her clothes when she heard a muffled shout. Stepping to the door, she opened it and saw Mickey and Lyle coming out of their dressing rooms. "What's wrong, Lyle?" she called out.

"Don't know," he answered. "It sounded like Jonathan."

Dani left the dressing room, and as she sped along the rear of the backdrops, she saw Ben moving toward Ainsley's dressing room from the other side. They reached the door at the same time, and he let her go in first.

Ainsley was standing in the middle of the room, staring at the mirror with eyes wide open in stark fear.

Dani followed his gaze and saw a note taped to the mirror. Moving closer, she read it. Like the last one, it was made up of letters cut from magazines and glued on a single sheet of paper.

> "DEATH, A NECESSARY END, WILL COME WHEN IT WILL COME." IF THE PLAY GOES ON, A LIFE GOES OUT. MEMBERS OF THE CAST, WILL YOU DIE FOR A MONSTER LIKE JONATHAN AINSLEY? ONE OF YOU CERTAINLY WILL HAVE A "FINAL CURTAIN" IF THE PLAY GOES ON!

The bulky policeman suddenly appeared, commanding, "Don't touch that note! Not until the fingerprint men see it!"

Ainsley's face was pallid and his lips pulled tightly together. He shook his head but said nothing. He seemed about to faint, and Trask whispered, "Not again! Not again!"

"I'll call the station," Dani offered. As she went down the hall to call Goldman, she felt some of the weakness that had stricken Ainsley. She knew he would still insist on staging the play, and for the first time she realized that she herself might be the murderer's next victim. Her nerves under normal circumstances were firm, but as she walked quickly through the murky backstage area, she felt her shoulders tighten and quickened her pace.

Eight

A NORMAN ROCKWELL WORLD

Nobody left the theater, and Carmen spoke for them all when she said, "Now we go through the whole bit with the cops again!"

She wasn't wrong, for when Goldman arrived half an hour later he directed the print men to get what they could, then commandeered Ainsley's office. "Ainsley, you and Nero wait in another office while I see everybody else."

Dani waited in the lobby while he spoke to Lily. Mickey was flitting around nervously, asking questions no one could answer. So she was glad when Lily appeared, bearing the message, "He wants you next, Mickey." Trask went in and was out in less than five minutes. He left hurriedly, saying, "Hey, Ringo, Goldman says for you to come on in."

One by one the cast entered the office, none of them staying very long. Finally the Lockridges came through the door, Goldman having taken them together. As they passed by her, Sir Adrian said, "You can go in now, Danielle."

"What did he ask you?" Dani questioned.

"Oh, nothing really," Sir Adrian answered. "Where were you during the performance? Did you see anyone go into Ainsley's dressing room? Do you suspect anyone?" He shook his head, and a sudden gust of anger touched his eyes as he guided Victoria toward the exit door. "It's all quite hopeless, as I told him. Good night, my dear."

"Good night," Dani said and made her way to the office, where she found Goldman standing by the window looking outside. He turned as she entered, nodded, and greeted her. "I'm wasting my time. Anybody could have put that note on the mirror." He lit a cigarette, staring at her through the rising trail of smoke. "I don't suppose you want to confess?" he asked with a slight smile.

"Well, as a matter of fact, Lieutenant, I do."

His eyebrows lifted, and she found it difficult to tell him any more. "You're going to be very upset."

She paused, and he prodded her sharply, saying, "How about if I decide if I'm going to be upset. Just let it out."

"All right." She looked him straight in the eye and said firmly, "My name is really Dani Ross, and I'm a private investigator from New Orleans. Ainsley wanted someone to find out who was sending the threats, so he hired me to join the company. He, or actually we, thought it might be better if I stayed undercover."

Goldman pulled the cigarette from his lips, stared at it thoughtfully, then lifted his eyes to meet hers. "Nice, the way you let the police in on it," he said evenly. "We just love it when private eyes sneak into town to help us solve crimes."

He was very angry, she saw. She decided to make whatever defense she could. "At first there were only the letters. You wouldn't have been able to do much about it, would you? I know how overworked policemen are."

"It's good to know you're thinking of my welfare," Goldman answered flatly. "And when someone *did* get killed, you didn't think it was worth the trouble to let me know about yourself?" He turned and crushed the cigarette into a glass ash tray, then gave her an angry look. "I wonder how much influence I have. Like, do I have enough to get your license revoked?"

Dani attempted to placate him. "I can't blame you for being angry, Jake. I was wrong not to tell you earlier."

Her words surprised Goldman, and he stared at her for a long time. Finally he shook his head, but the anger had changed to irritation. "All right, I guess you can keep your two-bit license."

"Thanks, Jake," she said, then added rapidly, "One of my operatives is on the job with me. Ben Savage, or Ben Davis, as he's known here. He came in to take Miller's place with the sets. Ainsley thought it would be good to have some muscle on the stage, and Savage is good at that."

"Any more little goodies for me?"

Dani smiled in relief, for he was past the angry stage. "No, that's all. And really, Jake, you'll get it all from now on—everything we turn up." Then she frowned and shook her head. "Which isn't going to be a lot unless we do better than we have."

"What about the note? Any way you can pin down who put it there?"

"Not a chance! It's pandemonium behind those sets during a performance—the actors and the stagehands all falling over one another."

"But the note wasn't there when Ainsley first got to the theater, was it?"

"No. It was put there sometime during the last act. Jonathan doesn't go to his dressing room at all during that time. He's onstage almost the entire act, and usually he just stands in the wings and waits for his entrance. This was only a rehearsal, of course, but he wouldn't have had any reason to go to his dressing room."

"Somebody went there," Goldman growled. "People didn't go there much, did they? Into Ainsley's dressing room?"

"Oh no. And if I had seen someone going in—other than Jonathan, I mean—I would have noticed it."

"Well, I asked everyone about it, and each person says nobody went into that room."

"One of them is lying," Dani commented.

"Sure, but which one?" Goldman shook his head impatiently. "I've got a feeling about this thing. Whoever killed the woman, and tried to kill Lyle Jamison, isn't going to retire. These serial killers who write notes are playing games. 'Catch me if you can.' Got to be a big ego involved here," he said thoughtfully. "He's betting he's better than anyone else, that he can kill and get away with it."

"I suppose there's enough ego in this play to stock the world, Jake," Dani pointed out. "All show people have it."

"Yeah?" he grinned suddenly. "You too, Danielle?"

"I suppose so or I wouldn't be in this lousy play!"

He sobered, then asked, "Any ideas at all?"

"No, Jake. There are only two people in the cast whom *I know* are innocent—Ben Savage and me."

"What about Ainsley and Jamison? It was a close call with that chandelier, and they couldn't have cut that rope themselves."

He saw a flicker of doubt run over her features and waited until she framed an answer. It came slowly, reluctantly, as though she hated to put it into words. "I'm used to thinking objectively about crime, Jake. Always it's about somebody else. But now the thought keeps coming to me, *I'm one of the cast. I might be the next to be killed!* So it makes me a little overcautious. But I'm not letting anyone get behind my back until we have this killer behind bars."

Goldman nodded. "You have the right idea there. I'd hang on to it if I were you. Now, two things. Will you have dinner with me tomorrow night?"

"No. I go to church in the morning, and we rehearse in the afternoon, maybe until late."

"You have to eat." He shook his head, saying innocently, "I think you're anti-Semitic, Danielle."

"No, I'm not!"

He smiled lazily. "Only way to prove that is to have dinner with me."

Dani tried to think of an answer but couldn't. Though she knew he didn't mean what he'd said, she laughed and gave in. "All right, Jake. But I've never been out with a rich cop. I'll try to spend all your money."

"Fine with me. Now, tell Savage I want to see him. If he's tough enough and smart enough, maybe I can use him. I'm always in the market for good volunteers."

Dani left, calling to Savage, who was talking to Julio and Earl. "The lieutenant wants to see you, Ben." She moved away, wondering how the two would get along; she made a quick guess they wouldn't.

When Savage walked into the office, Goldman at once voiced his opinion. "Your boss just told me about your little setup here. Let me give it to you like I gave it to her—you two better let me know anything you find out, or I'll have you back in New Orleans eating fish bait so quick your head will swim!"

"Did you scare her as much as you're scaring me, Goldman?"

The lean policeman studied Savage, finally stating, "You must have been a cop at one time or another. There's always a little arrogance in cops."

"It's the way with us cops, isn't it?" Ben questioned in a bored tone. "You want to scare me some more with your fierce manner, or can I go get something to eat?"

Goldman studied him, then said, "Go eat. But first, I don't suppose you have any nominees for the psycho who's all set to knock the cast off?"

"This is going to be a tough one, Lieutenant," Ben noted soberly. "You could put a man to watch each member of the cast all the time, but that's a little impractical. As for clues, you've got the notes, the cut rope, and the gun that killed Amber LeRoi. But that's not enough, is it?"

"No." Goldman shook his head, admitting almost angrily, "I hate this kind of thing! Nothing to hang your hat on. Let me know if anything comes to light."

"Sure, Lieutenant." Savage left the office and found Carmen Rio talking with Earl and Julio. "You guys ready to eat?" he asked.

"You mean we ain't gonna get rousted by the law?" Earl demanded in mock amazement. "The revolution has come true, Julio!" He grinned. "This honkey gets pulled in by the cops, and us brothers don't even get questioned!"

"Honkey?" Ben asked, taking no offense. "I haven't heard that for years."

"I ain't kept up with the white folk cussin' like I should," Earl confessed.

"Yeah," Ben grinned facetiously, appreciating the man's act. "Now let's get those steaks I promised you."

"You fellas going to eat?" Carmen broke in.

"I bet them a steak I'd be as good as they are on the sets," Ben explained. "I lost." He gave her an inviting look. "Like to come along? You can keep these birds from picking on a poor redneck lad from the hills."

Carmen smiled, saying, "I'm starved! Let's go to Benji's."

"Benji's!" Julio answered at once. "That place is too rich for my blood."

"I'll cash in my war pension," Ben offered. "Lead the way, Carmen."

"Thought you was Mickey's main squeeze now, Carmen." Julio grinned.

"He doesn't own me!"

They took a cab across town to a steak house that spent a great deal of money on decor. They were met at the door by a snooty young woman who allowed them to follow her into a room not much smaller than the Colosseum. She said something that sounded like "The waierill bewith yousoon," then stalked away.

"Why's she talk funny?" Julio asked with his brow wrinkled.

"I think she's got an adenoids condition." Earl nodded wisely.

"No, she's been to some expensive school," Ben corrected him. "All those high-toned college girls talk like that."

The waiter came all prepared to give a sales pitch, but Ben said, "Bring us four good steaks." His abrupt manner insulted the waiter, who ignored him, asking, "And your wine?"

Carmen ordered a Margarita, and Earl and Julio called for the same. Savage gave the sour-faced waiter an innocent look. "I'll have a root beer—not too strong."

The waiter gave him another look, then turned and left, his back straight. "You hurt his feelings, Ben!" Carmen laughed. Then when the drinks came, she asked curiously, "You're not drinking anything?"

"No. I'm a drunk."

They all stared at him, and Carmen asked cautiously, "You mean you have a drinking problem?"

"No, Carmen, I mean I'm a drunk." He took a sip of his root beer and noticed they were all staring at him. "What's the matter, you never saw a drunk before?"

"Oh, yeah." Earl nodded quickly. "I seen about a million, but I never heard anyone come right out and *admit* it."

"I guess you're trying to say you're an alcoholic, ain't you, Ben?" Julio said. He seemed eager to put the matter in the right perspective. "I'm one myself. It's just a sickness, you know, Ben."

"No, Julio . . ." Ben looked around the room with interest, then back to the other three. "I'm not an alcoholic. I'm a drunk."

"Well," Carmen asked in a puzzled tone, "what's the difference?"

"The difference is that us drunks don't have to go to the meetings." Ben shrugged.

Carmen leaned forward, her eyes searching Ben's face. "But if you're a drunk, why aren't you drinking?"

"Don't like the stuff," Ben explained. "Gives me a headache."

"So you're a drunk who don't get drunk?" Earl asked. "Now that's cool!"

The drinks came quickly and then the steaks. They all ate hungrily. After they were finished, Carmen asked, "How was the steak, Ben?"

"Real good," he said. "Better than the one I get at Mom's Cafe back home."

"Where's home?" Carmen wanted to know.

"All over. My dad died before I was born, and my mom's been in an institution for years. So I lived here and there ever since I was a kid."

"Me too," she murmured. The room was dim, but a small combo was playing, and three couples made use of a postage-size dance floor. "Dance with me, Ben," Carmen entreated.

He got to his feet, and she walked into his arms, saying nothing the whole time they moved across the floor. She was soft and fragrant, but he wondered what she was really like on the inside. She was short, and she leaned her cheek against his shoulder. She whispered, "I like a man who doesn't talk all the time. Actors gab too much, usually about themselves." When the music stopped and they went back to the table, she said, "It's too early to hit the sack. Let's go someplace else."

"Hey, Julio, we could take them to Jimmy's Hideout," Earl suggested.

They left and went to Jimmy's, then to three other places. By the time they left the last one, in Greenwich Village, Earl commented, "I'm starting to talk the way drunks do, you know?"

"Yeah," Julio nodded, observing the others with an owlish interest. "I think you *are* drunk, Earl. I'd better get you home before you fall down. Lemme help you."

As he said this, he sagged, and Earl grabbed him. Holding him in one mighty arm, he winked at the others. "Yeah, I can't stand up, Julio. You better help me." Then he added, "You two be okay? I'll see you at rehearsal tomorrow."

Savage and Carmen watched the two make their way down the street, Earl practically carrying Julio. "Pretty good eggs," Ben decided. "Where do you live, Carmen? I'm lost myself, so I might as well take you home and start from there."

Her eyes were slightly unfocused, but she drew herself up, commanding, "No, you first. Call me a taxi."

"You're a taxi!" Ben exclaimed, then laughed, adding, "I always wanted to say that!" A few minutes later, he helped her get in, then entered himself and gave his address to the driver.

She said little during the ride, but when he got out and paid the driver, she followed him, saying, "Let's go up to your place for a while."

The cab driver, a thin man with thick glasses, gave Savage a wink and took his money. "Some got it, some don't got it," the cabbie yelled out the window as he pulled away.

"It's pretty late, Carmen," Ben warned, but she shook her head. "All right, but you've got to go home soon."

"You sound like my old man," she muttered. She stumbled several times as they moved along the sidewalk. He held her up, guiding her into the elevator, then leaning her against the wall while he found his key. She followed him inside and looked around the apartment. It consisted of a combination sitting room and tiny kitchenette and a bedroom just large enough for one bed, one dresser, and a bath.

"I'll fix some coffee," he offered and moved toward the kitchen.

As he made it, she watched him sleepily. When the coffee was ready, he poured two cups. "Sugar?" he asked. When she answered, "Black," he took the cups carefully to the couch. She took hers, drank a swallow, then reached over for her purse, which was on the floor. She pulled a leather-covered silver flask from it and gave him a crooked grin. "I'm a drunk too, Ben." She removed the top, poured some liquor into her cup, and carefully put the flask down. "But I guess I really *am* a drunk. Not like you. You're lying." She swallowed the liquid, then said, "You're a funny guy, Ben."

"About average, I guess."

"No. It only took you about two days to learn all those sets. That's not average. And you don't make passes. I was waiting for that. We all were."

"Who's 'all,' Carmen?"

"Why, me and Lily and Danielle," she explained in surprise. "Lily and I made book on which one of us you'd hustle first." She picked up the flask, took a long pull at it, then lowered it. "I sorta thought it'd be me. But you don't make passes, do you, Ben?"

"Don't bet on that."

She sat there, her eyelids heavy. There was a pause between her sentences when she spoke, as though she had the lines down, but the messages from the brain had trouble getting through. With her smooth features and full figure, she was an intensely attractive woman. Her entire manner revealed that she was accustomed to being pursued by men. As she sat there, her dark eyes studied Savage carefully.

"I know men pretty well," she bragged. Taking another drink, she swayed slightly, adding, "Too well maybe." Her eyelids drooped, and she brought them up with an effort. Her eyes were slightly out of focus. "Whatsa matter?" she demanded suddenly. "I'm not good enough for you?"

Ben shook his head. "You're drunk, Carmen. Time to go home."

She seemed not to hear him and went on in a sullen fashion, "Not good enough! Not good enough for him!" She began to mutter and shook her head angrily. "Thinks he can get rid of me! But he can't!"

Ben asked quietly, "Who can't, Carmen?"

"You know! Everybody knows!" She began to cry, and he reached out and pulled her to her feet.

"Let me take you home, Carmen."

"No! Don't wanna go home," she muttered. She put her arms around his neck and whispered, "Love me, Jonathan! Love me like you used to!"

Savage held her up, and she held tightly to him. As he tried to figure out how he would get her into a taxi, she passed out, going limp in his arms. With a sigh, he placed her on the couch, then went to the bedroom and pulled back the bedcovers. Returning, he scooped her up, carried her to the bedroom, and deposited her on the bed. He pulled off her shoes and went to the closet for the extra blanket he'd stored there. Snatching a pillow off the bed, he went back to the living room and tossed both onto the couch.

For a long time he sat drinking coffee and thinking about the complications of the case. Finally he lay down and was just drifting off when he heard Carmen calling. He rolled off the couch and moved to the bedroom. It was dark, but he could see by the light from the living room that she was rolling around in a frenzied manner. When he stooped to take her arm, she cried out, "You killed her! You killed Amber!"

Ben stopped his attempts to awaken her. He asked softly, "Who killed Amber, Carmen?"

She shook her head, and her eyes were wide open. "I—I saw you! I saw you put the real bullets in the gun!"

A great tremor shook her body, and she cried out, "Sir Adrian! Sir Adrian! Why did you do it? Why did you kill Amber?" Abruptly she shut her eyes, moaned, and seemed to slip back into a restless sleep.

For a long time Ben stood there, looking down at Carmen. Finally he went back to the couch and sat there. He stared at the wall for ten minutes, trying to put what Carmen had said into perspective. But the more he thought about it, the less sense it made. Finally he lay down and went to sleep.

When he awoke the next morning, Carmen was gone. Rubbing his stiff neck, he thought about what she had said in her drunken stupor. *Not enough to convict anybody, but enough to make Lockridge a suspect*, he thought.

◆ ◆ ◆

Though she had only visited Tom Calvin's church a few times, Dani had gotten over the feeling of being a visitor. On the Sunday before the play was to open, prior to the service the pastor had come down the aisle and greeted her. Tom introduced her. "This is Danielle Morgan. She's in the cast of *Out of the Night.*"

"Oh, yes. I have two tickets for the performance tomorrow," Reverend Edwards exclaimed. "I'm an old fan of Jonathan Ainsley's. I wish you'd ask him to come to church with you."

"I will," Dani agreed confidently. She expressed her appreciation for his sermons and sat with Tom during the service, contented and at peace. Afterward they went to eat at a nearby cafeteria that featured Italian food. As Dani downed a healthy serving of spaghetti, she said, "I love to go to church. I know many find church to be outdated or irrelevant, and some even think God is no longer around to hear or help us, but they're wrong, aren't they?"

Calvin grinned at her. "Yes. God hasn't abandoned us. I thought so for a long time, but when I was converted, it was like someone had turned on a light."

Dani leaned back, thought about that, then nodded. "What a

nice way to put it, Tom!" Then she looked at her watch, saying ruefully, "Time to go to rehearsal. I wish we didn't have to."

"You're a funny kind of actress, Danielle," Tom remarked as he helped her put on her coat. "All the Broadway breed I've known have been totally self-centered."

"Oh, I'm not much different," she quickly protested. When they were on the street heading toward the theater, she asked idly, "What about your family, Tom? Do you have a large one?"

"No, just one sister and a few cousins."

"What about your father? You said once that he and Jonathan were great friends."

"Yes, I guess they were once." Tom clenched his hands so tightly, they turned white. Grimly he continued, "Dad was a very gentle man. And when Jonathan was an unknown, my father took him in."

"How nice!" Dani affirmed. "You must have loved him very much." Then she asked tentatively, "How did your father die?"

"Of neglect!" Tom's lips quivered, and he said nothing for a few moments. Bitterly he cried out, "Dad got sick, and we were always pretty broke. He called Jonathan and asked for help. I was there when he called. I'll never forget it, Danielle! Dad spoke to him, and when he hung up the phone, he had the most beautiful smile on his face. He said, 'It's all right now, Tom! Jonathan is going to help me!'"

Dani waited for him to go on, but when he remained silent, she prompted him, "What happened, Tom?"

"Nothing!" he snapped, his eyes narrowing. "Dad died without a word from his good friend, the great man Jonathan Ainsley! He promised to help but didn't do a thing."

Tom suddenly shook his head. "I—I didn't mean to dump all this on you, Danielle. I've never told anyone else about it."

She put her hand on his arm. "That must have been terrible. The hardest thing for a Christian is forgiving a person who's hurt someone you love, isn't it?"

He seemed anxious to change the subject, and they talked about the play. When they got to the Pearl, it was time for rehearsal to begin, and she had no further chance to speak with him.

It was a good rehearsal. Afterward the cast gathered to listen to Nero tell them briefly about opening night. Then Jonathan gave them a few words of encouragement.

Dani went to her dressing room and changed out of her costume, then left, thinking about the opening performance. As she passed from backstage to the outer stage, she heard a woman speaking angrily, then saw Carmen being held by the detective, Jack Sharkey.

"Let me go, you dirty cop!" Carmen cried as she tried to break away. But the big man held on tightly. Dani moved toward them, but Ben was already there.

"Let the lady go," he ordered quietly.

Sharkey moved with amazing speed for a big man. He let loose of Carmen and threw a punch that caught Ben high on the temple, knocking him to the floor. Ringo Jordan appeared suddenly from the left side of the stage. He moved toward the policeman with a slight shuffle, his left fist raised and his right arm bent close to his body.

Sharkey laughed hoarsely. "Come on, you has-been! I'll cream you!" He threw a vicious punch at Jordan, who picked it off easily with his left hand, then sent a solid right into Sharkey's stomach. The blow made a slight booming noise, and the policeman's mouth opened, but no sound came out, and his lungs began to heave as he tried to breathe. Ringo grabbed him by the shoulders, whirled him around, and hauled him off as easily as if Sharkey had been a ten-year-old.

Carmen ran to Ben, who was getting up slowly. "Ben, are you hurt?"

"No," he assured her. "What was that all about?"

Seeing Carmen step to Ben's side, Dani wanted to go to him, but she knew that would expose their undercover roles. She was about to go her way but heard Carmen say, "Oh, nothing. He's just a womanizer." In a lower voice, Dani heard her add, "Ben, I left my purse in your apartment. Did you find it after I left this morning?"

Dani missed a step, then hurried off, not hearing Ben's reply. She didn't look back, and when two or three people spoke to her she didn't hear them. Outside she turned and walked blindly down the street, heedless of her destination. She came to a red light and waited for it to change. As she started to cross, she felt a hand on her arm.

Whirling, she turned to find Ben standing beside her. The streetlight cast uneven shadows over his square face. He was looking at her intently, and she felt like a fool. "What is it?" she demanded.

"You're going the wrong way," he pointed out. "Your apartment is the other way."

"I'm going to do a little shopping," she said. "Let go of my arm."

"I need a few things myself," he commented. "But isn't this a bit pricey?" He stared into the window of an exclusive dress shop. "When they're this fancy, not even daring to have price tags, you have to watch out, boss. I bet this little number would take your whole paycheck." He nodded at a white evening outfit.

She stared at him, then shrugged. "All right, so I'm angry."

"No, you're *jealous*," he corrected her. "You don't want me, but you don't want any other woman to have me either. Kind of like that dog in one of Aesop's fables—he wouldn't let the oxen eat the hay even though he wouldn't eat the hay himself."

"Jealous!" Dani's voice cracked a little, and she forced herself to laugh. "You have the most enormous ego, Ben Savage."

"We did this scene once before," he commented. "Reminds me of when I first worked for you—on the Case Bearings affair. I had to get some information from a woman. Remember what happened?"

Dani did remember. She had gone to Ben's room and found him with a coarse woman of the street—and had fired him on the spot. Later she discovered he had been getting the woman to agree to testify for one of their clients.

Ben saw the memory come into her eyes.

"All right, so Carmen stayed all night at your apartment," she said, forcing herself to be calm. "I'm not interested in your personal life!"

"You're not?" he exclaimed in surprise. "I'm interested in yours, boss. But do we have to stand here in the middle of the street? Can't we have a cup of coffee or something?"

She nodded stiffly. They found a small cafe around the corner. The coffee wasn't very good, but the place was almost empty. As they sat in a booth in the rear, he gave her the details of the preceding evening. "She was pretty well out of it, but she fingered Sir Adrian. You can make whatever you want of all that."

Dani sipped the bitter coffee, then shook her head. "I don't buy it."

"Why not? Lockridge had a motive. Matter of fact," Ben pronounced slowly, "he had *two* motives. He hated Ainsley for the way he's treated him, and he admitted to you that Amber almost ruined his life and his marriage. Now Amber's dead, and Jonathan's been charged with murder."

Dani shook her head. "I know, Ben, but . . . do *you* think he did it?"

Savage looked down at the tablecloth. "I don't know, Dani. Carmen hates Ainsley too. She could have staged that scene last night."

"But she doesn't know we're detectives."

"No, but she knows the police are looking for a nice suspect to fry, and she might hope that I'll spill the beans to Goldman."

Dani bit her lip, thinking hard. "This can't go on for long, Ben. Either somebody will figure out we're undercover or the killer will get Ainsley."

"You've got that right," Ben agreed slowly. "Look, I have an idea. If we can prove that Lockridge had some live .38 shells, we could tell Goldman. Sir Adrian has insisted all along he's never bought any shells, never even shot a gun."

"How can we find out a thing like that?"

"I can burgle his apartment, of course," he announced.

"Ben, you'd go to jail if you got caught!"

"Then I'd better not get caught," he said. "Look, it's easy. You lure the Lockridges out of their apartment, and I'll burgle it. They like you, don't they? Take advantage of that."

"Ben, I don't like it."

"It's the only game in town. And here's something else—I might just come up with the typewriter that was used for the first notes." He saw the hesitation in her face and insisted, "Look, boss, it's time to play hardball. I like the old couple too, but that doesn't mean a thing. They say Hitler loved dogs. We've got to dig up something!"

Dani sighed, then nodded. "You're right, Ben. I'll do it. Maybe I can get them to go out for lunch Tuesday."

"Tell them you're nervous," he suggested. "They're too nice to turn you down."

"And while I'm buying their lunch, you'll be looking for evidence that will send Sir Adrian to jail for the rest of his life."

Ben stared at her. "You're all mixed up again, boss. This is the real world, not the one Norman Rockwell painted. He always showed the kind of world he wanted—nice old ladies saying grace at the truck stop, puppies, kids in love. But he never once painted a picture of some drunk on Skid Row or a teenage girl shooting heroin."

Dani dropped her head, then lifted it. "I know the world's hard, Ben. I just like to see the other side of it."

He grew gentle then and patted her hand. "Sure, so do I, but a killer is on the loose, boss, and the best thing we can do is put him away. That's the way we make our living." He sat there, staring at the street. "Better hang on to that Christian faith you have, Dani," he warned. "It's tough making it work in the Big Apple!"

Nine

A SLIGHT CASE OF BURGLARY

The hours seemed to race by for Dani, and Monday night found her standing in the wings, waiting for the curtain to go up. Nothing seemed real, though, and a thought floated through her mind, one that made her remember the old *Twilight Zone* reruns. Her real world had gotten lost in some sort of time warp, she imagined, and she and all the other members of the cast were caught in some sort of terrible situation for all eternity, playing the same role over and over again.

Then Jonathan's voice broke through, and her mind returned to the sounds and smells of the Pearl Theater. "You'll be fine, Danielle, just fine." Jonathan's face was filled with excitement, the way it always was when he was about to perform. The curtain went up, and he moved onto the stage and was greeted by a sudden explosion of applause. Dani watched as he stood there in the bright lights, a handsome, dramatic figure, his head inclined as the ovation swept over the theater.

Dani caught a movement to her right and saw Mickey Trask caught in a moment's repose. His still face and the turn of his lips showed bitterness, a dissatisfaction that was reflected by a sudden gesture. He slapped his hands together, and she heard him mutter, "The great man!" When he realized Dani was watching him, he smiled cheerfully, then frowned and said, "He's an awful man, but most people don't see that, do they?" He looked out on the stage again and said quietly, "They don't have to work for him."

Reflecting on Mickey's words, Dani felt his hand on her shoulder and heard him say, "Go get 'em!" She walked out into the light, and for an instant her mind seemed to stop. Jonathan walked toward her, kissed her cheek, and spoke his first line to her, and then it all fell into place.

She spoke her lines and moved around the stage, unconsciously falling into the patterns Simon Nero had drilled into her. He had asked her once what she thought about when she was performing, and after a moment's reflection she explained, "Why, nothing, Simon—I mean nothing except the lines and the movement."

"That the way it's supposed to be." He had nodded. "It's what all the great ones can do. The ones who aren't great are busy in their heads with their own business—what they'll do after the performance, or *How do I look in this new costume?* But a real actor or actress is able to set all that aside for a brief moment and live the character. When it becomes real for an actor or actress, it becomes real for the audience."

Dani didn't think of that now as the scenes rolled by. She left the stage at the right moment, waited for her next cue, then went back again. With part of her mind during her moments offstage she was aware that several policemen were watching including Goldman and Jack Sharkey, and the stagehands were in constant motion performing their complicated art. From time to time someone spoke to her, but so great was her concentration that when the play moved to its end and the curtain fell, a slight shock passed over her as she returned from the world of make-believe to reality.

Jonathan took a bow and moved toward her. Taking her by the hand, he led her onto the stage, announcing to all, "You so often hear the line I am about to say that you may automatically discount it. I beg that you do not, for it is truth, right from my heart." He suddenly kissed Dani's hand and went on, "If it were not for this young woman, I doubt that I would be on this stage at this moment, for her courage and talent have given me the heart to continue."

Dani curtseyed as applause filled the theater, then moved back as the rest of the cast was introduced. *He handles himself so well on stage*, she thought. *No one would ever believe the tensions that exist between Jonathan and most of the cast.*

Finally the curtain closed, and Dani went to her dressing room. Goldman stopped by to say, "I'm impressed." He stood there, a handsome figure, sharp-eyed and competent. With a smile he admitted, "I was pretty nervous tonight, and I don't usually get that way. But you were as cool as a piece of ice. No fear at all."

"That's not hard when you have something else to think of, Jake," she rationalized.

"Go out with me for a bite?" he offered.

"I'm pretty tired," she said. "Another night perhaps."

"Sure." He left at once, and she appreciated his recognizing her fatigue. She changed into her street clothes, and as she was putting on fresh lipstick, a knock sounded. "Come in," she invited.

Savage opened the door, came in, and said quietly, "Everybody's going to Twenty-One. Ainsley's got some sort of celebration planned."

"That club's not quite my style," she hedged. "Are you going?"

"No," he said, then grinned. "Not to change the subject, but don't forget—I'm going to burgle the Lockridge place tomorrow at noon. You want a report on what I find?"

"They won't be there," she assured him. "They turned me down because they have a previous date. Come to my place when you're done. And be careful," she advised. "We don't need you in jail, Ben." He slipped away, and Dani finished her makeup, then left the Pearl with Jonathan, who had agreed to drop her off on his way to the club. In his excitement the actor wanted to talk about the performance, but Dani was a poor audience since her mind kept thinking about Savage and his planned breaking and entering.

The next day Ben got into the year-old Escort he had rented. He had gotten tired of subways and taxis and had already made one trip to the Upper East Side apartment building where Lockridge and his wife lived. It was a large, buff-brick high-rise with a tight security system.

Now, parking the car a block away, he moved down the street, walking right by the front entrance without so much as a glance at the uniformed doorman who stood just inside the glass doors. As soon as he was out of sight, he moved rapidly to the side entrance, where a sign indicated SERVICE ENTRANCE. The door was locked, as he had expected. So he rang the bell, then waited.

The door opened, and a middle-aged woman in a dark blue uniform opened the door. She wore thick glasses and asked in a voice that had a faint English accent, "What is it?"

Ben opened his wallet and held it up for her to see. "Bell Security Systems, ma'am. Time to replace the solenoid batteries."

"We didn't send for you," she said with a puzzled frown.

"No, ma'am, but this is part of our regular service. The batteries are good for two years, but we like to check them every quarter just in case. If they go out, the whole system is out of working order."

He had spent half an hour making the card with a set of rubber letters that fit into a stamp. The words BELL SECURITY SYSTEMS were printed on the back of his regular card, ROSS INVESTIGATION AGENCY. It was one of the handiest pieces of his equipment, and he had often wondered that a piece of paper had so much power and authority. Once he had told Dani that he thought it was possible to get into the War Room of the Pentagon with a handmade card.

He stood there, looking bored, and as he expected, the woman said, "All right, come on in."

"It'll take about an hour to check all the systems," he told her as he stepped inside.

"Do you need keys for the apartments?"

"No, ma'am."

"Well, I can't go with you. Let me know if you need anything."

"Sure will." Ben walked briskly away, and the woman went to

a door marked MANAGER. At once he took the elevator to the tenth floor, got off, and saw that nobody was in the hall. Going to apartment 1004, he bent down and peered at the lock. He took a small leather case from his inside pocket, then removed several stainless steel picks. As he worked on the lock, he thought of Manny Sears, the cat burglar who'd taught him to pick locks. He'd helped Manny defend himself against a bum rap, and Sears had been glad to pay him off by giving him a course in picking locks. He moved the sliver of steel carefully until a tiny *click* sounded. Quickly he turned the knob, opened the door, and stepped inside.

When he turned on the light, he saw that Sir Adrian and Lady Victoria lived very well indeed. The apartment was spacious, with one wall cloaked by a large velvet curtain. He looked behind it and saw that it was a nice view of the New York skyline. A pair of double doors opened onto a small balcony that had a round, wrought-iron table and four chairs.

The other walls were lined with walnut bookcases and wainscoting made of the same material. Pale mauve walls, above the wainscoting, held original paintings, mostly landscapes from an English school. The furniture was white leather, and the tables hand-carved rosewood.

Savage went through the living room efficiently, finding nothing of interest, then passed through a door that led to a suite composed of a very large bedroom, a study, and a bath. The bedroom had two full-sized double beds, more bookcases, and walls lined with pictures of the couple. Many of them were enlarged snapshots of the Lockridges with famous people. Moving from print to print, Ben recognized Peter Sellers, Laurence Olivier, a young Richard Burton, and a great many others he didn't know.

He moved into the bathroom, not expecting to find much, but going through the motions. There were two medicine cabinets. One, apparently Victoria's, was sparsely furnished, containing only aspirin, some shampoo, and a laxative. But the other was crowded with pill bottles of every size and shape. Ben read the labels on some of them but didn't recognize most of them. But one marked *nitro-*

glycerine caught his eye. "Maybe Sir Adrian has heart trouble," he muttered, putting it back.

The study he saved for last. Piles of magazines and newspapers were stacked along one wall; on a small table lay a scrapbook, a pair of scissors, and rubber cement. He flipped over the scrapbook and saw that it was filled with articles about their plays. What surprised him was that the magazines were not just on drama but on a variety of subjects. He moved his eyes toward the desk, and the first thing he saw was a new portable typewriter. The threatening notes had been typed on an old typewriter. "It's never as easy as you want it to be," he muttered, beginning to search the drawers of the rolltop oak desk. One of the Lockridges was methodical, for everything was neat and in order. Receipts, insurance notices, and warranties were all neatly tagged in place. The checkbook showed a lower figure than he might have guessed, but they probably had stocks and bonds.

There were no signs of guns or ammunition in the chests or bedside table, but in the small study he saw a glass case with an old revolver, a .38, and a strange-looking knife with an odd, wicked-looking curve. He opened the case and, using a handkerchief, examined the revolver. It was ancient and dry, with a few flecks of rust on the cylinder. *Probably wouldn't even fire,* he thought. But he found no ammunition, not even a box of pellets. Savage carefully replaced everything and went toward the door. With his hand on the knob, he stood there, thinking hard. He hated to be defeated, and somehow he had been certain that he'd turn up *something*. He let his mind wander over the apartment, trying to come up with a hiding place. Nothing.

As he turned the knob, he thought, *Receipts all tagged and in place.* It was a long shot, and he was beginning to fear that the pair might come back before he left, but he quickly returned to the study and opened one of the drawers. A thick sheaf of small slips of paper was bound together by a rubber band. He slipped it off and saw that the receipts were chronologically arranged beginning with January 1. He skipped the first two months, then began looking at each slip. He let himself hope a little when he found a receipt from a drugstore for thirty-seven cents. That meant they didn't throw *anything* away. Carefully he thumbed through the stack, noting that some of them were cash register slips that gave no legible reading of the actual purchase. Most of these, however, were from shops that wouldn't sell ammunition anyway.

His eye suddenly picked up the words *Empire Sporting Goods*, and then he saw the words "box of Remington .38 shells." The date was March 12. *Just a few days before LeRoi was killed*, Ben remembered. He took down the date of the sale and the time, replaced the receipts, and left the apartment.

On the way down in the elevator, he saw nobody and left by the service entrance. He drove straight to Dani's apartment and parked the Escort. A new Lincoln Town Car was parked right in front, and he recognized it as Goldman's. After hesitating briefly, he entered the building and went to her apartment. When he rang the bell, Dani opened at once.

"Come in, Ben," she said. "I've got coffee on."

"Hello, Ben." Goldman nodded. He sat on the single easy chair, holding a cup in his hand. When Dani came back with Ben's cup of black coffee, Goldman said, "I'm off duty. How'd your visit go?"

"No ammo in the place," Ben said. He took a sip of the hot coffee, then added, "But there was a receipt from Empire Sporting Goods for a box of .38 shells."

"When were they bought?" Dani asked quickly.

"Two-fifteen in the afternoon on March twelfth."

"You brought it with you?" Goldman questioned.

"No."

Goldman looked relieved. "Good! As long as he doesn't get rid of it, we can get a search warrant and pick it up."

"He's a real methodical guy." Ben shook his head. "I'd guess he keeps every scrap of paper he gets his hands on."

"Pretty dumb to keep this one," Goldman said. "But they all do something dumb." He looked at the pair and shrugged. "The receipt doesn't give us enough to nail him, of course."

"No, but it's enough to make us watch him, Jake," Dani pointed out. "That was a good idea, Ben. Do you have anything more?"

"Well, I guess it wouldn't be too smart to search everybody's place, would it?"

"No." She smiled. "But at least now I feel as if we've done a little something to earn our money."

"Will you tell Ainsley?" Goldman asked.

"Oh, yes, it's his money."

Ben was staring at the wall. "There's something else about that place that should mean something, but I can't get a handle on it." He frowned, then rubbed the scar on his forehead. "Maybe it'll come later." He finished his coffee, rose, and turned to the door. "See you later."

Surprised by the detective's quick departure, Goldman asserted, "He's pretty swift, Ben is." A question framed itself in his eyes, and he asked, "You two are pretty close, I guess?"

"Well, in a way, Jake. Ben saved my life in that Maxwell Stone case. I'm grateful to him for that."

"That all of it?"

She shifted her body, and he saw that the question had disturbed her, which didn't surprise him. Goldman had been intrigued by Danielle more than by most women. He liked women, and his good looks and quick wit alone would have assured popularity with them; but his money made him even more sought after. Keener than average discernment made him an excellent police officer, but it also helped him read the smiles of the many women in his life. Most of them were shallow, and he could never be certain if they loved him or his money.

But he realized that Danielle was different. At first he had written her off as simply cold, but he quickly corrected that first impression. She was quiet for the most part, but he was aware that beneath her smooth manner lay a hunger for life. Some of this was reflected in the expression of her gray-green eyes that at times seemed too large for her face; when she was excited, they took on a special sparkle. Her mouth was large and sensitive, but her nose was too short for real beauty, he decided, and her face a little too squarish.

He asked suddenly, "Do you think of me as a man you might fall in love with?"

Taken off guard, she stared at him, finally shaking her head firmly. "I don't really believe in 'falling in love,' Jake." Dani leaned back on the couch and drew her feet beneath her in a girlish way. She said no more but let the silence run on. That was one of the things about Danielle that intrigued Jake Goldman—her ability to allow silence in a conversation. Most women, he had noticed, felt that somebody had to be talking all the time.

"You don't believe in love?" he prompted. "I thought everyone did."

"I didn't say I didn't believe in love, Jake," she responded. "It's the *falling* part I have a problem with. It's the kind of word you use for a physical action, like, 'The carpenter fell down the cellar steps.'"

Goldman grinned. "Well, don't you think love can be like that? I have a few scars to prove it."

"It's too much like a Hollywood cliché," Dani explained. "You've seen the old movies. A man is walking along, and he sees a girl. Their eyes meet, and they fall in love. They've never seen each other before in their whole lives and know nothing about each other. He may be a student of Etruscan pottery who spends his life in pursuit of knowledge, and she may be a brainless chorus girl, but that doesn't mean a thing! They've fallen in love!" She smiled at his expression, but she meant her words seriously. "According to that kind of thinking, love is some sort of chemical reaction."

"Well, there's something to that, I think." He leaned forward, his eyes alert. "Don't some men repel you from the first and others turn you on?"

"Turn me on?" Dani responded. "That's just as bad as 'falling in love'! What am I, some kind of light switch?"

"Come on now! You'll never make me believe that some guys haven't had that something that awakens the woman in you. The new feminists have finally admitted that gals get some sort of sexual charge from looking at men."

Dani met his gaze and said evenly, "Yes, there's that. God made us that way, didn't He? We have all kinds of hungers, and a hunger is made to be satisfied."

Goldman shifted uneasily, then asked, "Let me put it bluntly. Do you ever feel what the preachers call 'lust'? And remember, I'm a trained policeman accustomed to getting the truth out of suspects."

Dani's eyes were bright, and she asked with a trace of humor in her voice, "What do you suspect me of, officer? Being human? I plead guilty. Do I get hungry? Yes, I do. Do I eat anything that falls before me? No. Do I feel desire for a man? Certainly! I'd be worried if I didn't."

"I'm glad to hear that!" Goldman said. He came across to the couch and with one swift, practiced movement put his arms around her. She lifted her head to speak, but he put his lips on hers. Her perfume was faint but enticing, and the closeness of her body as he held her stirred him. But she pulled back, saying, "You're a good kisser, Jacob. I can tell you've had lots of experience."

He stared at her, frustrated but not angry. "You're a piece of work, Danielle!" he exclaimed; then he grinned. "Why do I feel so good when I've been thrown to the wolves?"

"You haven't been thrown to anything, Jake." Dani smiled. "But you have lots of bad ideas about love."

"Really?" he asked, leaning back to watch her. "Give me a quick rundown on the nature of true love."

"Oh, don't be silly!" she exclaimed as she stood to her feet. "Go home, Jake. I'm ready to drop with fatigue."

"No lesson from the teacher?" he pleaded as he rose.

She pushed him to the door but paused as a thought touched her. "Well, maybe just one. Love is not a single thing, Jake. It's not just physical, and it's not just emotional or spiritual."

His dark eyes studied her. "I think you're trying to tell me that I'm a carnal person, aren't you, Danielle? That all I know about is bedding down with some broad."

She shook her head. "I don't know you well enough to make that judgment, Jake. But I know love isn't a case of flu, which is what Hollywood and the writers of those awful 'romance' novels try to project."

"A case of flu?"

"Sure. Ask most guys or gals what love is, and they'll say, 'Well, it's when my knees get a little shaky, and I breathe hard, and I feel feverish, and I can't think very well.'" She opened the door and pushed him out, explaining, "That's the flu, and you get over that in a few days." Then she grew very serious, her eyes fixed on him. "I'm saying, Jake, that when I love a man it'll take more than a healthy body. I've got to have what's on the inside. Then when the outside begins to get old, I'll have the man who's real! End of lesson. Good night, Lieutenant."

Goldman walked out to his Lincoln, got in, and turned the key. But before he pulled away, he looked upward to where a light burned in a window and grinned. "A case of flu!" he murmured. Then he laughed and drove away at top speed.

Ten

MIDNIGHT ENCOUNTER

Tuesday afternoon the cast met at the Pearl at the request of Simon Nero. He worked through some rough spots, but they were interrupted by Tom Calvin, who came in with the papers. "Review time!" he cried, and they all gathered around, grabbing at the editions of the various New York papers.

Dani took no part in the excitement, but she saw that for the others the reviews were almost a life-and-death matter. On the whole they were very good, and Ainsley, of course, attracted the most praise. He read aloud a flattering review, his face beaming with happiness. "Look here," he shouted. "Maynard Hines says we'll be sold out for the rest of the year! I never could stand Maynard, but I'll always like him now."

Calvin came over to stand beside Dani, noting her lack of participation. "Not interested in what the critics have to say about your performance, Danielle?"

She shrugged. "I'm not sure I want to know, Tom."

"But it's *good!*" he said in a pleased voice. Spreading the paper out so she could see, he read aloud:

> One of the surprise treats was the performance of Danielle Morgan, who played the role of Marian Powers. The role itself is not difficult, but stepping into a play at the last minute—and in such trying circumstances—is always a challenge. The most one can expect, in most cases of this sort, is adequacy. Miss Morgan, however, possesses at least

> a trace of intensity, which carries over into her role. She never once fell into the trap of overplaying the part (which would be a temptation even for a veteran!), and in the scene where she is shot by the star, the audience held its breath. It was impossible not to think that the last time this scene was enacted, it resulted in the death of Amber LeRoi. But Miss Morgan refused to succumb to the temptation of trading on that bit of human drama, relying instead on a range of expression both in voice and body action that has great promise. The only flaw in her performance was the love scenes with Jonathan Ainsley, which proved rather insipid.

Dani gave Calvin a quick smile. "That 'trace of intensity,' Tom, is unmitigated nervousness."

"I don't think so," he disagreed.

Ainsley had come over, smiling at her. "So our love scenes are 'insipid,' are they? Well, we'll have to put some fire into them, won't we, Danielle?"

"Congratulations, Jonathan," Dani offered. "I'm glad the critics appreciated your play and your performance."

"Critics!" Ainsley said with contempt. "I like what Mark Twain wrote about them: 'The trade of critic, in literature, music, and the drama, is the most degraded of all trades.'"

"But we all grab the papers and stand around reading their reviews, don't we, Jonathan?" Lily objected. She had gotten reviews almost as good as Ainsley's. Her face glowed, and bright animation filled her eyes as she looked up at him.

"Why, I suppose we do," he admitted, putting his arm around her. "But I feel about critics as I suppose statues in the park must feel about pigeons!"

A laugh ran around the group, and Dani began to read the reviews for herself. The most intelligent one, she thought, was written by a rather ferocious sort of man with the formidable name of Slaughter. He ignored Ainsley and stated flatly that the skill and presence of Sir Adrian Lockridge made the play hang together. Dani privately agreed and went at once to where Sir Adrian and his wife were standing more or less to themselves. "Sir Adrian, I know you must be pleased with this review," she commented. "It's a very penetrating analysis, and I couldn't agree with him more. Congratulations!"

"Thank you, Danielle," Sir Adrian beamed. "It is rather unusual for Slaughter to be so complimentary. He's generally like a scorpion!"

Lady Lockridge patted his arm, and her smile was triumphant as she said, "You are a perceptive young woman, my dear!" She cast a sly look at Jonathan, adding for her husband's benefit, "My darling husband, I would think that now you won't have to put up with more of that man's impertinence! He's livid with jealousy, you know," she confided to Dani. "Can't bear to have another actor get any credit!"

"This can mean great things," Sir Adrian said, staring at the review. "It will mean a long run for this play, of course. But I'm thinking—"

Dani had been reading the article, but glanced up when Lockridge broke off abruptly. His face was pale, and his sensitive mouth was twisted in pain. "Sir Adrian, are you ill?" she asked quickly.

He seemed not to hear her but, holding his hand on his stomach, moved away. "He'll be all right, dear." Victoria confided, "He's been having digestion problems lately."

Dani watched as the pair left the set, disappearing through the wings. "What's the matter with Lockridge?" a voice broke in, and she turned to see Mickey Trask with a curious look on his face. "He sick or something?"

"I don't think so," Dani said. "Just a stomachache. I think they went to get him something for it."

"He sure is a hard guy to get to know," Mickey observed. "In a second he can go from being real nice to being mean as a snake!

Just today he got sore at Ben when something went wrong with the props, and I thought he'd light into him!"

Trask usually wore a smile, but now an angry look covered his smooth face. He held one of the reviews in his hand and with an angry gesture smashed it with his fist. "Did you read the garbage that stupid ape of a critic wrote about me?" Without waiting for her reply, he began harshly cursing the critic, a man named Larry Selby. Finally he pulled himself up short, saying bitterly, "I don't have to take this, Danielle. If Ainsley had kept his word, I'd be directing this play instead of that oaf Nero!"

Dani hardly knew how to respond. She had often thought of Mickey as a cheerful, happy sort. He had a drinking problem, of course, but she had seldom seen this vicious streak. The expression in his eyes as he spoke of the critic and of Jonathan Ainsley had been a flash of pure hatred. For the first time Dani wondered if the happy-go-lucky actor might be more of a suspect than she had thought. Although she had known from the beginning that Trask resented both Nero and Ainsley, not until this moment had he revealed the depth of his antagonism.

We have to consider them all guilty until they're proven innocent, Dani decided as she moved around the stage, studying the cast and their reactions to the reviews. She came to stand beside Lyle, who was absorbed in his reading. When he looked up to see her standing there, he smiled happily. "Looks like the play is a hit, Danielle. Are you glad?"

"Why, of course, Lyle," she answered. "I'm happy for the good reviews you got."

"I was pretty worried, to tell you the truth. Everyone's been so uptight in this play, I'm surprised I've been able to remember my lines."

"It has been rough, hasn't it?" Dani looked around, then added in what she thought was an innocent tone, "Poor Mickey! He feels awful about what that critic wrote about him! And of course he blames Jonathan for it all."

"Mickey's got a real hate building up against Jonathan. I've thought a couple of times he might be the killer."

"Why, Lyle, you don't think he'd kill Amber just to get even with Jonathan, do you?"

He shrugged. "Somebody did."

"I find it hard to believe Mickey would be capable of murder."

Lyle bit his lower lip, thought about it, then reasoned, "Actors are a funny breed, Danielle. Most of us are egotists, buried up to our necks in self-worship. That makes for pretty unstable personalities. When somebody jostles us, we tend to explode."

"Oh, but just verbally, you mean, Lyle!"

"If the ego is big enough, Danielle, it's like a time bomb. You know how those things are. Somebody puts one on an airplane, and it just sits there, ticking away. Nobody knows about it or thinks about it. But when the clock runs down—boom!—it explodes."

"You paint a grim picture," Dani commented sadly. "Do you really think anyone in this place is as bad as that?"

He dropped his head, studying the floor, then looked up, and Dani was shocked to see the depth of anger in his brown eyes. "Sure, I do. I've never said much to anyone, Danielle, but when Lana was murdered, I hated everyone! She was going to divorce Simon and marry me. It was as if the sun had been ripped out of the sky! I was so filled with hate . . ."

"It's hard to lose someone we love," Danielle murmured.

"Yes." He hesitated, then in a bitter tone, exclaimed, "Nero says he thinks I killed Lana, but I know *he* did it!"

"Lyle!"

Jamison nodded. "He's insanely jealous, not just of Lana, but of anything that's his. He didn't kill Lana by his own hand—he's too clever for that! But he was behind it."

Dani admitted, "Well, it's clear he hates you. Maybe that would be the motive for trying to drop that chandelier on you. But why would he kill Amber or try to ruin Ainsley? That wouldn't make any sense. His career hasn't been going too well, but if this play makes it, he'll be back on top. It wouldn't be reasonable for him to try to stop the play."

Lyle laughed shortly. "No, but psychotics aren't reasonable, Danielle. You've never seen Simon when he's in one of his rages. He'd kill anything that got in his way. Ainsley promised him he could direct the film version of this play. Maybe he changed his mind, and if so, I'm telling you Simon Nero would kill him with pleasure." He would have said more, but at that moment Nero called out, "All right, rehearsal time. Places, everyone!"

Nero kept them at it for three hours, and that night the performance went much more smoothly. Jonathan took it on himself to give the love scene he had with Dani a little extra, whispering in her ear, "Merely trying to keep the critics happy, Danielle!"

As usual, after the performance most of the cast was ready to go home. Dani said good night and left the Pearl, but when the cab pulled up in front of her apartment building, she discovered that she had left her script and Nero's new notes in her dressing room. "Take me back to the theater," she directed the cabby. When she got out at the theater the driver said, "My shift's over, miss. But there's always a cab near this location."

"All right." Dani paid him, then went to the stage-door entrance. Stan Waltoski, the custodian, was just leaving. "Just pull the door shut, Miss Morgan." He nodded. "The lock is set."

"Thank you, Stan." Dani went at once to her dressing room and found the manuscript. One of the changes had displeased her. Sitting down, she found the note that Simon had made. Carefully she read it, then tried to think of another way to get at the change he wanted. Her concentration was so complete that she sat there for five or ten minutes, immersed in the problem.

A faint sound, not loud at all, but clear, attracted her attention. Getting up, she went to the door and listened. The sound seemed to come from the left. Her dressing room light was on, but the rest of the theater was dark except for a single bulb casting harsh shadows over the tangle of ropes and gear behind the stage.

Then she heard another noise, and this time she identified it clearly as the sound of feet moving across the floor. Ignoring her first impulse to get out of the theater, she steeled herself and moved into the murky backstage darkness. Her high heels made a tapping noise, so she paused long enough to slip them off her feet. As she moved silently across the cold floor, her heart began to beat so hard, she was afraid it would be heard.

But heard by whom? The cast was gone. Stan would not leave until everyone got out of the theater. Dani hadn't felt frightened before, but something in the silence and darkness of the theater put a lump of fear in her stomach. Her mouth was dry, and her hands were sweaty. Finally she paused, straining to hear something.

Once she thought she heard a faint sound from the outer section of the theater, something that sounded like a door closing. But she couldn't be sure. Carefully she continued across the cold floor, poised to flee at the slightest alarm.

She reached the end of the backdrop and moved around into the wings, and suddenly her foot touched something soft and yielding!

A gasp of fear broke from her as she yanked her foot back, and Dani almost ran away. Whatever it was on the floor remained silent, and suddenly she bent forward and peered at what seemed to be a bundle of sorts. Then she saw that it was a man lying on his side, a man who was moving slightly. Her heart pounding, she knelt down and by the dim light studied him. Shocked, she whispered, "Ben!"

The sight of Savage's still face jarred her nerves. By the dim light she could see that his eyes were shut. But when she reached out and touched his face, the flesh felt warm.

She carefully ran her fingers over his head, at once finding a large swollen area over his left ear. It was also damp, and she knew that he was bleeding. Her first impulse was to run for help, but that would mean leaving him alone. Her lips tightened, and she sat down on the floor. Taking his head in her lap, she sat there in the darkness, straining to hear. Nothing broke the silence, and after a while Ben started to stir.

Leaning forward, she saw his eyelids begin to flutter. Quietly she whispered, "Ben? Can you hear me?"

He rolled his head slightly, grunted at the pain, and opened his eyes. For a moment he lay there, his dark eyes expressionless; then he reached up and touched her face. "Dani?" he asked thickly. "What . . . ?"

"Don't try to talk, Ben," she urged. "You've been hurt. Just lie there a few minutes longer."

He studied her as she bent over him, not speaking. Finally he reached up and touched his head gingerly. "I think I can stand up now," he muttered.

She helped him to his feet. "We have to get you to a doctor, Ben. You might have a concussion."

"No, I'm all right."

Ignoring his statement, she walked with him to her dressing room, nudged him through the door, and demanded, "Let me see your head. Sit down here." He sat down obediently, and she carefully examined the bump. The skin was broken, but only slightly. "Doesn't seem too bad," she murmured. "Let me get you some aspirin." She went to her dressing table, got two aspirin, filled a cup with water, and brought it all to him. "Does it hurt much?" she asked as he downed the medication.

Handing the glass back, he blinked at her, then tried to smile. "It's not as bad as a root canal." Then he wondered aloud, "How did you happen to find me?"

"I came back for my script. Everyone was gone, and while I was sitting here, I heard a noise." She laughed somewhat nervously. "I wanted to leave the theater in a hurry, but I prowled around and found you lying on the floor."

"See anyone?" he questioned.

"Not a soul. Once I thought I heard a door closing, but I couldn't be sure."

Savage nodded, then winced as pain laced through his head. "Glad you didn't find him, Dani. Might have been bad."

"What happened, Ben?"

"I got to wondering if I could turn up something, so I came back to give the dressing rooms a going-over. I told Stan I'd lock up when I left, and as soon as he left, I started looking around. I didn't find anything, but I really didn't expect to. Then I got a feeling that somebody was watching me. I've felt that a time or two before. So I tried to sneak up on whoever it was. But apparently he did better than I did."

"Did you get a look at him?"

"Not really. I was cat-footing along, and I glimpsed some sort of movement to my right. Tried to move away, but he nailed me." An odd light came into his eyes, and he said thoughtfully, "Takes a pretty good guy to do that to me, boss. I may have lost a step, but I can still hold my own, and this guy is good! Well, I went out like a light. Next thing I knew, you were cuddling me in your lap."

Dani ignored that, asking, "What was he doing, do you think?"

"Nothing good," Savage grunted. He got to his feet, swayed slightly, then ordered, "We'll have to check everything. And we'll have to find out who has an alibi."

"That'll be hard, Ben." Dani sighed. "We can't just demand that everybody tell us what they did after they left the theater."

"No, I guess not. But we can check around, see if he's left any little goodies."

"I'll help," Dani offered quickly. "But what are we looking for?"

"Don't know. Anything that looks out of place. First we'll go over all the props."

Together they went through every item in the prop room but found nothing unusual. Dani watched as Savage checked the ropes and cables that moved the overhead scenery, but that too seemed perfectly in order. Finally in desperation they wandered around the stage, randomly looking at objects and props.

Finally Savage said in disgust, "I can't find a thing out of place."

"Maybe you scared him off before he could do anything."

"Maybe." He got to his feet. "We'll have to let Goldman know about this."

Dani nodded and followed him as he left the stage. As they passed the prop room, she paused.

"What's the matter?" Savage asked.

"I don't know," she murmured. Struggling with some vague idea, she answered slowly, "Something was different about one of the props, but I can't quite say what."

"Let's have another look," he said at once. They went to the prop room, and Dani let her eyes run over everything. "Anything ring a bell?" he asked.

Dani was about to shake her head when her eyes fell on a package. "That's it, Ben," she told him. "The package I give to Jonathan in the second act." She moved to pick it up and studied it. "It looks just the same but—" She looked at him. "It's heavier than I remembered."

"Give it to me," he ordered at once and took it from her. "We'll let the police lab check it out." He turned, and the two of them went to the spot where he had been knocked down. Suddenly he stopped, bent over, and picked something up.

"What is it?" Dani asked.

"Don't know." Handing her a small item, he questioned, "Ever see anything like this?"

After looking at it carefully, Dani said, "Yes." Her mind ran back to the last time she had seen such an object. "It's a dove lapel pin. Christians wear them sometimes."

"How'd it get here?" he wondered.

Dani shook her head, not wanting to speak. Finally she had to admit, "The last time I saw a pin like this, it was on Tom Calvin's lapel. He—he wears one like it a lot."

Savage gave her a keen look. "He could have lost it anytime, I guess."

Dani nodded but suggested, "Let's go tell Goldman."

Neither of them said anything until they left the theater. They got into Ben's car, and as he started the engine, she admitted, "I guess Tom Calvin is last on my list of suspects, Ben."

"You really like the guy, don't you?"

"He's nice. I can't believe he'd kill anyone."

Savage pushed aggressively on the accelerator, sending the car leaping forward to catch a green light. "Maybe this one will turn out all right," he comforted her. But a thin edge of doubt in his voice depressed Dani, and she didn't say anything more.

Eleven

NERO CHECKS OUT

Goldman looked down at the paper, then glanced across his desk at Dani and Ben. "The package had a bomb inside," he told them. "Plastic job. Anyone opening that package would have been a goner."

"Any prints?" Dani asked quickly.

"No, and not much hope of tracing any of the components. Most of it was standard stuff. He knew what he was doing, all right. He knew something about demolitions."

It was early, and rare, bright sunshine broke through the single window in the lieutenant's office. Dani had spoken to him on the phone, then had taken the package to the station. She had not slept well, and even the sunshine did not cheer her up. "It was meant for Jonathan Ainsley, Jake. In the play I give him the package, and he opens it up. It's in the second act."

"What's inside?" Goldman asked. "I mean when the bomb's not there."

"A silk scarf," Dani said. "Usually it weighs almost nothing."

Ben put in suddenly, "I wrap the scarf up after every performance. That's part of my job."

Goldman considered that, then asked dryly, "But not this time?"

"I'd already wrapped it up for the next performance. I always do that."

"Then the mysterious slugger who put you down must have taken the scarf out and put the bomb inside."

"It must be," Dani interjected. "And it would have worked too!" She bit her lip, thinking of the horrifying near-tragedy. "Would the bomb have hurt me, Jake? I'm no more than four or five feet away when Jonathan opens it."

"Don't know." He shrugged. "My guess is that you might get hurt, but Ainsley would take the worst of it."

"Did you tell him about the bomb?" Dani asked.

"Yes. He was pretty shook up or at least seemed to be," Goldman said. "I told him again he ought to call the play off, but he insisted there's too much riding on it. Guess you two ought to ask for a bonus. You sure saved his bacon, which I pointed out to him."

Dani shook her head. "No, Jake, in a way it was blind luck—or actually God's intervention. If Ben hadn't been around to get in the killer's way, we'd never have suspected a thing. Ainsley would have been killed tonight at about 9:30." She got to her feet, walked nervously to the window, and stared down at the street below. She turned, complaining, "This thing is so complex! Almost everybody in the cast has a motive, and most of them have the opportunity for murder. But no solution we come up with hangs together."

"Let's go over it one more time," Goldman suggested. "First Ainsley almost gets run down by a car. Then somebody takes a shot at him. Of course, that's all on his say-so. Nobody actually saw that going on. And any one of the cast could have pulled both those little stunts."

"Exactly!" Dani nodded, her black hair stirring as she jerked her head. "But then comes the real thing—Amber's murder. What about the store, the one Ben found the receipt from—what was it?"

"Empire Sporting Goods," Goldman reminded her. "Nothing doing, at least for now. The clerk our man talked to said he was too busy that day to look into their records. They were having a sale on ammunition." He shook his head grimly. "Isn't that wonderful? The one day we need to check somebody, the store has a sale! Our man said the clerk was pretty uptight about cops for some reason, but he couldn't make the guy nervous enough to dig out the information we need. Not yet anyway."

"So anyone could have put the real slugs in the .38." Dani pondered that. "But it's Jonathan who's been threatened. Why kill Amber?"

"Two possibilities," Goldman answered. "One, somebody wanted to kill the LeRoi woman for reasons having nothing to do with Jonathan Ainsley and the play. Any ideas?"

Dani hesitated, trying to decide whether to relate what she'd heard from Sir Adrian earlier. Finally she said, "I don't think it means anything, but Sir Adrian had had his share of trouble with her."

"I heard about that," Goldman commented. "She put him through the hoops, didn't she?"

"But that was a long time ago, Jake!"

"So what? Sometimes that makes it worse. I mean, when a man can't get rid of something like that, it starts to fester."

"We have to count Lockridge as a suspect," Ben agreed. "But what about Ainsley himself? It would be a pretty cute way to get rid of excess baggage. And he made it pretty clear that's how he felt about Amber LeRoi. Everybody heard him say he wished she was dead."

"He was just talking," Dani objected.

"Maybe, but the man sort of loses it from time to time," Ben observed. "Let's say Amber told Ainsley that her sugar daddy who was footing the bill for the play was about to pull out. Then he gets the idea of using the gun with live ammo to knock her off before she can tell her boyfriend to back out. Who's going to believe he did it deliberately? Even you don't believe that, do you, Jake?"

"It'd be a hard thing to prove in court, the district attorney says," Goldman admitted. "But I'm not ruling it out." He shifted in his chair. "It's that blasted chandelier thing that bugs me!"

"Me too," Dani chimed in. "I guess because it was aimed at Lyle. Nero hates him, but Nero was standing not five feet away from me when it happened. He *couldn't* have cut that rope!"

"That bothers me too," Goldman agreed. Reaching to his left, he pulled open a cabinet door and removed a paper bag. "Here it is," he said, taking out the rope. "I've looked at it so much I'm tired of it. Either one of you see anything at all funny about it?"

Dani took the rope and stared at the end carefully. "It's just a cut rope," she contended. "The only peculiar thing is that it's not exactly a clean cut."

"Yeah," Ben said quickly. "Half of it is a clean cut, but the other side is sort of frayed. But that could be explained by the weight of the chandelier."

"I see what you mean." Goldman nodded. "The knife sliced through the rope cleanly for the first half; then the weight of that big lamp just snapped the rest of the strands." He stared at it, shook his head, then added, "I guess that could be so. I'll run it by the lab again, but I don't think they'll be much help."

"Remember, it was Jonathan who shoved Lyle out of the way of that chandelier," Dani put in.

"He said he couldn't tell if it was falling right on top of him or Lyle Jamison," Goldman reminded her. "Anyway, once we've crossed those two off the list, everybody else is accounted for. You were close to Nero, so he couldn't have cut the rope. We've talked to everybody in the cast. None of them was alone when the thing fell."

"I keep remembering what Sherlock Holmes said to Dr. Watson." Dani smiled grimly. "'If everything that seems possible will not explain the circumstances, Watson, you must look to all that remains—the impossible.' Which in this case would be the Phantom of the Theater that the tabloids are having such fun with."

"It might be an outsider," Ben noted doubtfully. "But I can't see how. It's a small world back behind that curtain. Anybody who doesn't belong would be spotted at once. No, it *has* to be an inside job."

"I think you're right, Savage." Goldman took a folder from the cabinet. "Here are the letters. Not much for us there. No prints at all."

Dani studied the letters carefully. "I wish Jonathan had kept the first two threats. Did you ask him if they were like these?"

"He said he thought so." Goldman asked suddenly, "Why

would the killer use two different styles? These two typed, the next ones made of words glued on paper?"

"I've wondered about that," Dani told him. "And there's more than that. Something's different about the style—the way he says things. The first two notes are pretty straightforward." She read the first note aloud:

"'Ainsley—I am going to destroy you. A man such as you doesn't deserve to live. You have ruined my life, so now I do not propose to let you live. You escaped this morning, but you cannot escape forever.'" She tossed it onto the desk, stating that the next note was pretty much the same. "As you say, the physical appearance of the later notes is different, letters glued on paper. But what hits me is the difference in style."

"What do you mean, Danielle?" Goldman inquired.

Dani read the next note that Jonathan had received aloud: "'You have chosen to ignore my warnings. Now it is put out the light, and then put out the light. You owe God a death. You have twenty-four hours to live.'"

"What's all that stuff about putting out the light?" Goldman asked.

"It's from *Othello,* and the part about owing God a death is from one of the history plays of Shakespeare, *Henry IV*." She picked up another sheet and read it to them: "'Death, a necessary end, will come when it will come.' That's from *Julius Caesar*. 'If the play goes on, a life goes out. Members of the cast, will you die for a monster like Jonathan Ainsley? One of you certainly will have a "final curtain" if the play goes on!"'"

"So those two notes have lines from Shakespeare, and the earlier two don't," Goldman said slowly.

"There's more—I was with Jonathan when he got the note about putting out the light." She narrowed her eyes, thinking about it. Slowly she added, "He literally slumped down, almost fainted! It really hit him hard. And the last one affected him just as badly."

"He didn't seem as affected by the first notes," Ben recollected. "Is that what you're getting at?"

"Of course we weren't there when he received them," Dani admitted. "But when he told us about them, he treated them much more lightly."

"Can't make anything of that in court," Goldman said. "The man's an actor, isn't he? He can put on any front he wants to. The only hope is to find the typewriter that these first two were typed on or the magazines that the words were clipped from for these other two."

"Small chance of that, I would think," Ben muttered. He gave Dani an uncomfortable glance, then asked, "What about the pin?"

"The pin comes from a Christian organization called the Overcomers," Goldman said. Removing the pin from an envelope, he stared at it. "They give them out by the handfuls, they tell me. They also said that Tom Calvin is a member."

Dani nodded. "He wears one of those most of the time. I think it's sort of a test for him. The cast and crew at the Pearl are a pretty worldly bunch, so he wears the pin to make a statement about being a Christian."

"Any other Christians in the cast?" Goldman asked.

"Well, just me."

"Of course he could have dropped it anytime," Goldman stated. "But I'll go see him, try to find out where he was at the time you were getting your brains scrambled, Savage. Well, that's all for now."

Dani left the office with Ben, but as he got into his car, he said little. She watched him drive off, then roved the streets for a while, taking in the huge canyons created by the towering skyscrapers. She decided to have a talk with the clerk at Empire Sporting Goods. That meant a taxi ride, and as usual she felt she was being overcharged, but in less than half an hour she entered the store.

It was a fairly large place, packed with weight machines, football equipment, skin-diving gear, and just about every other sort of sports equipment a man or woman could want. She made her way to the gun department in a back corner of the store. A thin young man with a bad complexion was just concluding a sale. He handed a package to a man in thick, rubber-soled boots. "You're gonna like this little number, Mr. Meyer. Appreciate your business!"

He turned to Dani. "Help you, miss?"

"I need a little information," she told him quickly. Giving him a warm smile, she explained, "I have a friend who's having a problem—a pretty serious one. The police are even involved."

His face went stiff, and she knew she had approached the right man.

"For myself, I try to stay as far away from the cops as I can," she added.

"You got that right, lady!" the clerk agreed. "Hey, is this about the .38 shells? A cop was in here yesterday tryin' to pump me."

"I guess so. There was some trouble, and the law is trying to pin it on my friend. So what I need to do is talk to whoever made the sale."

The clerk hesitated, then leaned forward. "That'd be Benny Allen," he whispered. "I didn't tell that to the cops though. I don't tell them nuttin' for reasons I'd rather not give!"

Dani said quickly, "I understand. So, can I talk to Benny?"

"Naw, he ain't here. He won a trip to London a couple of weeks ago. He left day before yesterday."

Dani let the disappointment show in her face. "Oh, I wish I could have talked to him before he left. When do you think he'll be back?"

"Next Wednesday. I know 'cause I'm havin' to work double time while he's gone." He gave a quick look around, then added, "I think Benny told me about the .38 shells though."

"Really?"

"Yeah. We get all kinds of people in here, but Benny said this customer was kind of strange. Said she didn't know beans about guns."

Surprised it had been a woman, Dani almost said something that would have given away her undercover status.

After giving her an odd look, the clerk went on, "Benny said she came in looking sort of—well, guilty, you know? Like she was doin' something wrong. Benny told me, 'She acted like she was gettin' the ammo to knock somebody off.'"

"Did Benny say what she looked like? I need to know whether it was my friend."

"Benny didn't really describe her. We didn't talk about it much. He just mentioned it as he was leaving to catch his plane." The man leaned forward, and curiosity sharpened his eyes. "Sounds like your friend's got big trouble, huh?"

"Could be." Dani opened her purse and wrote her name and number on a page from a small notebook. Giving it to the clerk, she flashed her best smile. "Will you give this to Benny when he gets back? I think I could make it worth his while if he has any definite information I can use."

"Sure, I'll give it to him."

Dani left the store, wondering if she had stumbled onto something. A woman had bought the ammunition. That could be Lily, Carmen, or Lady Lockridge. But it might be a false lead too. She knew from sad experience that most developments like this proved useless.

The phone was ringing when she opened her door, and she ran to answer it.

"Hello, Dani, how are you?" a familiar voice asked.

"Dad! I was going to call you today."

"I just wanted to give you a progress report," he said. "And it's good. Got two new accounts just yesterday."

"Dad, I hope you're not doing too much!" she exclaimed. "You know what Doctor Lovell said."

"I know more about how I feel than any doctor does," her father objected. "The new man we hired is working out fine. He's going to be a good one."

She sat down in the soft chair, kicked off her shoes, and curled up to listen as he told her about the agency. Then she asked about Allison, her fifteen-year-old sister, and her brother Rob, age seventeen.

"Well, Dani, they're having their problems," he said slowly. "I think every parent we know is having some sort of trouble with their kids. It's something about the times, I suppose. Never had that much trouble with you."

"Oh, yes, you did! You've just forgotten the bad times."

They talked about the family, and he asked about her case. "It could be a long-range thing, you think?"

She knew him very well and recognized what he would never come out and say. "Dad, if you need me, I can find a way to get out of this case and come home right away."

"No, don't do that," he answered. "But you don't sound too hopeful."

"I'm not," she admitted. "I can't find anything solid to hang on to. But it can't go on forever. We'll break this case yet. Keep a light in the window for me."

"Sure. We miss you."

A lump rose in Dani's throat, and she said, "I love you, Dad. I'll call as soon as I get some news."

Before long she was relaxing in a tub of hot water. As the tension drained out of her, she put the case out of her mind and thought about how badly she wanted to go home. But her stubborn streak wouldn't let her quit. She got out of the tub, dried off, and slept for two hours before getting up to prepare for the night at the Pearl.

That evening, in the scene when she handed Jonathan the package, he gave her an odd look and stumbled over his line. Afterward he came up to her dressing room, and she brought him up to date on the case. When she finished, he shook his head. "I don't mind admitting, Danielle, I'm getting scared. If you and Savage hadn't found that bomb, I'd be dead right now."

"Death is only a step away from any of us, Jonathan," she commented seriously.

He glanced at her, studying her face, and quietly asked, "You're not afraid of dying are you, Danielle?"

"I suppose I have some fear of the unknown," she responded slowly. "But you're right—I don't fear death. It's what comes after that we ought to think about, Jonathan. I'm ready to stand before God, and I hope you are too."

"Ever since all this began to happen, I've been thinking about life and how short it is." He pulled himself together, gave her a shamefaced look, and taunted, "Well, well, I guess you're going to try to make a Christian out of me now."

"I wish I could, Jonathan." She smiled. "Jesus has brought real joy into my own life. He can do the same for you."

Looking uncomfortable, he left abruptly, and almost at once Lily came in. "That policeman is here again, Danielle. He asked me a lot of questions. Won't they ever stop?"

"Not until someone goes to jail," Dani said. "What kind of questions?"

"Oh, the same ones as before. Where was I when this or that happened? Who was with me? Things like that." She stood there, watching Dani as though she wanted to ask her a question. Of all the members of the cast, Dani thought, Lily was the most vulnerable, and the least likely to be the killer. Finally Lily inquired, "Danielle, aren't you afraid?"

"Of being the next victim?" Dani asked. "Well, I'd rather not be, but . . . Lily, are *you* afraid?"

"Oh, yes!" Lily shivered at the thought. "I'd leave the play in a second if—"

Dani finished her young friend's sentence. "If it weren't for Jonathan?"

"I love him, Danielle." There was, Dani saw, a great dignity in the young woman. Lily drew herself up, and her eyes were honest as she announced, "Oh, I know about Jonathan—his women and all that. But I love him anyway."

Dani felt she had to say something. "Lily, men like Jonathan Ainsley act as though there are two standards—one for everybody else and a special one for them. Young ladies like you can really get hurt."

"That's true," Lily agreed quietly. "But what can a woman do when she's in love, Danielle? I can't just decide with my head to walk away, can I?"

Dani wasn't sure what to say but made one more attempt. "I can't advise you, Lily. I admire Jonathan tremendously, but the woman who marries him will have to be willing to be second in his life—to other women and to the theater."

"I know, and that's all right with me. As long as he loves me, that's all I ask." Lily gave Dani a teary smile. "Well, here I am crying all over you! I don't usually do that. You must have a motherly nature."

"I guess so." Dani smiled back. She gave Lily a brief embrace. "Anytime you want to talk about this, I'm available."

When Lily left, Dani looked at herself in the mirror. "You're getting to be quite the little counselor, aren't you?" Sobering, she asked, "But who's going to give the counselor some advice?"

◆ ◆ ◆

The bombshell went off twenty minutes before the curtain rose. Dani was chatting with Mickey Trask when Tom Calvin appeared. He strode straight over to Ainsley and said something. The actor's head flew back in shock, and he stared at Calvin unbelievingly. After a rapid conversation, Ainsley called out, "Everybody come out here immediately, please."

The entire cast assembled immediately, and Ainsley began to speak quickly, tripping over his words. "I have disturbing news. Simon has decided to leave the play." He waited until the cast's muttering died down before continuing, "I may as well tell you the reason. He has chosen to resign because he feels it's become too dangerous to be part of my play. This will make things more difficult, but we've come so far, I don't think any of us wants to stop now. I should have waited until after the performance to tell you this, but you have a right to know. Let's meet as soon as the performance is over. There are a couple more things we need to talk about."

The cast went back to their individual responsibilities and roles, everyone speculating on the new development. None of them had liked Nero, but as Mickey Trask put it, "He's hard to work for, but he was one of us."

After a somewhat ragged performance, they all met on stage. Ainsley's eyes scanned the crowd, then prompted them, "I know we're all disturbed about Simon's departure. But we can handle this, just as we've dealt with our other problems. We'll just have to pull together."

"Who will be our director, Jonathan?" Lyle asked with concern.

"A good question," Ainsley responded. "Though some of you may disagree, I have decided to direct the play myself. It was what I intended to do from the first, and now that we've become such a great team, I don't see any reason why I can't double as director."

Dani immediately saw a difficulty that Jonathan obviously didn't see. As he had spoken, she had watched the faces of the cast. Ainsley's decision to direct the play himself had definitely caught Mickey Trask off guard. His eyes narrowed, and Dani saw their fury. *He expected to get the job,* Dani thought.

"There is one more thing I must share with you," Ainsley went on. He looked around and smiled briefly. "I have no family, as you know, in the real sense. But I would like to think of you as being like a family. And in that sense I want to let you be the first to know—" He paused dramatically, and Dani suddenly knew what he was going to say.

He walked over to Lily, put his arm around her, and turned to face the cast. "I'd like to announce that Lily and I are officially engaged to be married."

At once most of the cast moved forward with their congratulations, but Carmen Rio wheeled and left the stage hurriedly. Looking at Mickey Trask again, Dani now knew what she had earlier only suspected: He was in love with Lily. Blankly, he stared at Lily, his eyes unbelieving. Finally he shut his mouth firmly and joined the others. Dani heard him say woodenly, "Congratulations, you two. I hope you'll be very happy."

As the actor left the stage, Dani saw that Ben too was watching Mickey carefully. Their eyes met, and Ben nodded slightly. Later Dani said, "I'd hate to think it was Mickey, Ben."

"You'd have good wishes for Attila the Hun," he answered gruffly. "You're always looking for the happy ending, boss, but I don't think this story's going to have one."

Twelve

LILY'S SCENE

The next few days were colder in New York, making Dani homesick for the mild climate of New Orleans. Thursday afternoon she went shopping and bought a bright red angora sweater, but when she got home and tried it on, she decided it wasn't a good color for her. "Should have worn it out in the daylight," she muttered, staring at herself in the mirror.

The doorbell rang, and she opened it to find Ben standing there.

"I picked up all the personnel folders from Ainsley," he said, pushing past her. "I thought we might look them over this afternoon." He laid a pile of thick manila folders on the coffee table, then glanced at her more closely. "New sweater?"

"Yes. It looks hideous, doesn't it?"

"I don't know," he said, staring at her with a judicial look. "On the whole it looks better than that old rag you wear when you give Biscuit a workout."

The thought of her rust-colored quarter horse turned Dani's memories toward home. "I wish I were riding him right now, Ben. We're going nowhere on this case. Dad called again, and I could tell he's doing too much."

Savage wasn't finished with the sweater. "No, it's not hideous, boss. An earthy type like you needs to dress flashy." Without a break he threw in, "You ready to give up and go home?"

Dani ran her hand through the mass of short black curls, threw herself into a chair opposite Ben, and gnawed at her left thumb. It was a habit he had noted long ago, a sure sign that she was worried. "I'd like to but we can't, can we, Ben? I mean, if we hadn't found that bomb, it would have killed Jonathan."

"Stop sucking your thumb," he ordered, grinning at the look of annoyance that his comment brought. "It'll make your teeth grow crooked."

"Never mind my teeth!" Her voice held a waspish tone. "Let's wade through these things and see if we can find anything that ties anybody to a murder." It had been Dani's idea to get the personnel folders. She hoped that something in the backgrounds of the cast members might throw light on the murder and attempted murders.

"What are we looking for, boss?" Ben asked.

"I don't know," she admitted. "Something that will give us a clue about why one of the cast would want to kill Jonathan."

"Shouldn't be too hard. They all hate his guts."

They sat in the tiny living room, poring over the folders and finding very little. Dani said, "Ben, Ringo once worked in the mines in Colorado. They use explosives there a lot."

"So you're thinking he could have learned how to make that bomb."

"It took some skill. The average person couldn't do it."

Ben snapped his fingers, riffled through the stack, and pulled one of them out. "This is Mickey Trask's folder. He was in the navy for a while. Could have learned something about demolitions there."

Dani nodded slowly. "Could be. Let's see what else we can turn up."

After they worked steadily for another fifteen minutes, Savage held up a stock photograph of a scantily clad Carmen Rio. It was a studio shot with curls of vapor rising from somewhere off camera. She had the usual sultry look used in such shots. As he showed it to Dani for her inspection, Ben said, "I think there's a clue in this photo somewhere. Maybe I'd better take it home and study it more closely."

"Push your eyeballs back in, Savage," she snapped. "I might

have known you'd give that one close attention." He didn't answer, and she glanced over to see that he was holding a single sheet of paper and staring at it intently. "What is it, Ben?"

He looked up with a peculiar light in his hazel eyes and handed her the sheet. "Bingo!"

Dani took the paper, a customary sketch of an actor's life. It included the usual information about the applicant's background and closed with a statement of goals. Dani ran her eyes over it, wondering what had aroused Ben's interest. Then she got it. "Ben, the E's and the O's are all raised!"

"Yes, indeedy, boss." He grunted with satisfaction. "This was typed on the same machine as the first two threats Jonathan showed us." He looked down at the photograph. "Carmen doesn't look much like a murderer, does she?"

"They usually don't," Dani said. She studied the note and nodded. "We need to compare this with the notes Goldman has. Do you think it's enough to make an arrest?"

"I doubt it. Even if she still has the typewriter, there'd be no way to prove she used it to write the notes. She could say someone else used it for that."

"First, we have to find out if it's her typewriter. But it almost has to be, Ben. We'll ask Jake to get a search warrant."

Savage rubbed the scar that ran down his forehead into his left eyebrow, thinking slowly. Finally he shook his head. "We need more than this, Dani. First we need to be sure she still has the typewriter. Maybe she gave it to one of the other actors."

"Are you thinking of going through her place, Ben? The way you did with the Lockridge apartment?"

"If I have to," he admitted. "But let me try something else first. If I can get her to ask me up to her apartment, maybe I could find out what we need to know." He grinned at Dani. "With my swift wit and muscular body, what woman wouldn't be thrilled if I asked her out?"

She ignored his jabs, warning, "It had better be soon, Ben. We can't afford to waste any time." Her eyes took on a worried cast, and she said, "I have the feeling we're playing with fire." She walked nervously around the room. "I was in a car wreck once," she said suddenly. "My brakes went out, and I ran into a bridge abutment. It was terrible! I saw that I was going to hit it, but there was absolutely nothing I could do! I feel like that with this case."

Savage nodded. "I kind of feel that way myself." He got to his feet and started for the door. "I'll find out more about the typewriter tonight. If my manly charm doesn't work, I'll burgle her place."

"Be careful, Ben," Dani cautioned. "Don't get yourself arrested—or killed."

He paused, giving her a serious look, then pointed out, "I'm just a stagehand, Dani. You're the one who's on stage. I want to nail the culprit before anything happens to you."

"Don't worry about me."

He said, "I do though" and left the apartment. Dani slowly walked back to the bedroom and pulled off the sweater, dwelling on his earlier comment. Looking at herself in the mirror, she asked her image, "Are flashy colors really right for me?" She started going through the stack of folders again.

She kept at it until it was time to dress for the evening. There wasn't much to be gleaned from them, she thought as she left the apartment. She wasn't sure how, but she knew Ben would find out about the typewriter. He was the most determined man she'd ever met; whatever he set out to do, he would accomplish.

Her thoughts turned to Carmen. She tried to think of the dark woman as the murderer they were seeking. *She hates Jonathan,* Dani thought as she rode through the busy streets, insulated by the cab against the crowds of the city. *Physically speaking, it's not impossible that she could have written all the notes, she could have tried to run Jonathan down, and she could have cut the rope holding the chandelier. But I can't imagine her slugging Ben—or making a bomb for that matter.*

Getting out of the cab, she went into the theater's side entrance, where Tom Calvin met her. The look on his face made her ask, "What's wrong, Tom?"

"Another threat," he said. "Jonathan found it on the floor of his dressing room. I guess someone must have slipped it under the door."

Dani walked toward the dressing room with Calvin, asking, "How did Jonathan take it?"

"Not too well," he admitted. "In fact, I think worse than the last time. He's been drinking some to steady his nerves, but naturally that hasn't helped much." As they reached the door of Ainsley's dressing room, Tom excused himself. "He's been pretty hard to live with, Dani. If you don't mind, I think I'll let you go in alone."

"Of course, Tom." Dani knocked on the door, and Ainsley said, "Come in." When she entered, Ainsley was sitting in the chair before his mirror. He turned, and Dani saw that he was half drunk. "Hello, Jonathan. Tom told me about the letter. Is this it?"

"Yes." Ainsley picked up a half-empty bottle of whiskey, filled the glass in front of him to the brim, and drank it down. He lowered the glass and watched as she read the letter. "I'd hoped we'd seen the last of those."

The new warning was nothing like the other two. The letters were all capitals, made with child's crayons, all different colors. The paper was plain white, with no watermark.

> AINSLEY, YOU CAN'T ESCAPE FOREVER. YOU'VE DESTROYED TOO MANY INNOCENT PEOPLE. YOU'VE LEFT A SLIMY TRAIL EVERYWHERE YOU'VE BEEN. BUT YOUR LIES WILL STOP SOON—BECAUSE A DEAD MAN CAN'T TELL LIES OR RUIN WOMEN. YOU CAN SAY GOOD-BYE TO THE THINGS YOU LOVE BEST BECAUSE YOU'RE GOING TO LOSE THEM ALL!

Dani lowered the letter and stared at Jonathan. His face was pale, and his lips were trembling. He looked ill. She asked, "What are you going to do, Jonathan?"

"What *can I* do?" he cried plaintively. "I can't quit because my whole life is tied up with this play. If I don't make it with this one, I'm finished!" He clasped his hands together and squeezed his eyes shut. When he spoke again, his voice was filled with fear. "But I don't want to die! And that's what will happen if this maniac isn't caught!" He suddenly opened his eyes and rose out of his seat. Grabbing her hands, he demanded, "Danielle, you've got to help me! You've got to!"

His grip was so strong, Dani's hands began to hurt, but she said quietly, "Jonathan, you have to pull yourself together. Sit down and let's talk." She maneuvered him into the chair and asked, "How much have you had to drink?"

"Not enough!"

"No, you've had too much. If you ever needed a clear head, it's right now. Have you told Goldman about this threat?"

"Yes. He said he'd be by later for the performance, but there are no extra men for guards. And it wouldn't work anyway. If the maniac wants to kill me badly enough, he'll find a way."

Dani stared at the note, read it again, then shook her head. "This note isn't like the others."

"No more taped-on words," he agreed. "It would be impossible to trace a set of child's crayons."

"I meant that it didn't have the same tone as the others. No quotations from Shakespeare—just a plain warning. He's getting smart, or maybe he always has been. Usually murderers get caught because they repeat a pattern over and over—a *modus operandi*. But this guy is as changeable as the wind. He never does the same thing twice, and he writes his letters in different ways."

"He's a maniac, that's all I know!" Jonathan moaned.

Dani read part of the note aloud: "'A dead man can't tell lies or ruin women.'" She looked at him, then asked directly, "How many women have you ruined, Jonathan—I mean women who would be connected to somebody in the cast?"

He shifted in his chair, then lifted his shoulders, saying, "I can't answer that, Danielle. I've known quite a few women. They play a game with me, and I play it with them. Sometimes I've been used by them, and sometimes I suppose I've hurt them."

"Women like Carmen?"

Ainsley looked at her suddenly, then nodded, his face unhappy. "Yes, like Carmen. She never really meant anything to me. As I said, it's a game."

"Maybe she didn't know the rules of your little game, Jonathan," Dani said evenly.

He saw the disapproval on her face, and when he spoke, his voice had none of its usual confidence. "I know you look at these things very differently from the way I do, Danielle. And I confess that lately I've been forced to think that my life has been—well, less than it should have been." He put his head in his hands, pressing his palms against his brow. Lifting his head, he continued, "The whole idea behind this play is that man can take care of his own troubles. But for the last few nights I—I've been asking myself just how true that is."

"'No man is an island,' Jonathan," Dani reminded him. "You've known that line for a long time. And none of us are whole within ourselves. That's why God made the first woman, remember?"

"I guess I'd forgotten about that."

"The Bible says that as soon as God made Adam, he said, 'It is not good for man to live alone.' That's what women are for, so men don't have to be alone. And that's what men are for, Jonathan, so women will have someone to love them."

He stared at her, finally commenting, "When you say that, it sounds very real and desirable. But I grew up in the world of entertainment, Danielle. There are no morals there that I've discovered. Oh, we hide that from public view, but life in my world amounts to 'get what you can'—at any cost and from anybody who gets in your way."

"What a terrible world," Dani said dejectedly. "Not one I envy." She took a deep breath and went on, "The only thing that keeps me going, Jonathan, is having a few people I can trust and having God beside me all the time."

A long silence followed her statement. Then Jonathan remarked, "I'm glad you're like that, Danielle. I hope you always will be. In my whole life I've never seen an example of what a Christian is. But knowing you has given me some hope—not much, mind you—but a little hope that maybe even for a fellow like me there's a chance for a better life."

Dani wasn't sure how far she should press him right then; so she prayed silently for him. "There's hope, Jonathan," she encouraged him. "Now, let's go over the list, and you tell me who would have the most interest in destroying you. Then I need to run home for a bit before coming back for the performance."

♦ ♦ ♦

Carmen was surprised to find Ben Savage standing in front of the door to her apartment. She had been putting her makeup on, getting ready to go and do some shopping before it was time to go to the theater, but the bell had interrupted her. She stood there looking at him. "Hello, Ben," she finally managed.

"Hello, Carmen," he answered. "Can I come in? It's getting cold out here."

"I guess so, but I'm in a hurry. Got some shopping to do."

He took off his overcoat and threw it over a chair, then turned to her. "Won't keep you long. Matter of fact, I'll go with you."

She studied him with practiced eyes, searching for some motive. She had known many men, and her experience with them had not built any great trust for them. "You didn't come here to help me do my shopping," she said tartly.

"Well, Carmen, as a matter of fact, there is one thing I wanted to ask you." Ben put his hands up in a helpless gesture. "That cop, Goldman? Well, he's been after me a lot. Asking lots of questions."

"About me?" Carmen demanded.

"About everybody." Savage shrugged. "But this morning it was about you. I guess somebody must have told him we were good friends because somehow he knew we'd been out together."

"One time," she contemptuously disclaimed. "That makes us bosom buddies?"

"I guess so, according to Goldman."

"You tell him I spent the night in your apartment?"

"Nope. None of his business."

Carmen relaxed when she heard that, and a softer expression came over her face. "You didn't take advantage of me, Ben, though I was expecting you to."

"I always like to have things fifty-fifty," Ben said. "I wouldn't want a woman that I had to get drunk before she fell for me."

Carmen bit her full lower lip and studied him. After a long silence she dropped her eyes. "Didn't know there were any men like you left, Ben. Most guys will do anything to get to a girl."

"You don't think too highly of men, do you, Carmen?"

"I've got no cause to!" She broke off her speech in anger. "Well, come on in and have some coffee. No use standing in the middle of the hall jabbering."

He sat down, and she poured coffee for the two of them. She was an attractive woman, he realized again, with her creamy skin, alluring figure, and coal-black hair. Her perfume was subtle but enchanting. She sat down at the table close to him. "Now, what did that cop say?"

"I think they're trying to find somebody to take the fall," Ben told her. "I heard that the police commissioner has threatened to lop off some heads if Homicide doesn't come up with something soon. And Goldman's got nothing."

"Why me?" Carmen wondered.

"You're the girl Ainsley dropped." Ben took a swallow of his coffee. "Hey, this has chickory in it. I love that stuff!" he rhapsodized.

But she was staring at him angrily. "Sure, I was sore at him. But not enough to kill him, or Amber either. She was out of the picture long before I came along."

"Goldman figures that you could've put the bullets in the gun, thinking that if he killed LeRoi he'd go to the chair for it."

"That's crazy, Ben!" Carmen slammed the coffee cup down. "And why would I try to wipe out Lyle with a chandelier?"

"Trying to get Ainsley, according to the cops," Ben explained.

"As for that bomb, anyone can buy one if he knows the right people. And that was aimed right at Jonathan."

Anger turned Carmen's face hard. Finally she asked, "What else did you come here for, Ben?"

He looked at her and said, "One thing, Carmen. Maybe you don't remember, but when you were passed out on the bed in my place, you started having dreams—bad ones. I went in to wake you up, and you were saying something."

"What did I say?"

"You said, 'Sir Adrian! You killed her—you killed Amber! I saw you put the real bullets in the gun!'" Savage watched her closely and thought he saw a break in her expression. "Did you see that, Carmen—Lockridge loading the gun with live ammunition?"

"No, I never saw that!" she cried out loudly. "I was drunk that night at your place, Ben! I was just talking crazy!"

Savage knew he had pushed her as far as he could. "Well, that's what I thought. That's why I didn't say anything to Goldman."

Relief flowed across her face, and she managed a weak smile. "Thanks, Ben! You're a good man."

He patted her arm, then got to his feet.

"You're not going to help me shop?" she asked, trying for a lighter note.

"No, I have things to do. But maybe we can go out sometime, just the two of us."

"Name the place," she said.

Ben nodded and started for the door, pulling on his overcoat. As he rammed his hand in the pocket, he was brought up short. "Blast it!" he said with irritation.

"What's wrong, Ben?"

He pulled a long business envelope from his pocket. "I need to get this in the mail right away. But I want it to look professional, so I'll have to go all the way to the Pearl to use the typewriter in Tom's office."

"You don't have to do that, Ben," Carmen said, "I have a portable. It's not much, but—"

"Anything you've got will do, Carmen." He waited as she disappeared into a bedroom. *Nothing is ever this easy!* Ben thought. When she came back bearing an old Royal portable, he had to keep his face from breaking into a smile. Once he had typed an address onto the envelope, he got to his feet. "Thanks, Carmen. That saves me quite a bit of time."

"I'll see you at the theater," she said. Leaning against him, she suddenly reached out and pulled his head down. Her lips were full and soft beneath his own, and he let her be the first to pull away. "Let's go someplace afterward," she whispered.

"Sure, Carmen." He smiled and left the building. "I wonder if I ought to take up acting?" he asked himself sardonically. "I played that scene so well, I might as well get paid for it!"

It was still too early to go to the theater, so he drove back to Dani's apartment. When he rang the bell, she opened it almost at once. "Well, the typewriter is there," he announced, moving inside.

"Are you sure?"

He pulled the envelope from his coat pocket and held it up. "I'll be surprised if this isn't a match."

Glancing at the clock, she suggested, "Let's go get a sandwich at Louie's. You can tell me all about it."

He drove her to a small sandwich shop they had discovered, far enough off the beaten track not to be crowded. Louie Martino made great lamb-and-cheese gyros and absolutely refused to make a hamburger. If a customer asked for one, he would look down his nose and declare, "I think they sell those down the street."

A tall, thin man, Louie himself met them and flashed Dani a smile. "Ah, just time for a quick sandwich before the performance, right, Miss Morgan?"

"Right, Louie." Dani returned the smile. "Make it two—and coffee."

They seated themselves at one of the booths, and Dani put her elbows on the red-and-white checkered tablecloth. "So tell me how it went," she demanded, her eyes bright.

"She has the typewriter in her apartment." Ben shrugged. "Goldman can get a search warrant anytime."

Her eyes blinked, and she objected crossly, "Ben, you gave me the headline, but I want the full story!"

He smiled at her. "Remember the first time we ever locked horns?"

"No. We've done that too many times! What was it about?"

"On my first job for you, I gave you a report you thought was too skimpy. You nearly blew my head off."

"Well, you *don't* make the best reports in the world!"

"Would you like me to put them into poetic form? Sonnets maybe?"

"Oh, Ben!" She tossed her head. "Don't make me beg. Tell me what happened—all of it."

"All right, boss. You sure know how to get the truth out of a guy!" So he told her all of it, including the highlights of the night Carmen had spent at his apartment. Louie brought their sandwiches in the middle of it, but he continued as soon as the restaurateur left. Finally Ben leaned back and asked, "That detailed enough for you?"

She was watching him with a strange expression in her large eyes. The short, black hair, arranged like a crown, made her eyes look enormous and very beautiful. He tried to read her glance but could make nothing of it. Finally she said, "I'm glad you didn't do it."

"Do what?" he asked, confused.

"Take advantage of Carmen when she was drunk."

He grinned, took a swallow of coffee, then quoted, "'My strength is as the strength of ten, because my heart is pure.'"

"Tennyson, eh?" She smiled briefly but shook her head. "Most people think their heart is pure, whether it is or not. I mean, you can beat a man until he can't walk or you can even shoot him, as long as it fits within whatever moral code you've made up for yourself."

He shook his head. "I just do what has to be done."

"Wrong!" she snapped. "There's more to it than that. You're

hard as nails, but somewhere along the line you've decided on some things that are right and wrong. You'll let yourself be pounded into the ground before you'll break one of your codes."

"I think you're describing you, not me."

She studied him, still possessed by a thought he couldn't read. Finally she said, "Someday you'll find out about right and wrong, Ben."

"Find out what?"

"You'll find out that before anything can be called wrong there has to be something called right. Any man who says there's no God and no moral law in the world can never say, 'That's not fair!'"

Savage was enjoying this, having been on the receiving end of several such conversations. He knew her convictions went to the bone. "Why couldn't he say that?" he asked.

"Because if there's no moral law of any kind—no God, in other words—what makes things wrong?"

"People do," he argued. "They make up laws."

"But they had to have an idea of injustice before they could come up with a system of justice. Can't you see that?" Her eyes were bright, and in her intensity she reached out and shook his arm. "If there were no moral force in the universe, it wouldn't be wrong for one person to kill another for his belongings. Which is what Darwin is really saying, isn't it? That we're all animals who take what we want whenever we're strong enough?"

"It seems to work that way in the real world, Danielle," Ben interjected.

"Yes, with madmen like Hitler," she said. "But what about people like Jim Elliot, who died as a martyr in Ecuador? He loved the people who killed him. And his wife went back later and told the very natives who'd killed her husband about the love of Jesus Christ. How can you explain things like that, Ben?"

He sobered and shook his head. "I *can't* explain them, Danielle. Maybe they're just different from common people like me."

"I don't believe that," she objected stubbornly.

"I know you don't." He moved his shoulders. "Guess we'd better go. Curtain time in an hour."

He paid the check, and they drove to the theater through heavy traffic. "I hope Jonathan's in better shape than he was when he got the latest letter," Ben commented as he parked the car. "Calvin said it took all the steam out of him."

Once they entered the theater they became enmeshed in a different world. Dani checked on Jonathan and was relieved to see that his eyes were clear. She went to her own dressing room and changed into her first costume.

A few minutes before the curtain call, she left the dressing room and moved toward the stage. She found Ringo slumped against the wall. "Hello, Ringo."

"Hi, Danielle. Did you hear about the new threat?"

"Yes. I've been praying that nothing happens tonight." She studied the big man, then commented, "It's like living on top of a powder keg, isn't it?"

"It's pretty scary all right." He nodded. "I don't think Ainsley can take much more."

They talked for a few moments, then Dani said, "Time for the curtain. Do a great job tonight, Ringo."

"You too, Danielle!"

The first act went smoothly enough, with Jonathan seeming cool and professional. Dani spotted Goldman and two other policemen backstage. As the play moved into the second act, she told Lyle, "All right so far" and got a grin from him.

Mickey Trask came to stand beside her toward the middle of the second act, a murder scene, which had been troublesome from the beginning. It called for the death of Lily's character, Diane Melton.

The difficulty had always been the timing. The murder, one of several in the play, was carefully staged—one of Trey Miller's favorite sets, a bedroom with high windows on three sides. In the middle of the room stood a large poster bed with a canopy. The scene called for Jonathan to be in the room with Lily at the end, but in the scene following Diane's murder, Ainsley had to enter almost at once in full evening dress.

After Jonathan would leave, Lily would go to bed, and the lights would dim so that almost nothing could be seen. Then a shadowy figure would appear at one of the windows, open it, and stand over the young woman. He would then remove a knife from his belt, raise it, and plunge it downward!

It was a key scene, and the audience was not supposed to know who the killer was. Since Jonathan had only just enough time to make the costume change for the next act, Nero had instructed someone else to do the stabbing. Usually Tom Calvin or Mickey Trask took his place, although neither of them wanted to do the scene. Calvin didn't like to be onstage at all, and Mickey disliked the fact that the killer appeared only as a shrouded figure and had no lines.

Mickey cried out in a low voice, "I hate this scene."

"Better go get your costume on," Dani suggested and watched as he nodded and disappeared into the thick backstage darkness. All lights were off, and she turned to watch Lily and Jonathan play out the scene. It was a love scene, and Dani couldn't help thinking, *Lily doesn't have to act in this scene—that's why she comes across so well.*

Finally Jonathan left. Lily slipped off her dressing gown, turned the lights off, and got into the big bed. Utter quiet filled the theater. It was, Dani realized, one of those moments in a drama that was bigger than itself. Lily's character had been the most sympathetic in the entire play, and her look of youthful innocence could win any audience. But the driving ambition of the central character made it obvious that she had to die.

When the shadow of a hand appeared, framed by one of the large windows, every spectator was pulling for Lily to survive, though without much hope. The suspense built as the sinister figure jimmied the window, then very slowly, carefully, and silently put one foot and then the other over the sill. The lighting was superb. Nero had fought with Pinkie, the light man, over it, until he got what he wanted, which was for the audience to see the face of Lily, the shadow, and nothing else. The light was on the head of Lily's bed, where it would fall full on her face.

And it worked, Dani saw. The dark figure of the intruder was a shadow and a shape, but the single light focused on the face of Lily as she lay quietly with closed eyes and a small smile on her lips.

Then the shrouded figure pulled a knife from his belt, and the same faint light that touched Lily's face made a dull gleam on the blade as it was lifted high.

The suspense was unbelievable, as always, and Dani watched as the arm suddenly swept downward.

The script called for Lily to die instantly, but as the knife fell, a piercing scream shook Dani's nerves, and Lily cried out, "He's killing me!"

Instantly there was the sound of breaking glass, and then the tiny light was extinguished, leaving the stage in utter darkness. Ainsley screamed for lights, but Pinkie, up in the balcony, was confused. Caught off guard, he sat there doing nothing.

Dani felt the press of bodies moving toward the stage, and Goldman's voice rang out. "Seal all the doors!"

Finally someone had the presence of mind to switch on a light, and Ben instantly closed the curtain. Dani ran to the bed, arriving there at the same time as Jonathan, who reached for Lily, crying out her name.

To the relief of all of them, Lily opened her eyes and whispered, "I'm all right!"

"Thank God!" Jonathan said and held her close. Then he pulled back, staring down at her. "You're bleeding!" he cried out.

Lily touched her left side, where a crimson stain was blossoming on her night dress. "He—he cut me, but I don't think it's serious."

Dani was pushed aside by Goldman. "Let me see," he commanded. She glanced over his shoulder and noticed that the blood was flowing from a gash no more than four inches long on Lily's left side. "Not bad," was Goldman's verdict. He turned and walked rapidly away.

Dani followed at once, relieved that Lily was all right. As they passed off the stage and made their way to the rear, someone called out, "Hey, Lieutenant, over here!"

Dani followed closely as Goldman moved behind the set. One of his men bent over a still figure. "You got him!" Goldman exclaimed in satisfaction. "Where's the knife?"

"He ain't got no knife on him, Lieutenant," the other man said at once. "And he's been hit on the head. Feel that bump!"

"He must have a knife!" Goldman leaned over to touch the side of Mickey Trask's head. "Get up on the stage and find it—*now!*"

"Yes, sir!"

Dani knelt beside the unconscious man. "That's a bad-looking bump, Jake," she warned.

He stared at her wordlessly, then looked back at Trask's face. Dani heard somebody dismissing the audience. Then the officer who had been sent to find the knife returned. "Lieutenant, there's no knife on the stage."

"Call an ambulance," Goldman snapped. His face was harsh, and he suddenly slapped Mickey's cheek twice. "Come out of it, Trask!" he ordered coldly.

"Goldman, the man is unconscious!" Dani turned to see Tom Calvin, who had come to stand beside her.

Jake stared at him, then down at the blank face of Mickey Trask. "Somebody tried to kill that woman," he announced slowly. "I don't care if there's no knife or if he's dead to the world. He's under arrest for attempted murder!"

Thirteen

WELCOME TO THE KINGDOM

Goldman insisted on meeting the whole cast on the stage at ten o'clock the next morning. Jonathan had called off that evening's performance until they could determine whether or not Lily would be able to act.

When Dani arrived just before 10, she went straight to Jonathan's office and found him looking wan and haggard. "How is Lily?" Dani asked at once.

"It wasn't nearly as bad as it could have been," he said. He lit a cigarette with fingers that were not quite steady. The lack of sleep had taken away his customary exuberance, and he sat there staring at the desktop for a long moment. Forcing a slight smile, he reported, "The cut was relatively superficial. She had several stitches, but the doctors say she'll heal quickly."

"I'm glad to hear that, Jonathan." Relief filled Dani's voice. "It could have been fatal."

"Have you talked to Goldman yet?" he asked.

"No."

"He's talking about closing the play down."

"That might not be a bad idea, Jonathan. Sooner or later this person is going to kill again." Dani studied the actor thoughtfully, then asked, "Would it be the end of the world for you if you did close the play?"

"Yes!" Ainsley snuffed out his cigarette nervously, got to his feet, and headed for the door. "Let's go see what Goldman has to say."

On the stage, they found the others already gathered. Mickey Trask was being carefully watched by a plainclothesman. The actor had a white bandage on the left side of his head and a look of outraged anger on his baby face.

Goldman waited until Dani and Jonathan moved onto the stage, then announced, "I thought it would be better to talk to you all at once than one at a time, and there's more room here than down at the station." Goldman's pearl-gray suit and wine-colored tie with a diamond that glittered whenever he moved made Dani think how unlike a police officer he looked. But anger ran below the surface of that smooth demeanor.

"Let me tell you upfront, I've tried to get this play shut down." He threw Ainsley a hard look. "But somebody's put pressure on in the right places, and my superiors tell me it can't be done. Civil liberties or something like that."

No one said a word. In the silence Goldman slowly lit a thin, brown cigarette. Snapping the case shut with grim anger, he said, "If one nut calls with a bomb threat, they ground airplanes, but you people don't seem to want to admit there's a real psycho just waiting to put some of you underground."

"I think we understand the seriousness of the thing, Lieutenant," Ainsley spoke up. "But we can't let this maniac rule our lives."

Goldman stared at Ainsley as if he had made a particularly stupid statement. "All right, let's get on with this," he responded calmly. "I understand Miss Aumont isn't seriously hurt, but the charge is still attempted homicide."

"You can't hang this on me, Goldman," Mickey said loudly. He glared at the policeman defiantly, adding, "I was never on the stage at all."

"Suppose you give us your version again, Trask," Goldman suggested. He had heard the story several times, but he wanted to check the reactions of the group.

"Again?" Mickey cried indignantly. "I've gone over it a dozen times. I went back to put on the costume like always. Then I went behind the set and started to go to the window when somebody let the roof down on me." He touched the white bandage on his head gingerly, then shrugged. "I didn't see anybody. Just boom! The next thing I knew, I was waking up with my skull bleeding and hearing that I'm under arrest."

"So who climbed in the window and tried to kill Lily Aumont?" Goldman asked.

"How should I know?" Mickey demanded. "All I know is it wasn't me! I was out like a light!"

Goldman suggested, "I want each one of you to tell me exactly where you were at the time of the attempted murder. *All* of you—men and women."

Ainsley said at once, "I was in my dressing room, getting ready for the next scene. I have to change into a formal tuxedo, and I have just enough time to make the switch."

"Anybody with you?"

"No. I was alone."

"All right." From his smooth features it was impossible to tell what Goldman was thinking. "Sir Adrian, can you summarize your movements at the time of the crime?"

"Y-yes, of course, Lieutenant." The older man nodded. He was sitting beside his wife on a pale green couch and looked ill. His face was drawn taut, and he seemed exhausted. "I was in the next scene with Jonathan, so I had to be in a tux as well. I can never tie my tie properly, so my wife has to help me with it." He flinched suddenly, as though struck by an unexpected pang, but quickly said, "As usual my wife and I were together, Lieutenant."

"Thank you, Sir Adrian." No one for a moment believed that he or his wife were physically capable of the crime.

"Miss Morgan? What about you?"

"Oh, come now, Lieutenant Goldman," Jonathan snorted. "Don't be absurd!"

"Why? Because she's a woman?" Goldman gave Dani a close glance, then contended, "It's not impossible for a woman to climb in a window and stab somebody."

Though she wasn't sure whether Goldman was just trying to draw the guilty party out or really suspected her, Dani sought to smooth things over. "It's all right, Jonathan. Lieutenant, I was standing in the wings watching the performance. I can't be sure whether or not anyone saw me."

"Yeah, I saw her," Ringo Jordan offered. "I was right behind her the whole time."

"And who was watching you?" Goldman asked.

"Nobody," Jordan admitted sullenly. "You think we stand around watching one another all the time? When the play is on, we have to move pretty fast to get everything done. What about your men—didn't they see anybody?"

Goldman ignored the question, demanding of the others, "Anybody see Jordan?"

"Well, I was with Lyle, just across the stage from Miss Morgan and Ringo. I saw them both before the lights dimmed," Tom Calvin offered.

"That's right." Lyle Jamison nodded. "I can vouch for that."

"But neither of you could see anything after the lights went out?" Goldman prodded. Neither of them spoke, so he moved on. "What about you, Miss Rio?"

Carmen was wearing a flamboyant dress that looked out of place for the setting. Her cheeks reddened as she answered, "I was where I always am at that point in the play. I have to come on in the next scene with a tray full of cocktail glasses. That means I have to go to the prop room and get them ready." She glared at him. "And no, I wasn't with anyone." Lifting her chin as though daring him to accuse her, she protested, "And if you think I could wiggle through that window in that tight maid's uniform, you're crazy!"

"That leaves the stage crew. You first, Davis."

Ben said at once, "Just as soon as the scene with Lily is finished, we have to move both wings of stage number one backwards. Then we have to run to the back and push stage number two to the front."

"But that's *after* the murder scene, isn't it?" Goldman asked.

"Yes. I go to the west wing. Earl goes to the right during that scene. The movable sets are shifted by means of a set of ropes that go through a reduction pulley. As soon as the murder takes place on stage, Julio closes the curtain. Then he runs around and gets ready to move stage number two in the slot created by moving the two halves to the right and left."

Goldman stared at him. "Let me ask it this way, Davis . . . Did anyone see you waiting to pull the stages?"

"I don't think so." Ben shook his head. "Earl and I get as far back as we can from the stages—we get better leverage that way. It was dark, of course, and I went to my station as the scene started. But I don't think anybody pays any attention to us—unless something goes wrong."

Goldman questioned Earl and Julio next, but they couldn't add to Ben's description. For the next twenty minutes he questioned them over and over until they were all sick of it. Finally Lady Lockridge interjected, "Lieutenant, my husband is ill. I want to take him home at once."

Goldman immediately nodded. "Of course. Thank you for coming." Dani watched as the two left and noted that Sir Adrian seemed almost lost. As they left, he leaned heavily on his wife, not taking his eyes off the floor.

"All right then, we've got three basic possibilities. One: an outsider, somebody not in the cast, came behind the stage. It wouldn't have been so hard, not with the stage so dark. Two: one of the cast—besides Trask, that is—slugged Trask, went on the stage, and stabbed the girl." He considered that, then looked directly at Trask. "And number three: you did the job, Trask."

"You're crazy!" Trask cried loudly. "Did I knock myself out?"

"Maybe you did."

"With *what?*" Mickey demanded indignantly. "I couldn't have split my head open with my bare hands, could I? And your men didn't find a thing on me or near me, not even a chair that I could have brained myself with!"

Goldman had no answer for that. He had gone over every possible scenario, but none of them could get past the fact that Mickey Trask had been struck on the head and they couldn't find whatever had been used to do it.

"And if I'd done it, I'd have the knife, wouldn't I?" Mickey said loudly. "I didn't have one, did I?"

The missing weapon had been the subject of an intense search. Immediately after the stabbing, Goldman had his men comb every square inch of the stage, but to no avail. Goldman hated sloppiness, and he knew that knife had to be there! He had scolded his men, but they swore there was nothing onstage to be found.

Now he finally took a deep breath, letting his irritation flow away. "We're going to be talking to all of you people some more, so stay available."

"What about me?" Mickey asked.

"You're not under arrest," Goldman decided.

Mickey's face broke into a smile, and he said to Ringo, "At last the cops do something right."

As the crowd broke up Jonathan announced, "I'll be getting in touch, but if Lily is up to it, we can go on again tomorrow night."

Dani went to her apartment and spent the morning trying to put the pieces together. She longed to have her father with her, for it was the sort of case he was best at. But it was too late to bring him into it, and in any case, for him to come to New York was impossible. The phone rang. When she answered it, Ben said, "I have two tickets to the rodeo at Madison Square Garden. Do you want to go with me, or do I need to find another woman?"

"Oh, Ben!" she exclaimed. "Just what I need. What time?"

"I'll pick you up at 6. We can eat something later."

Dani felt her load lift. This case had had her tied up for so long with no relief that she had become tense all day every day. She fixed a salad and was just finishing it when the phone rang again.

"Danielle? This is Victoria Lockridge."

"Oh, Victoria, how are you?"

"Well, I have a favor to ask, rather a large one."

"What is it? I'd be glad to help any way I can."

"I'm sure you noticed that my husband wasn't feeling well this morning. I brought him home and put him to bed, and he's been sleeping. But I need to run some errands. Would it be asking too much for you to come and stay with him for a couple of hours?"

Dani said quickly, "Of course not. What's your address?"

"It's not inconveniencing you too much?"

"Not a bit," she answered. "I have an engagement tonight, but not a thing this afternoon. I'll be right over."

Forty-five minutes later she was met at the door by Lady Lockridge, who drew her into the apartment. "I feel terrible, putting you to all this trouble, Danielle," she apologized. "But I don't like to leave him alone. And he doesn't like nurses."

"Don't think of it," Dani said. "Has he been to the doctor?"

Lady Lockridge looked very tired. "Oh, my dear, he's been to so many! He has a heart condition, you know, and we have to watch his medication very carefully." Her regal and usually formal face seemed distraught, and she shook her head with a gesture of futility. "He just won't take care of himself! I have to watch him like a hawk—his medicine, the proper meals, and not drinking too much!"

"He's fortunate to have a wife like you to take care of him."

The older woman gave her a quick look, an odd smile touching her thin lips. "Not everyone has said that," she commented quietly. "I was just having some tea. Come and join me before I leave."

The two women sat down at the kitchen table. When Lady Lockridge had poured Dani a cup of tea, she acknowledged, "I wasn't the wife most people wanted Adrian to have. He was at the top of his career when we met, you know, and I was just a struggling young actress." She sipped her tea, and a faraway look came into her eyes. "He could have married anybody, Danielle! He had everything—looks, talent, and presence!"

"But he chose you." Dani smiled.

"Yes, he chose me." Pride filled her eyes as she looked across the table. "Everyone said he was throwing himself away. His own family tried to talk him out of marrying me. But he did it anyway." She had been fiddling with the bracelet on her left wrist. Now she held it up. "Have you noticed this, Danielle?" she asked.

Dani looked at it. It was a woven gold chain with a single ornament suspended by a gold clasp. "That's not a ruby?" she exclaimed. "It's so large."

"No." Lady Victoria smiled. "It's made out of glass." Dani noticed now that it was a small flask shaped like a jug, with a tiny cork in the mouth. "It's filled with red wine, Danielle," she said fondly. Raising her eyes, she added, "Wine from our wedding supper. I've kept it all these years. Adrian says that our love, like the wine, gets only better as the years go by!"

"How sweet!" Dani exclaimed. "It's beautiful."

"My good luck charm. Like all stage people, I'm terribly superstitious," she admitted. "I'm never without it. We'll share it on our golden wedding anniversary."

"You've been very happy."

"I think we would have been happier if Adrian had been something other than an actor." Lady Lockridge spoke quietly. "It's a hard, glittering world, my dear. I don't think anyone ever walks away from it unscarred."

Dani sensed the pain beneath the words and quickly redirected the conversation. "I think this play will do great things for your careers."

"If we live through it," Lady Lockridge remarked bitterly. Her face turned hard. "Let me show you where my husband's medicine is." She took Danielle to the door leading from the living room and peered in. "Why, you're awake, Adrian!" she said cheerfully. "I have a surprise for you. I have to go out for a while, but I've brought you some company."

Dani followed her into the large bedroom, where Sir Adrian lay in a double bed. His lined face lifted into a smile when he saw her. "Well, I must be getting old!" he said to his wife. "There was a time when you wouldn't have left me alone with a lovely thing like this."

"I don't trust you an inch, Adrian," she teased, stooping down to kiss him. "However, I do trust Danielle." She moved to pick up her coat. "He needs two of those blue pills at three o'clock. Don't let him get out of bed."

"What a nuisance!" Sir Adrian snorted. "Nothing wrong with me that a good stiff drink wouldn't cure."

"You know what the doctor said," Lady Lockridge chided him. "I'll try not to be too long, Danielle," she promised as she left.

"Take your time," Dani responded. She came to stand over the tall man lying in the bed. "I'm sorry you're not feeling well, Sir Adrian."

He threw the bedcover back and swung his feet to the floor. "Hand me that robe, will you, Danielle?" He put his hands back, and she helped him into the velour robe. "Thank you. Now, let's go sit in the living room. I'm sick of this bedroom."

"All right." The two of them went into the living room. "Let's sit here where we can watch the city," Sir Adrian suggested. "It's a fine view, isn't it?"

They sat on the couch, talking about unimportant things. *How pale he is!* Dani observed. She had never thought of Sir Adrian Lockridge as an elderly man, perhaps because she had seen him in so many films as a young man. He was sixty-two, but one of her best friends, a shrimp fisherman named Henry Legrand, was ten years older and remained lean and strong. The actor's hand lay across the back of the couch, and Dani saw that it was thin and covered with liver spots, the wasted hand of a very old man indeed.

"Tell me about yourself," he said.

"No, that would be very boring."

Dani smiled. "Please, I want to hear about you—everything! Your whole life. I'm going to be telling my children someday that I spent the day with Sir Adrian Lockridge, and I don't want to spend it telling how I got braces when I was ten."

He laughed and leaned back on the couch. He began to speak

of his early days in show business, and she encouraged him from time to time. The time flew by. Once he had her get a book from the study and read to him. At the end of an hour she remembered. "Oh, it's time for your medicine. Let me get it."

She started to get up but suddenly saw that his face was twisted in an expression of pure agony. "Sir Adrian, what is it?"

He gasped, "Brown bottle—in medicine cabinet—get it!"

She flew to the bathroom, found a large brown bottle of liquid, and rushed back. "This one?" He nodded and reached out his hand.

"I'll get a spoon," she began, but he shook his head. Removing the cap, he lifted it to his lips and swallowed convulsively. Lowering the bottle, he sat there, biting his lower lip. Dani didn't know what to do, but she saw that the medicine was evidently very powerful, for the strain left his face, and he took a deep breath.

"Thank you, my dear," he whispered. "I think I'll lie down for a little while."

He got to his feet, and Dani walked with him. He seemed a little dizzy and leaned on her arm. She helped him out of his robe, and when he lay down, she pulled the covers over him.

"I'll just sit here for a while," she offered quietly.

He nodded. They remained silent for what seemed a long time. His eyes were closed, and that particular frozen stillness about his face reminded Dani suddenly of the face of a dead man. It was an unpleasant thought, and she pressed her lips together, forcing it out of her mind. *He's much sicker than any of us thought*, she decided. *I don't see how he can get through another performance.*

The silence ran on, and it was so deep that she was startled when he said, "Danielle?"

"Yes?"

"Don't tell my wife about the spell."

"Of course not." Dani realized that Lady Lockridge knew her husband better than he dreamed. "Have you been ill long?" she asked.

"Not like this. I had a bypass three years ago, but I seem to have gotten over that." His voice was thin, and she saw that his eyes were open, but he stared blankly at the ceiling. "For the past two months I've been having some sort of stomach trouble."

"What does the doctor say?"

"Oh, you know how those fellows are," he complained. "I've been to half a score, and they all poke and probe, then give you a bottle of pills and say, 'Here, old fellow, try this!'"

"There are some very fine hospitals here in New York. You ought to have a complete physical."

He smiled slightly and turned his eyes to look at her. "You sound like Victoria," he commented. "She's been at me for weeks. And I finally gave in. Went to one of the best just a week ago. My word, I didn't know there were so many things they could put a chap through! Medieval torture, that's what it is!"

"What did they say?"

"Say? What they always say—'we want to do more tests.'"

"You'd better mind your doctors." Dani smiled at him. She pulled the cover closer around his chin, adding, "We couldn't afford to lose you, Sir Adrian. You're a national treasure!"

She was surprised to see a tear glisten in his eye, and he moved his head from side to side. "You are a very comforting sort of person, Danielle." He hesitated before admitting, "I suppose we all have strange thoughts when we are ill. I've noticed that for the last few weeks I've been thinking more of—well, of what comes after, you know?"

"Everyone should think of that, Sir Adrian—sick or well."

"I suppose that is true, but life is so—so crowded!" His hands twisted together, and he stared at them. "When you're a young man, fighting to get to the top, you don't think it'll ever end. All you concentrate on is winning the prize. When you do gain a little recognition, you have to fight to keep it. After that—" He broke off suddenly and lay there, troubled but quiet.

Dani said quietly, "The best time for a person to find God is when he's a child. But most of us don't do that. We get excited about the world, but the world is never quite the prize we think it is. We go around and around on the carousel, trying to grab the brass ring; but when we get it, we discover it isn't what we really wanted at all."

He looked at her with a strange expression, as though he'd never really seen her. "You are a strange young woman!" he commented slowly. "They told me you were religious. I suppose that's why you think of these things."

Dani thought about that, then asserted, "I've always thought about God, even when I was a very little girl. I always assumed that everyone thought about God. Didn't you think about heaven and hell when you were a child?"

"You know, I really did!" he confessed with surprise in his voice. "It was a long time ago, of course, but I can remember quite clearly asking my father about those things. Who made me? Who is God? That sort of thing." He fell silent, then added with a touch of sadness, "Too bad we let those things slide."

Dani sat there, feeling inadequate. She had heard so many sermons stressing the need for sharing faith in Christ, but somehow this time she wasn't sure what to say. Once she had taken a five-day course, with books, instructions, step-by-step procedures, and so on. Dani had memorized the appropriate responses to all the questions that might come up. Then they had gone out to witness.

But all her training could not have prepared her for this encounter with Sir Adrian. Others had told her how they'd just met someone by chance, told him of Jesus and how He loved him, and then had seen that person get saved.

Dani had felt a little bitter that such things never seemed to happen to her. Now, looking down at the sick man, she prayed, *God, let me say the right thing!* For a moment her thoughts swirled, and then a strange sense of peace came upon her, and she recognized that the Lord was present.

"Sir Adrian," she said quietly, "may I tell you about what Jesus Christ has meant in my life?"

"Why, certainly!"

Danielle began speaking about her life, how mixed up and confused she was as a child and later as a young woman. She spoke of the sin and rebellion that she'd fallen into. Once it would have been very hard to say such things, but in the quietness of the room, it was not difficult at all.

"I was so mixed up, and the guilt was terrible," she remembered. "Every night I prayed that I wouldn't die and go to hell, but the next day I'd go out and do the same things again. It was like being trapped on a treadmill. I got so sick of life, I thought of ending it."

"Why, you can't have been such a terrible sinner, my dear!" Sir Adrian exclaimed.

Dani shook her head ruefully. "We have a peculiar way of looking at sin, I'm afraid. We have a list, and some sins are terrible, others not so bad, and so on. But God doesn't look at our wrongdoing like that. The second chapter of the book of James, the tenth verse, says, 'For whosoever shall keep the whole law, and yet offend in one point, he is guilty of all.' The Bible says that the fact that we are sinners grieves God. He isn't cataloging our sins according to some sort of scale. All sin separates us from Him."

Sir Adrian lay there silently, then shook his head. "But it hardly seems fair. Do you mean to say that a chap who's led a fairly decent life, paid his bills, and been good to his family—that chap is no better off than a monster who abuses children?"

"It doesn't sound fair on the surface, but God is doing a marvelous thing, Sir Adrian." Dani's eyes glowed as she spoke. Though she didn't realize it, she was presenting an attractive and compelling picture to the sick man. "The world was lost to God when Adam sinned. He set out to win it back, to take that which was lost and make it all good and pure again. That's what Romans 5, verse 12, is all about. It says, 'Wherefore, as by one man sin entered into the world, and death by sin; and so death passed upon all men, for that all have sinned.' The whole world was lost," she repeated. "But I like a verse that comes after that, Sir Adrian. It says, '. . . If through the offense of one, many be dead, much more the grace of God, and the gift by grace, which is by one man, Jesus Christ, hath abounded unto many.'"

He lay there silently. Finally he confessed, "I'm afraid I don't get all that, Danielle. I was never very good at abstract thinking."

"It *is* complicated," she replied, "because it's a cosmic thing, the struggle of good against evil in the cosmos. But I like to bring it down to the place where I can grasp it." She leaned forward, and her face was intense. "Mankind has sinned and is under God's judgment, for God cannot abide sin. So He bought it back, so to speak."

"Bought it back? How in the world could He do that?"

"Sir Adrian, you have undoubtedly heard John 3, verse 16: 'For God so loved the world, that he gave his only begotten Son, that whosoever believeth in him should not perish, but have everlasting life.'"

"I remember that," the sick man said quietly. "My father quoted it often. But I've never understood how that could be. How can a man who died 2,000 years ago do anything for me?"

Dani began to explain the nature of the Incarnation in very simple terms. She had no Bible in her hands, but she quoted freely from the Scriptures, pausing from time to time to make a point clearer.

"When I was a long way from God," she said finally, "I tried everything to please Him. I joined a church, sang in the choir. I lived as good a life as I could, but nothing worked."

She paused and sat there for so long that Sir Adrian asked, "So what did you do, Danielle?"

"I finally realized that God didn't require those things. Anyone can do them. What He really wanted was me. That's what God really loves, Sir Adrian. In John 3:16 the thing He loves—the world—isn't the planet we live on. It means all the people of the world. He loves *me*! He loves *you*! That's the miracle of the Bible and of the cross, Sir Adrian, the fact that Jesus loves us!"

He saw that tears had gathered in her eyes and reached out to take her hand. "My dear, I envy you!"

She let the tears run down her cheeks. "There's no need for that. I don't have any special clout with God. He loves us all. If you want Jesus Christ for your Savior, you can know Him."

He stared at her. "You mean right now?"

"Yes, right now. He asks you to do two things. The first is to repent—that means to turn away from those things that are wrong."

"I'm a little old for that, I'm afraid." Then he gave her a haunted look and added, "I've not led a good life. I have done things that I—I could not even say aloud to you!"

"You can't shock God, and it's not a matter of age," she explained. "It's a matter of turning loose. When you and Lady Lockridge were married, you had to turn away from all other women to her, didn't you? Well, the turning from the things of this world is like that. I know you've never regretted losing other women because you love her. It will be like that. You'll have so much in the kingdom of God, you won't regret the things you left behind."

He lay there, thinking hard. "And the second thing?"

"The second thing is also like a wedding, Sir Adrian. Remember when the minister asked you if you would have the bride as your own? Well, Jesus is waiting for you to receive Him. The Bible says, 'Whosoever shall call upon the name of the Lord shall be saved.'"

She saw that he was tremendously moved and asked softly, "Sir Adrian, would you do what I did when my life seemed hopeless? Would you just turn loose of the world and ask Jesus Christ to make you a new person?"

He lay there so long that she was beginning to wonder if he was offended. Finally he slowly lifted one trembling hand and took hers. "I would like very much to do that," he said.

Dani took his hand, bowed her head, and began to pray. Once she paused and urged him to ask God's forgiveness, and he did so with all the simplicity of a child. Then they both were quiet, and she looked down to see tears running down his cheeks. As she pulled out a tissue from the box on the table and began to wipe the tears away, he whispered, "If I had only done this years ago!"

She lifted the tissue, smiled at him, and spoke encouragingly. "You've come into the kingdom late, Sir Adrian, but Jesus said once that the last shall be first and the first shall be last."

Fifteen minutes later, when Lady Lockridge returned, she found them like that. As Dani rose, Victoria apologized, "I'm sorry I was gone so long."

Dani smiled. "It doesn't matter. Call me anytime." She went over and put out her hand to Sir Adrian, then impulsively bent and kissed his brow. "God bless you," she said, then left the room at once.

"Did you have a good talk with Danielle?" Victoria asked.

He pulled himself up to a sitting position and reached out his hand to her. When she came to take it, he exclaimed, "I have something to tell you, Victoria—something quite wonderful."

Fourteen

SIR ADRIAN'S FINEST PERFORMANCE

The rodeo, Savage decided, was just what the doctor ordered. Though not an avid fan himself, he got his money's worth by watching Dani as the events in the arena unfolded. They had good seats in Madison Square Garden, and he smiled as she lost all inhibitions, yelling and clapping and booing along with the rest of the fans. He flinched when a cowboy was thrown from the back of a huge, tawny Brahman bull, and insisted, "I wouldn't do a stunt like that if they gave me the Washington Monument!"

Dani looked at him oddly. "When you were on the trapeze, Ben, you risked your life two or three times a day."

"Maybe, but I'd rather fall and break my neck than get stomped by one of those monsters!"

When the bucking-bronco event was underway, he asked, "How does a guy win? By staying on until the whistle blows?"

"That's part of it, Ben, but there's lots more. A good rider has to rake his horse with his spurs in perfect time to the animal's moves. He can't grab leather or hold on to anything. It's a matter of style."

To Savage it all looked about the same, but then he wasn't a fan. It was the barrel racing that he'd brought her to see, and it was worth it. Again she explained the rules, though she'd done it before, and he listened as if it were new to him. She looked as excited as any schoolgirl, with her black curls tumbling around her face. "See those barrels forming a big triangle?" she asked. "Well, the idea is to take the horse around the barrels without knocking them over. Oh, look at that horse, Ben! Isn't he beautiful?"

They stayed to the end and afterward went to McDonalds for quarter pounders and chocolate milk shakes. Dani stuffed her mouth full, talking around her food, reliving the rodeo.

"You should have made a career of barrel racing, Dani! You like it so much," Ben told her.

"I wanted to, Ben. And I almost did. But it didn't work out."

"Why not?"

"Well, it's so competitive. There are only a fixed number of rodeos and about half a million girls who'd like to win the national. It's like all sports, I guess. For every 5,000 who try to get in, only one really makes it big."

He studied her through half-shut eyes. "Doesn't sound like you—quitting because the odds are tough."

She cocked her head and thought about that. "I was good," she admitted. "But there were 200 more just as good. I could have gotten by, I think, but that's about all. It's a pretty rough life too."

He grinned at her suddenly, his eyes catching the gleam of the outside lights. "Not like this piece of cake we've got going, I guess."

Her mouth went tight, and she nodded. "Good point. It's terrible, Ben. This whole mess with Jonathan is like an avalanche. I sometimes think nobody can stop it."

"You finished?" he asked, sorry he'd brought up the case. It had been good to see her lose herself in something more enjoyable, but now the moment seemed to be gone. On the way home he tried to steer clear of the mystery they couldn't seem to solve, but she was obviously thinking about it. As he walked with her up to her door, she explained, "The terrible thing is, I've gotten to know these people, Ben. They were just names once, but now they're all real!" She unlocked the door. "Come on in. I want you to go over some things."

She got the coffeepot going, and for half an hour they sat at the table, filling several legal pads with notes.

"Ben, what would it do to you if you found out that Carmen was the murderer?" Dani wondered aloud. "How would you feel if she was put in jail for life and you knew you were responsible for catching her?"

He lifted an eyebrow in surprise, then shrugged. "I'd feel sorry for her."

"But you'd do it?"

"Sure, I would. That's my job." She looked down at the pad in front of her, thinking hard.

"What would you do if it turned out it was Calvin?" he asked suddenly.

"Calvin? Why, that's out of the question!"

"No, it's not. But for the sake or argument, say it was him—would you lose sleep over sending him to the slammer?"

Dani narrowed her eyes, concentrated hard, then nodded. "Yes, I would." She straightened her back, and a faint light of anger entered her eyes. "Anybody would, Ben. Even you!"

He studied his coffee cup silently, then lifted his head. "A cop named Bates was on the take when I was in the department in Denver. I turned him in. He got kicked out and went to the pen for two years." Then he said evenly, "He was my partner. Got me out of a tight spot once or twice."

Dani stared at him, fascinated. "Didn't that bother you later?"

"I couldn't afford to let it." He shrugged. "Bates knew what he was doing."

"You're a hard one, Ben," Dani said slowly. "Too hard. One of these days you're going to learn about bending a little bit."

He only admitted, "Could be." He got to his feet. "Anyway, the rodeo was fun. I always liked to see guys get their brains scrambled by a dumb horse."

She laughed and rose to escort him to the door. He slipped into his coat, and for a moment they were so close that he could smell the faint aroma of her perfume. Her eyes were enormous.

"You'd better fire me," he advised her.

"Fire you?" She looked confused. "What in the world for?" Dani wondered what was going on behind that rough exterior. He had tried her patience time after time, and more than once in their stormy encounters she had come to the brink of firing him, but had never actually done it. Each time the thought of going on a case without his support caused her to cut him some slack.

"Why would I fire you?" she demanded.

"I am about to break a rule," he said.

"You don't usually notify me beforehand! What rule?"

Savage reached out and pulled her close. His voice softened as he whispered, "The rule that says I can't kiss my boss the same night I take her to a rodeo."

The corners of his lips curved upward, and she knew he was waiting for her to pull away. "Well," she answered softly, moving even closer to him, "are you going to break your silly old rule or not?" He had kissed her twice before, and both times had been light and carefree. She wasn't quite sure what to expect or do. She suddenly put her hands behind his head, drew it forward, and put her lips on his.

The pressure of his lips was faint, then grew stronger. His arms tightened around her. For a moment she held him, then slid her lips away. Stepping back, she smiled. "So you broke the rule, Ben. Good night." He stepped into the hallway, and she closed the door gently.

The kiss had shaken and somehow angered him. She had gotten the best of him. Staring at the door, he asked, "So am I fired or not?"

"Not!" came her faint reply, and he heard her giggling. Happy but irritated, he glared at the door, then whirled and walked down the stairs. But by the time he got to his car, his mood had changed. As he looked up at the lights in her window, a smile broke across his lips. "Well, she won that time!" He got into the car, whistling a cheerful and dreadfully off-key version of "Mama, Don't Let Your Babies Grow up to Be Cowboys."

♦ ♦ ♦

"The call came from Richard Jurgens while you were gone, Jonathan." Tom Calvin handed him a note. "That's his offer for doing the screen version of *Out of the Night.*"

Ainsley had just come into his office. It was only six o'clock, but he had asked Calvin to meet him to go over some financial matters. He looked at the note, smiled, and handed it back. "I got a call from John Simpson yesterday. He offered almost twice that, Tom."

He sat down at his desk, and for the next fifteen minutes the two men went over the finances. Finally Ainsley leaned back, saying, "Well, it looks good. Better than I'd hoped even."

"No play ever had so much free publicity, I guess," Tom commented. "But maybe it's all over."

"I think so," Ainsley admitted. "Whoever was doing it all must have been scared off." It had been a week since the stabbing incident, and since then everything had gone smoothly.

"How long a run do you want to shoot for, Jonathan?" Calvin asked.

"Not too long. I want to do the movie version as soon as possible. Then I have another idea that I think will fly."

Calvin hesitated, then prodded, "What about Sir Adrian? He's not doing very well."

"I've asked Dave Tolliver to learn the role." Tolliver was an actor of some stature who was a good friend of Ainsley's. "I've been worried about the old man. He's ill, and I told Dave to be ready to step in at once."

"I hope it doesn't come to that," Calvin wished regretfully.

"So do I, but we have to be prepared."

♦ ♦ ♦

Most of the cast felt concerned for Sir Adrian, who was barely able to make it through each performance. "You'd never know how bad he feels," Dani said to Lyle as they watched him go through his final scene in the play one night. "He gives it all he's got, but when it's over he's ready to collapse."

"He ought to quit, I guess," Lyle remarked.

"That's hard to do when acting is all you know," Dani murmured. She had grown very close to the old man during the past week. Twice she had gone to the Lockridge apartment to visit, and she could tell that the strain of her husband's ill health was getting to Victoria.

"Did you ever get the reports from the physical Sir Adrian had?" she asked once.

"Oh, it was the same as all the rest," Victoria quickly explained. She placed her hand on Dani's. "You're very good for him, Danielle!"

"I only wish I could do more."

Ben spent most of his free time checking props. "These people seem to have forgotten there's a killer loose, Dani," he complained one evening before the performance.

"I think we'd all *like* to forget it, Ben," she answered. He was prowling around, reaching under an old-fashioned bathtub. "What are you doing?" she demanded.

"Checking to make sure there's not a trapdoor under this tub. I'd hate to see you disappear right in the middle of the play." He gave her a quick grin. "This is my favorite scene in the whole play."

"It would be!" she snapped. The scene bothered her, for in it she appeared to be taking a bath on stage. In one of Miller's ornate sets, the huge tub was filled with a few inches of water. Then a machine whipped up suds to make it bubble over. She wore a workout suit and was in the tub from the time the curtain opened on the scene until it closed.

Mickey, who played her lover, came in, and they had a long dialogue, but no more than her head and arms were ever revealed. She would put on the workout suit in her dressing room, throw a robe over it, then go to the set. Earl always had the water just right with the bubbles all the way to the top. She would simply toss her robe to one side and get in. When the scene ended, she would get out, put on the robe, and go change for the next scene.

Ben had teased her about the scene from the first. "What will your parents think?" he mourned. "And what will all the guys back at the office think—Dani Ross taking a bath in public?"

Dani had put up with the gibes, but now as he felt around under the tub, she asked, "Ben, I'm feeling pretty jittery. I—I guess things are going well, but I feel as if we're in the eye of a hurricane."

He straightened up and nodded, his face serious. "I know what you mean. These people are living in a fool's paradise. It's just a matter of time until the murderer tries again. Be careful, boss!"

The performance that night was off, primarily because Sir Adrian was not able to keep pace. He missed several cues, and some of his lines came out so garbled they could not be understood. Jonathan was unhappy, they all saw, but he said nothing to Lockridge.

The next day Dani met Charlie Allgood at the theater. He was reading a paper, and when he saw her, he came forward at once. "You know anything about this?"

Dani looked at the story he indicated. The headline stated: "Tolliver to Replace Sir Adrian Lockridge in Play." The brief story explained that due to ill health Sir Adrian Lockridge was leaving the cast of *Out of the Night* and would be replaced by David Tolliver. "No, I didn't know about it," Dani murmured.

"I don't think Lockridge knew either," the reporter said. "He came in early this morning and had a real run-in with Jonathan."

"Excuse me, Charlie." She hurried to Jonathan's office. He was with Tom Calvin, and some of her anger must have shown in her face.

"Now before you start on me, Danielle," he said defensively, "this story is all wrong. It's completely out of order."

"Did you hire this man Tolliver to take Sir Adrian's place?"

"I certainly did not!" Ainsley stated emphatically. "I did talk to Tolliver on the phone. Asked him if he'd be free to take over if Sir Adrian couldn't continue, but that's all!"

"That's true enough, Danielle," Tom insisted. "I expect Tolliver told someone, and the reporters took it from there."

"How terrible that must have been for Adrian and Victoria!" Dani exclaimed. "Reading such a thing in the newspapers!"

Ainsley nodded grimly. "I know that better than anybody. The same thing happened to me once. I found out I'd been fired from a part by reading the paper. It was ghastly!"

"Sir Adrian was too upset to listen, Danielle," Tom said. "Why don't you go talk to him. Explain the way it was."

"Yes, and tell him I said he can stay in that role until he's a hundred as far as I'm concerned," Jonathan added.

"I'll do that." Dani nodded. "But, Jonathan, I think you should make a statement to the papers. Give it to Allgood. He's outside right now."

"I'll take care of it, Danielle," Jonathan promised.

She went at once to the Lockridges' apartment and was met at the door by Victoria. The older woman's eyes were cold, but when Dani asked, "How is he, Victoria?" she seemed to shake off the emotion that grasped her. "Not very well, Danielle. It came as such a shock."

"I can imagine, but I have good news. Can I talk to both of you?"

"Of course. Sit down and I'll get Adrian."

She left the room, but Dani paced the floor nervously. She had grown fond of Sir Adrian and of his wife as well, though she was much harder to get to know. When the pair came back, she began at once. "I must tell you, it's all been a horrible mistake. Ainsley has made no contract with David Tolliver. He told me to tell you that you can stay in your role until you're a hundred years old as far as he's concerned. Those were his exact words."

Sir Adrian was wearing an ancient smoking jacket. He had emerged with an angry look on his face, but slowly he relaxed. "There, you see, dear? I said it was all a mistake!"

Lady Lockridge was not so happy. "He's lying, Adrian. That man has never done an unselfish thing in his life. He'll never keep his word to you. He never has."

Dani stayed for thirty minutes, trying to calm them down. At one point she saw Victoria's shoulders slump, a rare sign of weakness in the strong woman. Dani went to her before she left, hoping to comfort her. "It'll be all right, Victoria, you'll see!"

Lady Lockridge kept her face averted for a moment. "It will never be the same, Danielle! Never!" she objected.

Dani went home for a while, then arrived at the theater in time to see Ben before she changed. "I talked to the Lockridges."

"How are they doing?"

"Not very well. I'm afraid for them, Ben."

She hurried to her dressing room to get ready for curtain time. She saw Sir Adrian in his costume, waiting to go on, and he looked better than he had for days. When he saw her, he promised, "Tonight, Danielle, you're going to see something special."

And she did. She saw a man dominate the stage in a way she could never have imagined. That night Sir Adrian Lockridge gave the finest performance of his life. He was flawless in every line. His body language was that of a young man, and the rest of the actors might as well have been made of wood for all the audience noticed them.

When the final curtain fell, Jonathan went to Sir Adrian, grinning. "The rest of us don't need to bother even going out there, Adrian. It's your show tonight!"

The audience simply would not let Sir Adrian go. He made eight curtain calls and finally lifted his hand for silence. When it came, he said strongly, "My life has been the theater. It is all that I have known. But now that I am older I see that I have left something out of my life. A dear young friend of mine has introduced me to something far better than anything I've ever known. Because of that, I can say with a feeling I never had before, may the Lord God bless all of you!"

He left the stage. Dani met him, tears in her eyes. "I love you!" she cried, and he held her close. The rest of the cast gathered to congratulate him, and Dani knew that as long as she lived she would never forget Sir Adrian's performance or his confession that he had found a better way.

Fifteen

THE LAST TOAST

I wish every performance could be as exciting as last night's, Ringo," Dani said wistfully. The two were drinking coffee in her dressing room, waiting for the first call.

"It was something, wasn't it?" The battered features of the big man were the marks of his hard life, but Dani had found that beneath the bruised form lay a sensitive person. Ringo gave her a quizzical look. "That stuff Sir Adrian said about some 'young friend' giving him something good—that was you, huh?"

"Well, yes, it was." Danielle picked up a brush and began to untangle her curls. "He's really a very lonely man. I just told him how I felt about God—how Jesus Christ has changed my life."

He leaned forward, studying her face. "You know, I've met lots of women, but never one like you. Guess if I had, I wouldn't have made such a mess of things." He sat back, reflecting on his past. "I was one of the first the cops questioned after Amber got killed. That's because I was sent up for manslaughter a few years ago."

"Your life's been hard, Ringo. Mine has been so easy that I feel guilty."

"No need to feel like that," he objected with a surprised look. "I had it tough, but it wouldn't have helped if you'd had a rough time too."

"How'd you get into acting?" Dani asked.

"Had to eat," he answered wryly. "After I got out of jail I tried several things. None of them worked though. Then I got a job as an extra in a movie an outfit was making in Denver. They needed a big, ugly guy to be a heavy, and when they saw me, they bought it. Since then I've been the bad guy in I don't know how many movies and plays. That doesn't call for much talent; I just look mean, that's about it."

"Did you have a family?" Dani asked. "Were you ever married?"

"Once," he said briefly. His lips closed over that single syllable like a steel trap; his attitude shouted NO TRESPASSING.

They heard Lyle call out, "Curtain in five minutes!" and got to their feet.

"Well, let's do it." Ringo smiled.

They walked together to the wings, and Dani saw Ben moving around, his eyes everywhere. He gave her a slight nod, but that was all.

The first two acts went well. Jonathan said in between scenes, "Well, Sir Adrian isn't as high as he was last night, but he's doing fine."

Earl came up to whisper, "Mr. Ainsley, Ben said that in the dining scene you're not to let the audience see that the food is artificial."

"Artificial!" Ainsley stared at him in amazement. "What's *that* supposed to mean?"

"We forgot to lay in fresh food," Earl stated apologetically. "So Ben says don't eat so much, and be careful because some of it's made out of plastic!"

"My sacred aunt!" Ainsley snorted. "Plastic food! Somebody will try to eat a plastic chicken leg and choke! Well, let's spread the word. I'll take the other side. You tell Mickey and Calvin."

"All right." Dani found both men standing together and passed the message along.

"Good thing we found out before we got into the scene." Mickey grinned. "It's always a shock to eat the real food—all cold and greasy! But it'd be worse to bite into a plastic biscuit!"

The scene took place in a large, ornate dining room, and at

one time or another every character in the play made an entrance, even Calvin and Carmen as the butler and maid.

"This scene," Jonathan had explained to them carefully, "brings all the members of the board together. The fate of the huge business empire is in the balance. The audience has a chance to meet every character, and we all have to project the spirits of those characters."

It was a long scene during which a meal was consumed, several debates took place, and emotions ran rather freely. At the end of the scene, all the cast exited except for Sir Adrian, who remained with Jonathan. The struggle narrowed down to these two men, protagonist and antagonist, face to face.

Dani had never liked the scene for the simple reason that she never liked the theme of the drama, had never believed in it. As always, however, when it was time for her entrance, she forced herself to stop thinking her own thoughts, trying to suit herself to the character.

The scene began poorly when Mickey knocked Victoria's champagne glass from the table. It shattered loudly, and he was forced to ad lib while picking up the pieces. After that false start, however, the cast caught the spirit of the thing, and it went well.

They seated themselves at a long dining table, with Jonathan at one end and Sir Adrian at the other. Lady Victoria sat to her husband's left, next to Mickey Trask, and finally Ringo, all facing the audience. Dani sat at Sir Adrian's right hand, directly across from Lady Lockridge. Beside her was Lyle. Lily sat at Jonathan's left hand.

The first part of the scene was dominated by Jonathan, who had a very long monologue that expressed the theme of the play: Man must make himself, for there is no other power that can help. The content of the monologue reminded Dani a great deal of a liberal philosophy professor's words to her during her junior year at college. "Man is just another onion," he had insisted. "You peel off layer after layer, and when you get to the center, there's nothing there!" She hadn't believed it then, and she didn't accept it now.

Since her back was to the audience, Dani was not required to reflect any particular emotion to the audience. Instead she watched

Lady Lockridge across from her and Sir Adrian on her left. Both of them looked pale beneath their makeup. Sir Adrian watched Jonathan, appearing, for the sake of the drama, to listen. But Dani could tell that the old actor's mind was far away. It hurt her a little to see him like that, for she still pictured him in her mind as the vigorous and youthful star who had blazed across the world of the theater decades ago. Dani wondered suddenly how actors felt when seeing their old films. Did they envy the slim bodies, the unlined faces, the careless air of being on top of the world? Or did it seem as if another person had played that part?

Since she had spoken to Sir Adrian about Christ, they had not had any long talks, but several times he had given her a warm smile. Once he exulted, "Danielle, our day together has made all the difference to me!"

Dani's glance shifted to Victoria, and she noted again how different she was from her husband, so much harder to get to know. *I wonder if Sir Adrian told her about his conversion?* Dani wondered. She determined to at least try to share the Gospel with Victoria.

Jonathan gave the line that was the cue for the toasting scene. "Jefferson, we'll have the champagne now."

Tom Calvin had been standing at attention, with his back to the wall. "Yes, sir," he murmured and went to the long, ornate liquor cabinet located to the right of the dining room table. At the same time Carmen, also waiting to serve, took out some crystal champagne glasses and put one before each of the guests. As she did, Ringo read his line, a challenge to all that Jonathan had said: "You're wrong about all this, Leo! Dead wrong!" He then drew Jonathan into a heated argument that required all those at the table to pay careful attention to the encounter. Dani turned halfway around in her seat, and the others too were careful to let their faces reveal what they felt about the conflict. As this was taking place, Calvin popped the cork, waited until the overflow stopped, then proceeded to go around the table. Beginning with Lady Lockridge, he filled each glass. Then he turned and put the bottle back in the iced container on the liquor cabinet.

"A toast!" Jonathan proclaimed, rising. He waited until they were all standing with glasses in hand. Then he said to Ringo, "Max, we do not agree on the methods, but we will agree on one thing—the strong will always be victorious! We can all drink to that!"

At those words, all of them lifted their glasses and drained them dry. It was only ginger ale, but Dani had always hated the taste of that beverage. It was suddenly her turn to respond. She ignored the unpleasant tingling in her mouth and began to speak her lines. After her monologue, Lyle and Mickey exchanged lines. Lily said nothing but stood looking at Jonathan with large eyes full of love.

Sir Adrian stood and said firmly to Jonathan, "We must talk more about this, Leo. I am not in agreement!"

At that point Jonathan drawled, "I think you and I must talk—alone. If the rest of you will excuse us?"

They all rose to make their exit. Dani took Lyle's arm and moved with him to the proper exit. Lady Lockridge stood for one moment beside her husband. Her line was "Don't be late, dear," but she seemed to have trouble getting it out. He kissed her, saying, "Wait for me. I won't be long."

She was the last to leave before the stormy confrontation between the two characters began. Ainsley had created the part of Robert Warren expressly for the purpose of being the alter ego of the protagonist, Leo King. In this scene King, the driving humanist who believed in nothing but himself, battled Warren, who believed that man needs more than himself to reach his potential.

Dani watched as Jonathan played his role so well. First he tried diplomacy. Inviting his adversary to take a chair, he said, "Now, Robert, let's have some sherry and talk this over." Going to the liquor cabinet, he took out a new bottle, poured two glasses full, and brought them to where Sir Adrian sat. "First, let's have one more toast." He smiled at him. "To the victory that each of us so clearly wants!"

Sir Adrian raised his glass, commenting sternly, "Yes, to victory—but only the proper sort of victory."

"Let's drink to that," Jonathan suggested, and the two men

drank their champagne. From that point on an argument built between the two strong characters; neither would capitulate. The scene had brought down the house the previous evening, with Sir Adrian rising above the text to express his outrage against a philosophy that was to him abominable. It had been a defeat for Jonathan in one way, Dani had realized, for Sir Adrian had taken the words written by Jonathan—words that stated the *opposite* of Jonathan's convictions—and made the audience accept them!

As she watched the scene, Dani saw that the rest of the cast was huddled together with Ben and his men. All of them had been thrilled by the performance of Sir Adrian the previous evening and longed to see the old man do it again.

But midway through the scene the script called for Sir Adrian to rise from his chair and walk back and forth in front of the table as he recited his lines. Though he did get up, the actor took only a few steps, then seemed to falter. A few of the cast caught an almost imperceptible break in his voice. Dani thought, *He's having another of those awful spells, like the one he had the day I stayed with him!*

That seemed to be the case, for Sir Adrian was not only struggling to get through his line but was bent over sideways. Suddenly he grabbed his stomach, uttered a muted cry, and staggered toward the chair. He fell against the table, sending the champagne and the glasses flying. The sherry bottle shattered as it hit the floor.

Jonathan lunged forward, trying to help him to the chair, but Sir Adrian's right hand caught at Jonathan's sleeve and fastened to it, causing Ainsley to fall heavily as the older man collapsed.

Suddenly Lady Lockridge was beside them. Ignoring the audience, she took her husband's head in her arms. Dani heard Ben cry out a command to drop the curtain and at the same time move toward the three on the floor. Sir Adrian's whole body arched backwards. His wife held his head, burying her face against his hair.

Without warning his feet became still, and the terrible arching ceased. It was as though Lockridge had suddenly relaxed and gone to sleep.

When Dani saw Victoria raise her head, she had never seen such emptiness in anyone's eyes. Her lips moved, and Dani heard her say clearly, "Well, Jonathan Ainsley, you've killed him at last! Now are you satisfied?"

Then came the pounding of feet and the confused cry of many voices. Dani tried to shut out of her mind all that was sure to follow—the police, the investigations, the accusations. She knelt and picked up the still hand of Sir Adrian Lockridge. Thinking of the moment he had prayed with her, she lifted that hand and kissed it.

Sixteen

A LEAP OF FAITH

The blustery winds of early April ravaged the city on Wednesday, the day of the funeral. All morning Dani had walked the streets aimlessly, thinking of the turmoil of the past week and of the ordeal that would take place that afternoon at one o'clock. Cold bit at her as the sharp wind, intensified by tall buildings that forced it through man-made canyons, swept her along.

She had always had an orderly mind—"Neat and organized as a filing cabinet," her accounting professor had proudly hailed it. Dani had always been able to analyze a problem, label information, then sort it into logical little stacks. But unlike many, she was equally able to reach into different, often completely unrelated fields, select details, and make them fit into the larger picture.

Her father had told her, "Most detectives are good at analyzing the facts of a case, Dani. The trouble is that most of the time we don't even have all the facts. We're like the men who find a few tiny fragments of bones and from those little pieces reconstruct an entire skeleton of a ten-foot-high mastodon! Anyone with patience could fit all the bones together if they were available; that would be just a large jigsaw puzzle. But to guess, to deduce, to reach out and pull something out of the mind when the physical facts aren't there—that's what a good detective can do."

"But how can you do that, Dad?" she had asked.

"I can't tell you," he had cheerfully responded. "Someone asked

Mozart once how to write a concerto. He told them he couldn't tell them how. When his questioner reminded him that he'd written a concerto when he was only twelve, Mozart said, 'Yes, but I didn't ask anyone how to do it!' It's the sort of ability some people just have, Dani, and you're one of those people."

She thought of that as she walked along the windy streets, hands stuck deep in her pockets to protect them. But it brought her no comfort. "Why can't I make any sense out of this crazy case if I'm so smart?" she wanted to scream. The shops that lined Fifth Avenue were full of the new spring fashions. From time to time she stopped to look at them. The designers had decided to use earth tones this year. Most of the styles featured garments that were baggy, and they hung on the mannequins awkwardly. When a covey of modish, upwardly mobile young women came down the street wearing the sort of bulky gear featured in the window, Dani thought waspishly, *They look ridiculous!*

Finally she returned to her apartment, took the phone off the hook, and filled the tub with hot water. Throwing her clothes into a heap, she immersed herself and gave a sigh of relief. She loved a hot bath; it was the most useful thing Roman culture had given to women. Slowly the fatigue flowed out of her body and from her mind as well.

From time to time the water grew tepid, and she would turn the scalding water on, then settle back to soak a little longer. Closing her eyes, she went over the past few days since the death of Sir Adrian. She thought of the angry response of the police, and she didn't blame them one bit. It was not Jake Goldman but Chief of Police Tim Flannery who had called the cast together—at the station, not at the Pearl, where cast members were interrogated separately.

She thought about Jonathan, who had stood firm despite the threat of being charged with murder, again. That Flannery longed to make the charge was clear to all of them. But as Dani lay soaking, she went over the evidence.

1. Sir Adrian Lockridge was poisoned. The autopsy proved that.

2. The poison could not have come from the first bottle, for the entire cast at the table drank from that.

3. The poison *might* have come from the bottle of sherry, but Jonathan drank from that same bottle. (The sherry bottle and both glasses were broken when Sir Adrian upset the table, and everyone's milling around after Sir Adrian's collapse had trampled the spilled sherry into the floor; so there had been nothing for the police lab to analyze.)

Summary: The victim was poisoned, but there was no physical evidence to prove how or when the poison was administered.

The chief would have liked to have made the charge but knew from experience that he couldn't make it stick without more evidence. He went back to his own office in a fury, saying he'd have every lawyer in the city government look for some way to end the fool play!

The warm water soothed Dani's body, but not her mind. She kept thinking of the countless times she'd gone over the murder, every detail of it, with Jake Goldman and Ben Savage. But they knew no more now than they did when they'd started.

Finally as she got out of the tub, she remembered how Jonathan had called them together the previous day, begging for unity. "We can't quit now," he had said, barely holding on to his composure.

After toweling off with a huge pink towel, more like a beach towel than anything else, Dani lay across the bed. Because she had slept so little recently, and because the warm bath had washed away her tension, she fell asleep.

At noon she awoke with a start and hurried to dress for the funeral. *What do I have that I can wear to a funeral?* she thought as she went through her clothing hanging in the small closet.

She found one black outfit but didn't want to wear it. Thoughts of Sir Adrian's death brought sadness, but the memory of the time he'd said, "Danielle, our day together has made all the difference to me!" brought joy. She believed Lockridge had truly given himself to Jesus Christ, and that gave her the courage to select a green and white outfit from her closet—colors of life, not death. The spring dress was a bright green that picked up the color of her eyes. The long-sleeved jacket was pure white except for a small embroidery over the left breast—a green and gold lion. She had seen the outfit in a shop window and at once wanted it—a rare experience for her. When she tried it on and found that it fit her perfectly, she asked the price, then stared in unbelief when the clerk told her matter-of-factly, "Only 350 dollars, dear. A real bargain."

Though stunned at the price, seeing how tall and regal it made her appear, she thought, *I'll bet Sir Adrian would like this one!* So she bought it.

The doorbell rang, and she went at once to answer it. Tom Calvin stood there. "I'm all ready, Tom," she said. "Just let me get my coat and purse."

As they walked outside, she looked around with surprise. "It's warmer than it was this morning, isn't it?"

"Yes, it is. The weatherman says the cold front is moving on through."

As they drove to the chapel, Tom said little about the play but seemed genuinely concerned about Sir Adrian's death. "I wish I had been a little more . . . I don't know, *friendly* I guess is the word," he remarked.

"All of us do, Tom," she agreed. "People are always at their best when tragedy strikes."

"Too bad a house has to burn down or something before people become kind!"

"It's not too late to be kind to Victoria."

He nodded as they turned down a side street. "That's right—say, look at all those cars!"

The street was lined with automobiles, and uniformed policemen were everywhere directing traffic and moving people along. "It looks like a football game!" Calvin moaned gloomily. "Vultures! That's what they are! They're just showing up because Sir Adrian was so famous."

Dani agreed for the most part. She too hated funerals that drew "spectators," her term for people who attend a celebrity's funeral.

After being identified by one of the officials, Tom was able to park in the crowded lot. Getting out of the car, they went toward the brick church, where they were greeted by a long-faced man in a dark suit. "Miss Morgan? Lady Lockridge has requested that you sit with her."

Dani followed him inside, down a short hall, and into what looked like the drawing room of a southern plantation. The attendant left silently. Lady Lockridge looked up from where she sat in a large green plush chair. Coming to Dani, she asked, "Would you stay with me, Danielle? Just for a little while?"

Dani put her arms around the woman and held her close for a long moment. She could feel the tremors going through the small frame and whispered, "It's not wrong to weep, Victoria."

Her words were more effective than she could have imagined. Suddenly the form in the plain black dress was shaken with a great gust of grief. No wild, unrestrained weeping, for there was enough strength in the woman to hang on to some control. But the tears flowed, and not Victoria Lockridge's only, for Dani felt tears on her own cheeks.

Finally Victoria took a long breath and moved away. She cleaned her face with a tissue, hastily removed from her purse, then turned to face the younger woman. Her face, never full, was accented now with sharp planes that etched the fine bone structure. Her lips were compressed, and her eyes were puffy. But her voice did not break as she said, "Thank you, my dear. I don't think I would have let another human being see me cry like that."

Dani empathized, "I understand. But you have to learn, Victoria—people want to help, but sometimes we won't let them."

"That's always been my weakness." She smiled slightly. "Adrian didn't hold people away. We nearly quarreled about that at times.

He'd say I was too distant, and I'd accuse him of being too friendly." Then she nodded. "He was right though."

Dani pulled a chair close to the one Victoria had sat in, and for the next few moments they talked quietly. Dani asked, "Have you thought about what you're going to do?"

"No. There really isn't much to think about. We have no real family ties, neither of us," Victoria responded sadly. She looked down at her hands, then lifted her eyes to Dani. "My world was Adrian, and his world was the theater. It's all I've known."

"Perhaps you should go away for a time," Dani suggested. "Then you and your friends can get together and decide what's best."

A strange expression swept over Victoria's face. She sat quietly for so long that Dani wondered what was going through her mind. Finally the actress broke the silence. "It's strange—Adrian and I knew so many people. Everywhere we went, people knew us. But we made almost no friends. I blame myself for that," she added, avoiding Dani's gaze.

"You probably have more friends than you realize, Victoria," Dani encouraged. She put her hand out and squeezed the hands of the older woman. "Many people really care about you, and they'll help you see this through."

Victoria lifted her head and studied the young woman. Finally she commented, "I can see why Adrian put such faith in you, Danielle. You really love people, don't you?"

"Of course."

"No, not of course," Victoria interjected at once, shaking her head almost angrily. "I've known so many people and seen so little love."

"I know it must seem that way." Dani was filled with a great desire to help this broken woman find the peace of God. Hesitating just a moment, she considered carefully, then explained, "Sir Adrian said almost the same thing to me once. That's when I told him about how I had found real love. Would you mind if I shared it with you too?"

For a moment Dani, seeing a defensive hardness reflected in Victoria's level gaze, thought she would refuse. Then the older actress seemed to change her mind, saying in a low voice, "Yes, I'd like to hear what you said to Adrian."

For fifteen minutes Dani spoke, going over her conversation with Sir Adrian. She used the same Scriptures she'd used with him but was careful not to pressure Victoria in any way. Finally she said, "So I asked him if he would ask Christ into his heart." She couldn't stop the tears that filled her eyes at the thought and wiped them with a tissue. "Then we prayed together. It was a wonderful time, Victoria. I believe he found peace at that moment."

"He *was* very different after that," Victoria agreed, her eyes thoughtful. "More relaxed and accepting of things." She reached over and squeezed Dani's hand. "He told me about your talk, but I didn't really understand what he meant, not then anyway. Thank you for telling me again, my dear, and for all your kindness to Adrian. You meant a great deal to him."

"It wasn't hard to love him." Dani quietly added, "I hope you can find the same peace that Sir Adrian found, Victoria."

Dani waited expectantly, but the moment was broken when the door opened and the man who had brought Dani in announced, "I believe the service is about to begin. If you're ready, Lady Lockridge . . . ?"

The two women followed him and took their seats in a side gallery. There were several people there, including several other famous performers, so Dani sat off to the side. The chapel was packed, and she spotted most of the cast of the play. Ben was seated close to the front, sitting beside Earl and Julio. Tom Calvin sat beside Jonathan in the second row.

The service was mercifully brief—a prelude of Gregorian chants, followed by the reading of the obituary, then a solo by a well-known soprano from the Metropolitan Opera. An Episcopal priest, a large man with a high tenor voice, delivered the funeral address, a eulogy that stressed Sir Adrian's professional accomplishments. Little was said of his private life, and Dani realized that the speaker had never known Sir Adrian personally. The sermon closed with the reading of several Scriptures, and Dani prayed that Victoria would be moved and comforted by them. The body was to be cremated, so there would be no graveside service.

She kissed Victoria, whispering, "I'll call you in the morning." Then she turned to Jonathan, standing beside Calvin. Trask and Lyle greeted her, and Mickey said, "This place gives me the creeps!" He left quickly, followed by Lyle who added, "Call me when you know anything, Jonathan."

"What a ghastly thing to happen!" Ainsley muttered, his eyes bloodshot from lack of sleep.

"We're all going to have to help Lady Victoria," Dani commented.

Jonathan looked at her sharply but agreed, "Yes, we must. But I don't how much help I can be—she's quite filled with contempt for me, you know."

"We must try," Dani insisted. "Do you still intend to go on with the play, Jonathan?"

"It may not be up to me," he told her. "The police want to talk to all of us tomorrow. Not Goldman—it's gone beyond him," he added bitterly. "It's the chief of police we're dealing with now. Along with the mayor's office, the police are trying to shut us down. Newspapers have had a field day with these stories, and the city is starting to get some negative publicity."

"*Can* they shut you down?" Dani asked.

"I don't know, but I want you at the meeting," Jonathan said quickly. "It's at two o'clock, at the theater. I'll come by for you."

"All right." She glanced around. "Tom, you don't have to take me home. I have an errand to run."

The two men watched as she and Ben left the chapel. "I wonder if those two are cooking up something?" Tom demanded.

Ainsley exclaimed, "I hope so!" and Calvin him a confused look.

Outside, Ben got into his car and asked, "What's up, Dani?"

"I'm not sure, Ben," she said slowly as they drove out of the parking lot. "It looks as if the play's going to be closed unless something happens to prevent it. But more importantly, we just have to crack this case."

He turned to look at her. He knew her very well, and something in her determined expression made him ask, "What's going on inside that head of yours? I can almost hear the wheels grinding!"

"Ben, I need some information, but I can't think of any way to get it—legally, that is." Usually it was Ben who suggested illegal or unethical methods and Dani saying no. But in this case she was beginning to feel so desperate that she didn't know what else to do.

He grinned suddenly, swerved to avoid a silver Thunderbird, then exclaimed, "You've got the mind of a cat burglar, Dani Ross! All right, let's have it."

He listened carefully as she spoke at some length. When he pulled up near her apartment, he promised, "I'll either get it or you can see me on visiting days, Tuesdays, 9 to 5—and don't try to smuggle a file in."

"Ben, don't get caught."

"I'll try my best. What are *you* going to do?"

She got out and closed the door. "I have a little chore of my own to do. Then I have to talk to Jake. He just has to give us a hand."

He said with a straight face, "Better wear that red sweater that looks so good on you. You'll need all the edge you can get with that dude."

♦ ♦ ♦

Head nurse Edna Pulaski, aware that a man had entered the room and had come to stand in front of her, continued dressing down the newest addition to her staff with blistering authority. "Never—and I mean *never*—let a patient out of bed when the attending physician has forbidden it. Do you understand that?"

The young woman in front of her was no more than twenty, and her cheeks were dead pale. Speech seemed to have left her, and she could only nod in a jerky fashion.

"All right, get to your work!" Nurse Pulaski did not even watch the girl scurry off but turned to look at the waiting man. "Yes? What can I do for you?"

Her tone was somewhat polite, for she could not decide if he was part of the administration—in which case she would have to be nice—or if he was only the relative of a patient. She was usually able to sort the two out, but this one didn't look worried enough to be the relative of a patient. On the other hand, he looked too efficient to be one of the bumbling administrators, who seemed determined to invent stupid rules that kept her and the staff from getting their jobs done.

He was no more than average height, trimly built, and athletic looking, which also was *not* true of the bookkeepers from the second floor! She studied his squarish face, noting the scar on the forehead and the steady hazel eyes.

"Nurse Pulaski? I'm James Dalgren." He reached into his inner coat pocket, removed a billfold, and spread it open to show her an identification card.

She bent closer, read his name, checked the picture, then read the name of his firm aloud: "Republic Communications." She looked up and stated flatly, "Never heard of it!"

"I hope not," he said, replacing the billfold. He smiled when she stared at him. "Our firm isn't looking for any publicity, lady. As a matter of fact, we do all we can to hide from it."

"What is it, Mr. Dalgren?" Pulaski demanded. "We don't have time for games or mysteries here."

"Neither do I. Do you know what a hacker is, Ms. Pulaski?"

"A hacker? Isn't that some sort of computer swindler?"

"Yes." He nodded. "I'm glad you understand the problem because a hacker is loose in your institution."

Nurse Pulaski stared at him, speechless. "Why—what in the world could he get from a hospital?"

"Information about patients." A middle-aged nurse came to the nurse's station, and he leaned forward, lowering his voice. "Can you imagine what an insurance company would give to have access to your records? They'd go right to wealthy patients or their families and offer just the policy they need. Sick people make quick decisions, you know, too quick."

"Yes, they do." Still confused, she asked, "What do you want from me?"

"I just need to run a check on one of your computers."

"Have you cleared it with the administration office?"

"No, I have not." He forestalled her vigorous protest with the words, "It's very likely that the hacker is working out of that office."

The nurse's mouth opened in a small O. *I wouldn't put it past them,* she was thinking, but being a professional, she objected, "We can't have the computer tied up for long."

"Won't take but fifteen minutes. I have to do a check at each station."

She hesitated, then nodded reluctantly. "All right, start with that one there. I can't stay with you though. I have work to do."

"Fine." Dalgren sat down and at once began running his hands over the keyboard.

Nurse Pulaski left the station and made her way to the elevator. Ten minutes later she returned with two large men in security uniforms. She looked around wildly and demanded of the nurse who was working inside the station, "Where's that man, the one who was working at the computer?"

"Why, he just left," the girl said, looking up in surprise.

"Try to cut him off in the parking lot!" Pulaski commanded, but by the time the two men had left, she knew they wouldn't catch him. She began planning how to shift the blame when the administration asked her why she had let an outsider have access to confidential information.

◆ ◆ ◆

Mr. Potter stared at the flashy blonde, then shook his head. "I'm sorry, but I can't do that," he said firmly. "It's against our policy."

The woman was wearing a fur coat, but it swung open to reveal an appealing red dress. She had a mass of strawberry-blonde hair and wore too much makeup. "Look, he's on his way over here anytime," she explained in a hard New York accent. "If he comes and I ain't here, he's gonna have your head in a box!" When Mr. Potter hesitated, her eyes grew small, and she lost her temper. "You think I'm gonna steal the TV? What's with you anyway?"

"I can't let a stranger into a tenant's apartment!" Potter complained.

"Well, I ain't exactly a *stranger*!" The blonde laughed, a harsh sound in Potter's ears. She warned, "I ain't gonna fight my way past you, honey. When he comes, *you* can explain why I ain't there. And you probably know he don't like excuses too much!"

She whirled and would have left, but the manager gasped, "Just—just a minute, miss." He caught up with her as she paused, tapping the toe of her high-heeled pump. "I'll have to ask to see some identification."

"Sure, pop. No problem." She followed him up a flight of steps and waited while he fumbled with a large set of keys. When he swung the door open, she fished in her purse, then came up with a card. "That's my driver's license, honey."

He looked at the card, fixed the name in his mind, and said, "Sorry about this, but . . ."

"Yeah, I know." She shrugged, then laughed. As soon as the door closed, the woman slipped out of the fur coat, tossed it onto the couch along with the purse, then surveyed the large apartment. She went to work at once, opening drawers and carefully examining every document she came across.

About thirty minutes after Mr. Potter had admitted the woman, he glanced out the window and saw her getting into what looked like a small rental car. As she drove away, he wondered if he should go check the apartment. When he did, he found nothing out of order.

Nobody can blame me for her not being here, he told himself firmly. *I let her in, but if she didn't want to stay, that's her business!*

♦ ♦ ♦

Chief Timothy Flannery, Dani decided, was straight out of an old movie starring Pat O'Brien and James Cagney. He was a corpulent, red-faced Irishman with a jovial smile and hamlike hands. A born politician, as any man would have to be to rise to the top of the loaf in his profession, he stood before the cast flanked by Mr. Denton Cranston, who represented the mayor's office, and a brace of homicide detectives. One of these was Jake Goldman, and his face was fixed in a noncommittal stare as Flannery spoke.

"I should not have to be making this speech," he said with a truculent air. "If you people had the sense of a chicken, you'd have dropped this crazy play a long time ago!" He chewed the end of a cigar angrily, then took it out of his mouth and aimed it at Ainsley. "You're supposed to be a smart man, Mr. Ainsley. Well, this isn't smart! It's stupid, that's what it is!"

Denton Cranston, the mayor's assistant, interrupted him smoothly. "Mr. Ainsley, the chief is a little irritated with this business, as you can see. So is the mayor, I might add." He studied the fingernails on his right hand, then lifted his eyes to meet those of Ainsley. "The publicity on this thing is getting out of hand. We have enough of a problem with violence in New York as it is. Now everyone in America can read the headlines: 'Murder—Live on the New York Stage'!"

"And how does it make the police look?" Flannery added. He shook his head. "I want the play closed until we catch the killer."

"But you might never catch him!" Ainsley protested. "Especially if he's a member of the cast. You can't follow all the actors everywhere they go after they leave the theater."

"So we're supposed to let somebody else get himself or herself killed," Flannery snorted. "And the papers can go on calling us a bunch of dumb cops! No way! You have to call off the blasted party!"

The argument raged on, but it was obvious to Ainsley that the officials lacked the power to close down the play. Finally Dani took a deep breath and gave Jake Goldman a slight nod. He stepped forward, saying, "Chief, may I have a word?"

Flannery stared at the slender officer suspiciously. He had never known what to make of Goldman. Flannery was automatically suspicious of any police officer who lived well, and Goldman went beyond all bounds. It was common knowledge that the chief had had Goldman investigated several times by various organizations, but the dapper policeman had never been connected with anything shady. By the same token, Flannery knew that Goldman was probably the best investigator on the force. He reluctantly said, "Go ahead, Goldman."

"This has been the most difficult case I've ever handled, mostly because of the isolation of the cast. They have their own little world, and no policeman is going to break through. At the very beginning of the case Mr. Ainsley had a very good idea. He decided to bring in a private investigator—an undercover agent."

At this statement Dani, who was watching the cast, saw looks of astonishment cross every face. "Who is it?" "I don't believe . . ." Goldman ignored the disgruntled chatter and raised his voice slightly.

"Usually I would insist on having one of our own people in such a position, but you can see that would be very difficult. The world of the theater is small, and an agent would be spotted almost at once. Therefore, after checking the qualifications of the investigator, I agreed to the plan." *Especially since it was already in place.* He chuckled to himself.

The chief was shocked. "I think you might have let the rest of us in on this, Lieutenant Goldman."

"Chief, you taught me some good lessons," Goldman said. "And one of the best was to keep your undercover man protected. You always stressed that, I think."

Trapped by his own words, Flannery could only nod.

Cranston asked, "Where are you leading us, Lieutenant?"

"Our man has been successful—or almost so. Evidence has been collected that will result in an arrest on the charge of murder.

However, there are still two items that must be nailed down. I'm asking that you allow the play to go on for just one more week. By that time the murderer will be in custody. I'll stake my reputation on it."

Flannery stared at him. Goldman was reputedly the most pessimistic man in the department. He never said a positive word about a case until the criminal was caught, tried, sentenced, and in jail. "Too many loopholes," Goldman often lamented. "It's not over until they're behind bars." But this time . . .

"You feel sure about this?" Flannery demanded. When he got a nod from Goldman, he looked at Denton Cranston. The two of them reached some sort of unspoken agreement, and the chief nodded. "All right, you have one week to get your man, Goldman."

He stalked off the stage, followed by Cranston and the two officers. As soon as they left, loud talk rose up like wildfire. Jonathan held up his hand, shouting, "All right! Hear me now—we go on in three days."

"What about the Lockridge roles?" Lyle asked.

"Just be at rehearsal tomorrow at 8," he said. "The roles will be filled. Now I've got a lot to do!"

The group broke up, the actors talking frantically about the new development. Dani demanded, "Jonathan, may I have a word with you?"

"Come along."

She followed him to the office and wasted no time getting to her point. "Two things, Jonathan. First, about Victoria's role—I think you should allow her to continue in it."

"Are you crazy, Danielle?" Ainsley almost shouted. "In the first place, she blames me for her husband's death. Second, this is the *last* place she needs to be. It would be too much for her. It's out of the question!"

"She has nowhere to go, Jonathan," Dani insisted. "Yes, she hates you, but that can change. Her husband hated you too, but he changed toward the last, didn't he?"

"Well, yes," Ainsley admitted grudgingly. "But she'd be on the very spot where her husband was murdered!"

"That's *her* problem, and I think she can handle it much better than her other problem, which is what to do with her life."

Ainsley didn't like the idea, but Dani wore him down. Finally he said, "Well, if she wants to do it, I reluctantly agree." He paused, then added, "The newspaper boys will love this one, won't they?"

Dani was disgusted with his callous attitude but ignored it. "One more thing—I want you to let drop to one person that I'm the undercover investigator."

"Dani, we can't do that!" Ainsley protested. "If the killer knows it's you, he won't hesitate to kill you."

"That's the idea, Jonathan. I'm the bait in the trap."

Jonathan sat down on the desk, stared at her, then shook his head. "Whom do you want me to reveal it to?" he asked quietly. When she spoke the name aloud, his eyes flew open. "Are you sure?"

"No. But we will be when he makes a try for me, won't we?"

"I don't like it, but it's your decision. When should I let it drop?"

"The day before we open the play again."

She left the theater and found Goldman waiting for her outside. "How'd I do?" he wanted to know.

She smiled at him, thinking of their last meeting. He'd been adamantly against the plan, but step by step she had convinced him that it was a certain way to catch the killer. "You ought to be in showbiz, Jake," she remarked.

He flagged down a cab and walked her to it. As he put her inside, he took her arm. "I don't want you to get hurt, Danielle. I've come to think a lot of you," he admitted.

"I'll bet you say that to all your undercover agents!" she quipped.

But Goldman didn't smile. "Listen, I have some extra manpower. Savage is on the job, and we're going to have you covered in every direction, but if you see or even think something looks wrong, don't be proud, hear me? Scream your head off!"

He slammed the door, and as the car moved away, she saw him watching her leave. As soon as the cab turned the corner and he was lost to her sight, she felt lonely, and tendrils of fear began to creep along her nerves. She made herself think of the portrait of Colonel Daniel Monroe Ross. Calling up the image of his fearless eyes, she murmured softly, "Well, Colonel, it's not Pickett's Charge at Gettysburg, but the way I feel it could be just as dangerous to your great-great-granddaughter!" The thought of that stern face braced her spirits, and she sat back as the cab dodged in and out of the traffic.

Seventeen

THE BAIT

The reopening of *Out of the Night* proved anticlimactic.

Nobody was shot or stabbed. There were no attempted homicides. As Charlie Allgood caustically put it in his column, "After all the sound and fury by the N.Y.P.D. about the dangers of a homicide in Jonathan Ainsley's hit play, the standing-room-only crowd had to be content with just solid performances and quality drama."

But Allgood was not aware of the intense preventive measures taken to halt another murder attempt. Three still-faced, rather unobtrusive men moved about the set before, after, and during the performance. Goldman had told Dani, "These three are the best SWAT men in the state. If the killer makes a move, they'll nail him!" In addition to the precautions inside the Pearl Theater, Dani was aware that she was being followed to and from the studio. And at the theater Savage was everywhere, his eyes constantly moving, like a frontier scout, with Earl and Julio as alert as bird dogs.

Ben had been dead set against the idea of leaking the information that Dani was the undercover agent. He had heatedly argued about it with Goldman and Dani. "You'll be a sitting duck!" he protested. "If you announce that you're the one who'll be getting the evidence to nail the killer, do you think he'll let that pass?"

Dani shook her head wearily. "Ben, we've been over this a hundred times! It's the only way to force his hand."

Savage stared at her, looking hard and tough in his dark stage clothing. "You know what this is?" he said suddenly. "It's a rerun of the action we had in the silo."

"What's that?" Goldman demanded.

Dani started to answer, but Ben interrupted loudly, "I'll tell you what it was. We were trapped in this sort of jail with a bunch of other prisoners. One of them was a killer. Guess who got the brilliant idea of using herself as bait so we could nab the murderer? Danielle Ross, girl detective, that's who!"

"It wasn't like that, Ben!" Dani objected angrily.

"It was like that!" he snapped. "What is it with you, Dani? Do you have a death wish or something? Or maybe you just like to hotdog all the time? Goldman, you ought to stop her."

The policeman had been taken aback by the fury of Savage's attack, but he looked at Danielle. "I think Ben has a point. Let's just let that part go."

Dani shook her head, and her stubborn streak surfaced. "Look, do you think he hasn't figured it out already? I think he has, but if not, we have to push him into the open! Jake, you promised me you'd go along with my idea. Are you going to welsh just because Ben's getting to be an old woman?"

Savage suddenly reached out and grabbed her arm. He ignored her wince of pain, dragging her close. "You've been around show-biz too long! Everything's got to be a big production, and Dani Ross has to be in the center of it!"

"Let me go!" Dani cried. She stepped back, rubbing her arm, and her face turned pale with anger. "Maybe you'd better remember who signs your checks, Savage! When I hired you, I thought you were a tough cookie. Now you're starting to fold just when the trouble's about to start! Why don't you get a job selling vacuum cleaners if detective work's too hot for you!"

"Maybe I will," Ben said, staring at her, his eyes blazing with anger. "After this is over, you can get yourself another man!"

He turned and walked away. "What's with you two?" Goldman asked. "You fight worse than a man and wife."

The words struck Dani, and she said bitterly, "Ben Savage thinks he's the only human being in the world who can do something right."

"And you're going to show him he's wrong?" Goldman shot back. "Look, Dani, this isn't some kind of game in which the one with the most points wins! This is life and death. I think Savage is right. Why don't we just change that one part of the plan?"

But she stubbornly refused to listen, and soon Jonathan reported that he had dropped the information.

After the performance Dani went to Ben, commenting, "See, it went all right."

His face was unsmiling. "He's not a complete fool. He'll wait until the SWAT team leaves!"

Dani had hoped Ben would soften his attitude, but as she walked away to congratulate Victoria on her brave performance, Dani wondered, *I don't know why I ever thought he'd change. He never has, and he never will!*

She pushed her way through a crowd to get to Victoria, who was surrounded by admirers, cast and audience alike. "You were wonderful, Victoria!" she whispered, hugging the older woman. Victoria held the embrace longer than necessary, but tears filled her eyes, and she could only nod.

As Victoria walked away, Dani thought about how simple it had been to get her to continue to be part of *Out of the Night.* She had gone to Victoria's apartment and said without preamble, "I think you ought to stay in the play, Victoria. It will be hard, but not as hard as being alone." It had taken very little more persuasion than that, for Victoria wanted an escape from her grief and her fear of the future. Within a day the details were set, and the newspapers had made a big thing of it—show business in the best tradition!

The replacement for Sir Adrian, Dave Tolliver, was an older man, of course, and an experienced actor. It had not hurt that he had been a long-time admirer of Sir Adrian, and his courteous and highly respectful attitude toward Victoria greatly helped her.

Dani accompanied the cast to a late supper to celebrate the reopening of the play. It was at an expensive supper club on the east side of town. She sat between Victoria and Tom Calvin, eating little and wondering why Savage had declined to attend the party. When she asked Jonathan, he quietly explained, "Partly because the stagehands don't usually come to these things. We may have given away your identity, but nobody needs to know about Savage. He'll be more effective that way. Anyway, he didn't want to come. He told me he was moving into the theater—he's going to sleep on a cot or something. Not a bad idea when you stop and think of it."

The party broke up, and Tom took her home. He came into her apartment for a while, and they drank coffee and talked until nearly two o'clock. Finally when he got ready to leave, he gave her a strange look and said, "Dani, what about me?"

"About you, Tom?"

"About you and me then," he said. "Is there any chance for me at all?"

Dani had not foreseen this development at all. She had become very fond of Tom, but not once had the thought of falling in love with him entered her mind. "Why, Tom," she answered slowly, "are you serious?"

"Why not?" He came toward her, trying to kiss her on the lips, but she drew back.

"Tom, this isn't right," she objected. "We don't even know each other very well. You've hardly seen me when I wasn't playing a role."

"I don't care about that, Danielle," he insisted stubbornly. "I only know that I've never met a woman as strong as you."

"Tom, you don't need a strong woman, if by strong you mean a woman who can tell you what to do."

"Do you think that's what I want?" he asked with sudden anger in his voice. "You think I can't take care of myself?"

"Do you really want to, Tom?" Dani saw that her question had struck a nerve, and she added gently, "Tom, you're a fine man, but I think you've always taken the easy way. You don't like Jonathan Ainsley or what he stands for, but you work for him. Why? I think it's because you're afraid to go out on your own. And that's sad, Tom, because you have so much to offer!"

"Like what?" he asked bitterly.

"You have courage, for one thing. I know it hasn't been easy living your Christian convictions in the world of the theater, but you've done it. I'm proud of you, Tom."

His face tensed, but slowly his eyes lost their anger, and he finally smiled slightly. "I guess I've known for a long time that I've been coasting. I suppose it's time to ante up, isn't it, Danielle?"

"Yes, Tom, it's time." She kissed him on the cheek, and he left at once. Shutting the door, she leaned against it and gave a deep sigh of relief. "Just what I needed," she murmured. "A thirty-year-old baby to raise!" But as she wondered about Tom Calvin's future, she thought too about Ben Savage, roaming the dark confines of the backstage area of the Pearl. Worried about her friend and associate, she prayed an old Scottish prayer she'd learned from her grandmother:

From ghoulies and ghosties and long-leggety beasties
And things that go bump in the night,
Good Lord, deliver us!

◆ ◆ ◆

Dani was just putting on her coat, getting ready to leave for the Friday evening performance, when the doorbell rang. Opening the door, she found Goldman standing before her, impeccably dressed but with an odd look in his dark eyes. "I'll drive you to the theater," he ordered abruptly, and she followed him to the car without asking any questions.

He didn't speak until they were underway. "My SWAT team won't be there tonight. They had to go to Albany on an emergency assignment," he commented as he wove a tight pattern through the traffic. "I probably won't be there either. A new case just came up this morning, and I have to get on it right away."

"Of course, Jake. I understand." She patted his arm, adding,

"You've done more than anyone could ever have expected. We knew you couldn't drop your other work just for this case."

"Sure, I could," he said. "I don't *have* to work for a living."

"Yes, I think you do, Jake," Dani responded. "What would a man like you do if he didn't have his work? Be a gigolo for some old lady?"

He said without emotion, "Not for an old lady. Maybe for you, Danielle."

When she made no answer, he turned to look at her. "I asked you once if I were a man you might love. All I got was a lecture. I'm asking again, and this time I don't want a lecture. I'm not asking you to marry me, not yet. All I'm saying is that I've never thought about a woman as much as I've thought about you. Maybe I'm going nuts, I don't know." He jerked the wheel viciously, missing a truck by inches, but seemed not to notice. "I thought I'd seen about everything there was to see in women, but you're not like the others."

Dani sat there, not knowing what to say at first. Finally she swallowed and explained, "Jake, I'm just a strange specimen to you. You're curious, that's all. You've been spoiled by all the women who can't wait to fall into your arms."

He swiveled his head around, peered at her, then shook his head. "No, that's not it. What I want is a beautiful woman as smart as I am, with a wonderful sense of humor, who can cook."

"Lots of luck!" Dani told him, then sobered. Thoughtfully she said, "Jake, you know why I won't even think about it, don't you?"

"Sure. It's because I'm Jewish and you're a Christian." He shrugged his trim shoulders. "That's no big deal! I'm Jewish by blood and by a little strip of land called Israel, but I have no God, Danielle. I gave up on Him a long time ago."

"That's not entirely true, Jake," Dani responded swiftly. "You're too much of a man to throw your heritage out the window. You know that's true!"

"All right, say I do," Goldman admitted. "What's wrong with me going to synagogue and you going to church? People do it all the time."

"I couldn't do it," Dani asserted. "How could a man and wife be one if they didn't agree on the single most important thing in human existence?"

Goldman said nothing for a time, then nodded. "I knew you'd say that. But there's more to it than that."

She stared at him. "Like what, Jake?"

"Like maybe you already have a guy lined up."

"No, I don't."

"I say you do," he insisted. "And I could put a name on him—Ben Savage."

"That's—that's not true!" she cried out a bit too loudly.

"Ol' Jake hit a nerve?"

"We're just business partners. Naturally we see a lot of each other. But I'd never marry him, Jake. Not unless—"

She broke off suddenly, and he said flatly, "Here's the theater." He got out and walked her to the door. Taking Dani's hand, he said seriously, "Watch yourself." Then he turned and walked away, getting into the car and driving off without a backward look.

The scene upset Dani so much that she walked by several people without speaking, which made them turn to stare at her curiously. She changed into her costume, then had a cup of tea with Victoria before curtain time.

"What is it, Danielle?" Victoria asked. "You seem upset."

"Oh, I . . . nothing really." Dani patted the older woman's hand. "I'm going to upstage you tonight if I have to eat the scenery! You've been stealing my fans!"

She kept the conversation light, hoping Victoria wouldn't ask any more questions. When Tom announced the five-minute warning, she went to her usual position. Mickey stood beside her. "You're getting better all the time, Danielle," he encouraged her.

"Thanks, Mickey." She looked for Ben but didn't see him before the curtain rose.

The play went smoothly. Dave Tolliver was no Sir Adrian Lockridge, but he was satisfactory.

As they passed in the wings once, Ringo said, "Did you notice—no guards tonight?"

"I know, Ringo. Have you seen Ben?"

"He was over by the light switches a few minutes ago."

"Tell him I want to see him."

The second act started and ended and still no Savage. Dani grabbed Jonathan by the arm. "Where's Ben?"

Ainsley, always totally immersed in his role, answered vaguely, "I don't know. Better ask Earl or the other hand."

She saw Julio lifting a chair onto one of the movable stages and asked directly, "Julio, where's Ben?"

"I dunno, Miz Danielle," he answered. "Me and Earl are having to make all the changes by ourselves. He better show up soon, or it's gonna be a big mess around here!"

Lyle suddenly appeared beside her, whispering, "You missed your cue! Get out there!" He practically shoved her out onto the stage into the arms of Jonathan, who staggered and ad-libbed, "My dear! We've got to stop meeting like this!"

The audience laughed, and Dani made it through the scene. As she went offstage, there was still no sign of Savage. Had the killer gotten to him? The thought that he might be lying dead chilled her.

Carmen Rio stared at her, then grabbed her arm. "What's wrong with you? You sick?"

"No, it's just that I can't find Ben."

"You don't have time to look for him," Carmen snapped. "Come on, you've got to change for the bathing scene."

It was the scene Dani liked least, but she went with Carmen to the dressing room. She put on the flesh-colored workout suit as Carmen urged her on. "Hurry up! You only have a minute. Here's your robe!"

Dani slipped into the floor-length robe and drew it around her as she walked rapidly toward the east wing, where Earl had maneuvered the big bathtub set into position. There was room enough in back for one person to squeeze through. Going around the hidden wing, she found that Earl had the tub bubbling over. "It's okay, Miss Danielle," he said, rising. "I got the water just right."

She took off her robe, tossed it into the wing, then got at once into the tub. The water was all right, not too hot, but the rubber mat she sat on was as rough and bumpy as ever. She sat there with only her head and arms out of the water, picking up a dainty white scrub brush.

The curtain rose, and she forced herself into her role—a woman who shows complete contempt for a man. She lifted the brush, then raised one soapy leg and began to scrub it. Carmen entered, followed by Mickey, saying, "Miss Marian, here's Mr. Charles. I brought him in, just like you said to."

"Thank you, Rosa," Dani said in a disinterested voice.

Mickey began his line. "You can't treat a man this way, Marian!" He stood in front of the tub, tense with anger. It was his best scene, and he did it well. Dani continued to brush her toes from time to time, languidly, giving the impression of a woman who enjoyed tormenting men.

Suddenly Dani realized that Mickey was standing farther away from the tub than was his habit, and she knew Trask was a nitpicker about details. His back was to the audience, so she alone could get a full view of him. Normally she felt amusement at the small actor's ability to throw a vitriolic stream of words at her as she lay in the tub while his baby face looked like a cherub's! He let his face match his words whenever the audience could see him.

But tonight as Trask said his lines, she saw that his face was twisted with hatred! His lips were pulled back, and his eyes were wide and staring. Suddenly a sense of danger swept over her, and her muscles tightened. She wanted to run, but she was in full view of the entire audience. And modesty had been so ingrained into her that the thought of scrambling out of the tub—workout suit not withstanding—was abhorrent to her.

She searched frantically for a solution, but nothing came. Trask raised his voice to a scream, and she knew that he was going to kill her and there was nothing she could do about it!

At that instant she heard a crash and swiveled her head to see a wall to her left suddenly give way, the wood and paper collapsing! A man dressed in dark clothing shot through the set and hit the floor.

Savage came out of the fall in one smooth motion. Dani saw his hazel eyes ablaze, and he drove himself right at her. He reached down, one arm beneath her legs, the other behind her back, and lifted her.

"Ben!" she screamed. "What are you doing?"

But he didn't pause. Taking three steps away from the tub, he practically threw her down! She caught her balance, then stared at him as he went straight for Trask, his arms held in the classic position of a master of the martial arts.

Trask at once fell into the same position and, with the skill achieved by hundreds of hours of practice, avoided Savage's chopping left hand. At the same time he launched a vicious kick that could have killed Ben if it had hit its mark. Savage took part of the force of the kick on his thigh, and that drove him to his left. As Trask aimed a kick at Savage's face, Ben swerved and the kick missed.

Dani heard the cries from the audience, and she thought she heard Jake Goldman shouting. But just at that moment Trask threw his whole body into a determined jab, his iron fingers aimed right at Savage's eyes. Ben caught the hand in midair and made a sudden twist, and the floor shook as Trask landed flat on his back. Ben yanked him to his feet and with a few short steps, holding Trask's arm behind his back, brought him to the edge of the tub.

"No, don't!" Trask shouted. He arched his body backwards, but the power of Savage's grip forced him forward until he was poised over the soapy water.

"What's the matter? You don't like bathing, Mickey?" Ben demanded. He looked up and caught Goldman's eye. The policeman had mounted the stage and now had his gun in his hand. "Just one little dip, Mickey!" Ben suggested.

He forced Trask downward until it seemed impossible for the

smaller man to keep from falling in. "No! Don't do it! It'll fry me alive!" Mickey whined.

"Did you rig the thing, Trask?" Ben demanded, giving the man a small push.

"Yes! I did it—I put the wire in there! Don't let me fall in!"

Savage pulled him back, whirled him around, and said, "You need a bath, Mickey!" and shoved him full-length into the tub.

Trask let out a great scream as he fell into the water. His head hit the end of the tub with a solid clunking sound, and he seemed to go limp.

Ben reached down and pulled his head up, then looked at Goldman. "He had a live wire rigged into the mat inside the tub. It was set to go off at 9:42. I found the timer at 9:39 plus."

Suddenly Dani realized what Savage was saying. The thought that she had come within seconds of being electrocuted hit her hard. Ben darted a glance at her and saw her face turn as white as the tub she'd been sitting in. Her knees began to buckle.

Savage grabbed her just in time to keep her from falling. As he stood with her dripping form in his arms, a flashbulb went off in his face, blinding him. He stood there, blinking and uncertain, while Goldman watched. When Ben made no attempt to put Dani down, the suave policeman asked slyly, "What are you doing, Ben? Trying to guess her weight?"

Ever the professional, Jake took a pair of cuffs from his pocket. He snapped them onto Trask's wrists, turned, and announced, "Ladies and gentlemen, this is the end of the play. Everybody go home." Then he turned again to where Ben stood, holding Dani. "I couldn't stay away after all, Danielle. I'd like a few words with you, Savage, if it's not too much trouble."

Ben looked down at Dani's face for a moment, then shook his head. "No trouble at all, Lieutenant."

Eighteen

THE GUILTY

Bright sunlight streamed through the high windows banked along the west wall of the large conference room that Goldman had commandeered. A long table with seven chairs on each side plus one at each end dominated the room. Ordinarily various law enforcement boards and committees used it, but this was the most convenient room Goldman had been able to find on short notice.

Goldman came in at precisely nine o'clock, accompanied by Chief Flannery. The two men walked to the head of the table, and Goldman quickly scanned the room, counting noses while Flannery sat down in the end chair.

Goldman glanced to his right, where Lady Lockridge sat, then on down the line. He counted off Lyle Jamison, Lily Aumont, Jonathan Ainsley, Dave Tolliver, Tom Calvin, and Carmen Rio. Shifting his gaze to his left, he saw Danielle Ross, Ringo Jordan, Ben Davis, Earl Layne, Julio Garcia, Trey Miller, and Simon Nero. Just as he completed his survey, a side door opened, and two armed guards ushered Mickey Trask into the room. "Put him at the end of the table," Goldman ordered, and Trask took his place in the single chair. He had not shaved, and his eyes were bloodshot, but he said nothing to anyone as he sat down.

The two guards stepped back against the wall, and Goldman briskly commented, "The chief thought it best that all of you be here for this meeting. Some things have to be cleared up, and before we leave this room they will be." He spoke confidently, his voice filling the room. "This is not a trial or even a hearing. Call it an interrogation if you wish. Formal charges have been filed against Mickey Trask, and bail will be set today."

"You can't make me stay in your rotten jail, Goldman," Trask stated angrily, his face pale with strain. "You can't prove a thing!"

"Trask, you'll have a lawyer and all the time you want to defend yourself, but this morning you'll speak when spoken to." Trask started to interrupt, but seeing the look on Goldman's face, he slumped in his chair sullenly. "Very well. Now I am going to turn this meeting over to Danielle Morgan, though we will use her real name now, Danielle Ross. By now you all know that she's been working with me very closely on this case, and since she's been on the inside, I've asked her to present the facts."

Goldman sat down, and Dani got to her feet. "I really feel that Lieutenant Goldman should be doing this," she admitted quickly. "Without his assistance, and that of Chief Flannery and his entire staff, solving this case would have been impossible. I've made this very clear to the press, and now I want to thank you all for your fine work."

Flannery's face flushed with pleasure. "Not at all, Miss Ross, not at all! We're always glad to work with reputable private investigators such as yourself." The chief had seen the morning papers' glowing quotes praising him, and he was euphoric. He had met with Denton Cranston, the mayor's assistant, and the two of them had congratulated each other over the victory they had forged, glad to accept credit whether it belonged to them or not.

"Now then," Dani said, "there are a number of crimes we have to consider. I've made a list on this board—" She walked to one wall, picked up an easel with a large board on it, and set it down to Goldman's right. "Not that I think you've forgotten any of these incidents, but I want you to see them in perspective." The pertinent information was written in large block letters:

1. Attempt to run down Jonathan Ainsley.
2. Attempt to shoot Jonathan Ainsley.
3. Attempt to drop chandelier on Lyle Jamison.
4. Death by shooting of Amber LeRoi.
5. Bomb attempt to kill Jonathan Ainsley.
6. Attempt to stab Lily Aumont.
7. Poisoning of Sir Adrian Lockridge.
8. Attempt to electrocute Danielle Morgan (Ross).
9. Six letters threatening Jonathan Ainsley—actually eight all together, but only six that any of us besides Jonathan have seen.

Dani read the list slowly, then turned to face the group, her face intent. She was wearing a simple gray skirt, full and long, and a long-sleeved blue blouse. The wide black belt matched the high-heeled shoes, and a single cluster of deep-blue sapphires hanging from her neck caught the light, flashing as she moved.

The room was as still and ominous as a crypt as she went on, "I want to leave the two homicides for last. The least serious matters, although they are punishable by law, are the threatening letters." She moved to the desk and picked up some papers from a small stack. "These six," she said, "were not all alike. Obviously they *could* have been written by the same person, but Lieutenant Goldman and I feel that they were not." She didn't look at Jake. If she had, she would have seen a slight look of surprise on his face; he quickly covered his surprise by firmly nodding.

"The first two letters came directly to Mr. Ainsley and were typed on an older model Royal typewriter. As most of you probably know, every typewriter quickly develops its own peculiarities. No two typed pieces are alike, and it's as easy for the police to match a message with a typewriter as it is to match a bullet to a specific gun, as Lieutenant Goldman can testify, can't you, Lieutenant?"

"Certainly, Miss Ross."

"We have located the typewriter. The lab has positively identified it as the typewriter belonging to Carmen Rio."

"That's a lie!" Carmen Rio leaped to her feet, her olive-tinted face pale. "I didn't send those notes!" She looked at Jonathan Ainsley and began to tremble. "You gave me that typewriter! Tell them!"

Ainsley stared at Carmen, then shrugged. "That is true, but I gave her the machine at least two weeks before the first letters came. I'm very sorry to hear this, Carmen, very sorry indeed."

Murmurs went around the table, but Dani broke in, "The lab report shows that the machine we're speaking of has two obvious flaws. One is a half-raised capital E; the other is a half-raised capital O. But when additional studies were made with other material typed from the same typewriter—letters written by you, Mr. Ainsley, while the machine was in your possession—the letter O was *not* raised. In other words, those other letters were typed on the typewriter *before* you gave it to Carmen Rio."***

Every eye turned to Ainsley; every ear waited for his answer. But Ainsley didn't move a muscle except for blinking his eyes. Finally he offered, "Well, it's rather . . . I mean, she must . . . she must have typed the notes when she was . . . well, when she was at my house quite a lot."

"But she would have had no reason for typing the notes at that time, would she, Mr. Ainsley?" Goldman interjected. "It was only after you dumped her for another woman that she had a motive."

Dani waited for Ainsley to answer, but when he only sat there, sallow-faced, she continued, "The next pair of threatening letters were completely different—letters and words pasted on a sheet of paper, in the old manner of kidnappers. And the tone of the letters was noticeably different. The latter were filled with quotations from Shakespeare, for example. Obviously, it's hard to find the words you want in printed copy. Common words such as *and* or *the* are easy, but others are not. In these letters the lines from Shakespeare were clipped in their entirety from a single book. This is the book they were clipped from." Dani picked up a thick, brown volume and opened it. "Without question, the clippings came from this book."

"And whose is it?" Lily asked.

Dani hesitated. In the silence Lady Victoria Lockridge's voice sounded clear and steady. "It is my book. I sent those two letters."

Goldman objected, "Lady Lockridge, do not incriminate yourself at this time! The court would call this entrapment."

"I freely admit I sent the letters," Victoria insisted. Her head was held high, and she looked directly at Jonathan Ainsley. "I have despised that man for years. When I heard he had received threats, I did what I could to make his life miserable. And I would do it again." She looked at Dani. "I know that you found that book in our apartment."

Dani forced herself to meet Victoria's eyes. "Yes, I did, Lady Lockridge. It was when I stayed with your husband. He asked me to read him something, and I found this book on your desk." She faltered, then went on, "It was difficult for me to decide what to do."

Chief Flannery said suddenly, "Lady Lockridge, don't you realize how this makes you look?"

"It doesn't matter. I didn't make any attempts on Ainsley's life," she explained. "Yes, I sent two threatening letters, but that's all I did."

"Which brings us to the last two threats," Dani announced. "They were written on white paper with crayons, the kind easily obtained. It is also very simple for a laboratory to match a crayon with a mark, and here we have the crayons with which these notes were written." She looked down the table and said, "The police found them in Mickey Trask's desk."

"It's a setup!" Trask shouted. He leaped to his feet, and at once the two guards began holding him back. But they couldn't stop his mouth. "You cops framed me! It wasn't no cops who went through my apartment—it was some tall, dizzy blonde! The apartment manager told me how he let her in, the stupid jerk!"

Goldman said evenly, "At five o'clock this morning two men from my office, Sergeants Rozell and Crione, went to your apartment with a search warrant. When the manager admitted them, they found the writing materials in question in your desk. Now sit down or I'll have you gagged!"

Ben leaned over and whispered to Ringo Jordan, "I wonder what tall blonde woman located that stuff for the cops?"

Ringo gave him a quick grin. "Wigs don't cost much, do they?"

Goldman explained, "What this reads like is this: Ainsley sent himself two threats, Lady Lockridge the next two, and Trask the last two. Lady Lockridge hates Ainsley, as she herself has stated. It's common knowledge that Mickey Trask is bitter on two counts—Ainsley stole his girl, and he didn't keep his promise to let Mickey direct this play."

"All right," Trask spoke up, "so I sent the dumb letters. So what? That don't prove I killed anybody!"

"No, it doesn't," Dani admitted. "Before we get to the actual homicides, let's look at the *attempted* killings. First, the close call when the chandelier fell. If it had hit Lyle Jamison, it probably would have been fatal."

"I can't understand why anyone would want to kill me," Jamison objected. "Except for Simon Nero, of course."

"I wasn't anywhere *near* that rope when that chandelier fell!" cried Nero. "Besides, it could just as easily have hit Jonathan."

Dani broke in at once, "It's true that you weren't near the rope when it was cut, Mr. Nero. But then again—" She paused and looked at the group with a glint in her greenish eyes, "Neither was anyone else!"

"Well, *somebody* did it!" Jonathan shouted. "It didn't cut itself!"

"No, it was cut all right, Jonathan," Dani agreed. "But it was a very odd sort of cut. Lieutenant Goldman, will you give us your findings on the rope?"

"I was never satisfied with that," Goldman said. He reached down and pulled a short length of rope out of a briefcase. "This is high-grade nylon, thousand-pound test. You could cut through nine-tenths of it, and it would *still* hold the weight of that chandelier! It just didn't make sense. Why wasn't the rope cut cleanly all the way through? One slash with a sharp knife would cut it completely through. But it was cut only halfway; the other half was frazzled."

Goldman looked at Dani and said with a straight face, "Miss Ross and I decided to have the rope tested in the police lab. We discovered that the frazzled half of the rope had been eaten away by a highly corrosive acid."

"What does that prove, Lieutenant?" Lyle Jamison spoke up, a puzzled look on his face. "If someone wanted the rope to break, why didn't he either cut it completely or let the acid do it all?"

"For a very good reason," Goldman answered. "He wanted the rope cut so it would look as though someone had slashed it, but he cut it only halfway through and then poured acid on it because it would take the acid some time to eat through the remaining strands. Our man would be elsewhere, perhaps even on the stage, when the rope broke."

"Ainsley!" Carmen cried out. "*You* planned that, just like you wrote the first letters!"

Ainsley started to speak, but Goldman broke in quickly, "Don't say a word, Ainsley. You might incriminate yourself. Though I will say that Miss Ross and I found a flask of highly corrosive acid in the back of your dressing-room closet. The name of the store where it was purchased was still on the flask, and the man who sold it is willing to testify that you, Mr. Ainsley, are the purchaser."

"Why would I try to kill myself?" Ainsley demanded, his voice rising. "I could have been hit by that chandelier as well as Jamison!"

"Actually, you were in a chair six feet from where it hit. You were looking up at it all the time," Goldman stated flatly. "The incident would have done two things for you. First, it would have thrown all suspicion away from you. The so-called Phantom of the Theater couldn't be you because you almost died at his hand. And the bottom line, and what we think caused you to come up with this scheme, was to sell tickets. Free publicity but two people dead!" he said in utter disgust.

"I never killed anybody!" Ainsley objected, his voice uneven.

His brow was wet with sweat, and he drew out a handkerchief, mopped it, then went on, "All right, I did write those first two letters, and then I hired Miss Ross secretly, so that if anybody suspected me and started digging, they'd find out about Miss Ross and I'd be off the hook. And I *did* rig that chandelier to fall, but nobody was hurt, right? I had it timed to the split second!"

When Goldman shook his head but didn't say a word, Dani forged ahead. "The next attempt was a bomb put in a package intended for Ainsley. Two things about this attempt would eliminate most people. In the first place the killer was surprised by my operative, Ben Savage, and managed to overcome him." Dani paused and looked at Ben. "Savage was trained in the Rangers in hand-to-hand combat. He holds a black belt in karate. No average man—and certainly no woman—would be able to take Ben Savage out! The second thing is that most people wouldn't know how to make a bomb like the one the police found in the package. Your men say— do they not, Lieutenant?—that the bomb was fairly complex, requiring a high measure of skill to produce."

"That's correct," Goldman agreed nodding. He turned and looked at the man at the other end of the table. "When my men searched your apartment, Trask, they found out two very interesting things. One, you were a Navy Seal—and thus an underwater demolition expert and highly trained in hand-to-hand combat. I believe you also are a black-belt karate man, or so your certificate reads from the Twa Mateo Academy of Martial Arts. And while we are at it, Mickey, you might as well know that we're on our way to proving you were the man who stabbed Lily Aumont."

"You're crazy! How could I hit myself in the head hard enough to knock myself out? Besides, I didn't even have a knife!"

"We're working on that, Trask," Goldman said. "But we already almost have enough evidence to put you away."

Trask began to tremble. "It—it's all a frame. That broad who broke into my apartment—"

"There was no 'broad' with my men this morning, Trask!" Goldman responded. "They also found the same sort of material used to make a bomb. Do you want to explain why you were making bombs in your apartment? Or do you want to save that for the jury?"

"Wait a minute now!" Trask gasped. He was breathing hard, and his chest heaved visibly. "I don't—"

"How do you explain the fact that your fingerprints were on the timer that was set to kill Miss Ross? Why did you confess to setting the trap in that bathtub if you didn't do it? Why would you have fought with Savage and done all you could to stay out of that tub if there was nothing in it but soapy water?"

"All right, all right!" Mickey yelled. "I sent the letters, and I planted the bomb and wired the tub, but that's not murder one! You can't hang the real stuff on me!"

Chief Flannery loudly announced, "You'll take a fall, Trask! Attempted homicide will get you off the streets for a long time!" A worried look touched his eyes. "But what about the two murders, Goldman? Trask might have hated Ainsley enough to kill the LeRoi woman and hope it would get blamed on Ainsley since he pulled the trigger, but . . ."

"Let's talk about the murder of Amber LeRoi," Dani said in response. "She had enemies—two of them in this play."

"Yes, I hated the woman," Lady Lockridge confessed instantly. "She ruined my husband and almost wrecked my marriage. But I didn't kill her." She spoke with quiet confidence, and no sign of guilt appeared on her face.

"Did your husband hate her, Lady Lockridge?"

Something changed in the face of the noble actress, a slight break in her confidence, just enough to be seen. "Adrian was a much kinder person than I am," she admitted slowly. "He . . . hadn't been well for some time, and there were times when he . . . resented what Amber LeRoi had done to him."

Dani stood still for so long that everyone turned to stare at her. Finally she asked in a muted voice, "Your husband owned a gun, didn't he, Lady Lockridge? He told the police he didn't, but that wasn't the truth, was it?"

"It was just an old relic!" Victoria protested. "Adrian's father had owned it, and he kept it for a memento! It hadn't been fired for years. Adrian said it would probably blow up if anyone tried it!"

"Was the gun a .38?" Dani asked. "And did you buy some .38 cartridges?"

"I—I don't remember."

"Victoria . . ." Dani forced out her words. "Mr. Benny Allen, a clerk at Empire Sporting Goods, will testify that you bought a box of .38 cartridges from him at 2:15 in the afternoon on March 12. He instantly picked your picture out of a group. He also said you were so nervous, you could hardly stand."

Silence fell over the room like a heavy curtain. Victoria's face grew tense, and her lips trembled. Tears came to her eyes, and she nodded faintly. When she whispered, "Yes, I bought them!" those at the far end of the table could hardly hear her.

Dani suddenly couldn't say a word, her own eyes filled with tears and her throat constricted as if a giant hand had closed upon it.

Goldman took a quick glance at her and cautioned, "Lady Lockridge, I must warn you that having a motive such as you have admitted to and confessing that you bought live ammunition for the gun along with having the opportunity to place the live ammunition in the murder weapon all make you look guilty."

"I cannot help what it looks like, Lieutenant," she said simply. "I did not do what you have suggested."

Dani had regained her composure and carefully questioned, "Why did you buy the cartridges?"

"Because Adrian asked me to," she replied. "He told me that with all the terrible things happening to members of the cast, it would be better to keep a loaded gun in our apartment."

"Did you believe that?" Dani asked quickly.

"No, I did not. I thought he might—!" She broke off abruptly, put her hands over her face, and began to weep.

For a while Dani made no further attempt to question her, but when the older woman wiped her eyes, the lady detective continued, "Your husband was a very sick man, wasn't he?"

"Yes."

"Sicker than he knew perhaps?"

Suddenly Victoria lifted her eyes toward Dani, and everyone saw the shock written across her features. "How did you know?" she demanded sharply, almost angrily.

"I have a report on his condition from the hospital where he took his last tests—"

"Those reports are confidential! No one but family is supposed to have them!"

Ben Savage slumped lower in his seat, but his eyes didn't flicker.

Dani said evenly, "Physicians have given their opinion on these tests, Lady Lockridge. But you know what they said, don't you?"

"Yes! Yes!" Victoria nodded. "They said he was a dead man! No more than a month, and in all probability a painful death!" She bit her lower lip, removed the last of her tears with a limp tissue, and sat up straight in the chair. "All right . . . I had hoped it would never come out, but I see it has to be told. Adrian's illness was terminal. I tried to keep it from him, but he knew! And it worked on his mind, his emotions. At the last he had terrible periods of black depression. Sometimes he would feel some hope, but never for long."

"I think we all can remember the mood swings," Lily offered gently. "We all thought it was from a drinking problem."

"No, it wasn't that," Victoria said. "It was as though he became another man, not the one I knew so well. When he was in one of his bad times, he insisted I buy the cartridges for the gun. I knew he wasn't telling the truth about why he wanted them. I was afraid . . . that he'd kill himself!"

"Did you ever think he might want to kill Amber LeRoi?" Dani had to ask.

"No. The thought never entered my mind! Adrian would never—"

"Well, he *did* do it!"

Everyone looked at Mickey Trask. The small man's eyes were

fixed on Victoria Lockridge, and he said loudly, "I saw him put the ammo in that .38!"

A rising cry of shock ran around the room, and Victoria's loud cry of "No!" was almost a scream.

"I'm not going take the fall for murder one," Trask stated flatly. "I was passing by the prop room, and I saw Lockridge. He'd opened the cabinet where the gun was kept. I saw him take the blanks out and put in live ammo!"

"You'll testify to this in a court of law?" Goldman asked.

"Yes!"

"It's just his word!" Victoria cried.

"No, it's not!" Trask shouted. "She saw it too!" He pointed at Carmen, who began to tremble. "Come on, babe!" Trask urged. "The woods are on fire—tell 'em what we saw!"

Carmen started to shake her head, but Dani promptly intervened, "We have a witness who will testify that he heard you say . . ." She picked up a sheet of paper and read, "'Sir Adrian! Sir Adrian! Why did you do it? Why did you kill Amber?'"

Carmen's eyes went at once to Savage. She held his gaze, then seemed to slump. "All right, I was with Mickey . . . and I saw what he said."

"You both saw Adrian Lockridge reloading the weapon used in the drama to fire at Amber LeRoi?" Goldman insisted.

They both agreed that was the truth.

Goldman said slowly, "So you both saw it and did nothing about it? The prosecuting attorney will love that!" His smooth face changed then, and compassion shone out of his dark eyes. "I think, Lady Lockridge, you will have to accept the fact that your husband was not himself—that he was temporarily insane when he did that."

"That is certainly true—he was not himself," she whispered. "All the years we were married, and I never heard an unkind word!"

Anxious to break the mood, Dani interjected brusquely, "And I think we now have the key to the attempted stabbing of Lily Aumont. The two of you did it, didn't you? Trask, you were supposed to stab her. Then someone had to give you a sharp blow on the head and take the knife. Carmen, I think you might as well admit to it."

"Yes, that was the way it was," Carmen confessed, her eyes dull. "He said it was foolproof! Now look at us!" ***

"Which brings us," Goldman said slowly, "to the death of Sir Adrian Lockridge." He stood there, his head down, staring at the table. "It's the most difficult part of the whole affair. The physical evidence is nonexistent!"

Lifting one hand he counted the points on his fingers. "Number one, he was poisoned. But the autopsy was unable to determine the nature of the poison. To put the matter bluntly, the victim's internal physical condition was so poor that it took very little to bring on death.

"Number two, the poison could not have come from the champagne bottle used in the dining scene. Everyone drank from that same bottle, with no ill effects. Everyone got a clean glass from the servant.

"Number three, the sherry bottle and both glasses used in the final scene were broken, and not enough traces remained for the lab to identify anything. But Ainsley poured both drinks into the glasses, in full view of the audience. There was no way Ainsley could have put poison in Sir Adrian's glass—no way at all!"

"Well, what are you saying, Goldman?" Chief Flannery spoke up. "*Somebody* must have put poison in that glass!"

"Yes," Goldman said slowly, and everyone leaned forward. "But the only person who could have put the poison in his glass was Sir Adrian himself!"

"He would never do that! Never!" Lady Lockridge objected defiantly.

"Not if he were in his right mind," Goldman agreed. "But you know, as do we all and as we have already discussed, Lady Lockridge, that your husband was a deeply troubled man. Isn't that so?"

Victoria bowed her head. "Yes, that is true."

"So that's it!" Chief Flannery got to his feet, a look of satisfaction on his face. "Take Trask back to his cell—"

"Chief Flannery, we're not finished yet."

Flannery looked at Dani, who stood straighter than usual. Her face was colorless, and her voice sounded forced as she added, "There is one other piece of evidence that must be brought forward."

"What is it?" Flannery asked in surprise. "Do you know of anything more, Lieutenant?"

"Why, no, sir." Goldman was watching Dani carefully, his eyes taking in the sallow cast of her face and the fact that her hands were trembling. "What evidence, Miss Ross?" he asked quietly.

Dani licked her lips, then said, "It concerns the death of Sir Adrian Lockridge. It was logical for us to think that the poison was put into the sherry. As Lieutenant Goldman has said, it was impossible for Ainsley to have done it. Knowing that Sir Adrian was a sick man, not in control of his faculties, it was logical for us to assume that he did it himself, hoping to throw suspicion on the man who had ruined him. But there was one time when the poison could have been given to Sir Adrian." Dani lifted her head and stared down the table. "At the dining table—*after* the champagne was served."

Goldman hesitated, not sure of her meaning. "Are you saying Sir Adrian put the poison in his champagne glass, but it didn't take effect until the next scene?"

Dani said slowly and emphatically, "I will never believe Sir Adrian Lockridge killed himself. For personal reasons—" She faltered here, then caught herself. "He was at the end a man who was filled with peace, perhaps for the first time in his life. Even if he knew he was going to die, I think he had the courage to face death. That is my opinion of him. What do you think, Victoria?"

Victoria Lockridge had been listening carefully to Dani. Then she said, "Yes, I think you are right." She smiled across at Dani—a strange smile, Goldman thought. "But how did he get the poison in his glass?"'

Dani said evenly, holding her gaze, "There was one point in that dining scene when every eye was drawn to Ringo Jordan at the opposite end of the table. At that moment it would have been possible for someone sitting at Sir Adrian's left hand to have switched glasses with him."

"He was left-handed, and I was at his left," Victoria commented. "It wouldn't have been difficult at all, especially with everyone's attention on someone else. But why would I switch glasses with him?"

Dani said as if the words were forced from her, "Because you had already put the poison in your own glass."

"How would I manage that, Danielle?" Lady Lockridge asked. She looked as if she and the young woman facing her were playing some sort of word game.

"From the small flask you wear on your wrist. The one you're wearing now."

"From this?" Victoria held her left hand up, catching the tiny flask in her right. "What would make you think that?"

"Because the flask was filled with red wine from your wedding, but now it's empty."

Lady Victoria lifted her arm and stared at the tiny container. Then she added in a conversational tone, "Yes, the wine is gone." She lowered her arm. "We've had the poison for a long time. It was something Adrian's brother brought back from India when he was stationed there. I hated it, but Adrian found it fascinating. It worked, just as they told Adrian's brother it would, in a matter of five minutes or so. The rest of it is still in the specimen case at home."

Goldman moved impulsively toward Lady Lockridge, as though she would bolt out of the room. But she did no such thing. Instead she removed the bracelet from her wrist and handed it to Goldman. He took out a handkerchief, let her lay it in the folds, then put it in his breast pocket.

"He hated hospitals and being sick," Lady Victoria explained quietly. Her eyes were dreamy, as though she were seeing something pleasant in her mind. "It would have been torture for him, having to be cared for by others, watching himself waste away." She opened her eyes and said, "Danielle, he said to me not long before the last,

'I wish men were like animals, that they could just crawl away and die alone—not be fussed over by everyone.' I knew him better than anyone. And I loved him—always. That's why I couldn't stand to see him suffer!"

She spoke no more, and every person in the room sat as if frozen. Lady Lockridge rose from her seat. She came around the table and stood before Dani. She reached out to touch Dani's cheek gently. "You must not grieve, my dear! You must not! I could not have kept it in. Sooner or later I would have had to testify that Adrian was not a coward who took his own life!"

She suddenly put her arms around Dani and hugged her fiercely. They both stood there stiffly, and Victoria looked into the younger woman's face, then moved to wipe away the tears flowing freely down Dani's cheeks. "Don't weep! You gave him life, dear. I saw it with my own eyes. He was never the same after you stayed with him and talked with him. Somehow you were able to pass your faith on to him! And I thank you for that! Adrian and I—we both thank you!"

She kissed Danielle and turned to face Goldman.

"Lieutenant, I'm ready now."

"Yes, Lady Victoria." Goldman looked as if he had been struck in the pit of the stomach. He moved falteringly around the table and put out his arm. "I'll go with you," he murmured.

Together they walked through the door in complete silence. Framed by the high doorway, Victoria turned and smiled, not just with her lips, but with her eyes. "Don't ever grieve, Danielle—you gave him life!"

She passed through the door, and it swung closed with a sigh, shutting her off from view.

Nineteen

BAYOU FUGITIVE

Ben Savage left New Orleans at 8, but the late April heat was already rising out of the earth, moist and thick. The Toll Causeway was mostly clear, so he set the cruise control on 65. Lake Pontchartrain lapped at the concrete pillars supporting the highway; shimmering heat waves already blurred the blue-gray surface. A flight of white egrets scored the steel-gray sky, and his eyes followed them until they dropped down into a reedy sandbank. Crossing Interstate 12, he caught State Highway 90 and held his speed until he passed through Houma. He had to slow down for the lights, so he pulled a piece of paper from his pocket, unfolded it, and studied the map that Daniel Ross had drawn.

"Go through Houma," Dani's father had said, tracing the route on the map. "But watch for the road marked Highway 57—it's a gravel road that bears left. Go through a one-horse burg, Dulac. Nothing much there but a store and a gas station. Watch your odometer. Exactly six and three-tenths of a mile, there'll be a dirt road on your right, between two live oak trees. It's easy to miss. Take that road till it plays out."

"What then?" Ben had asked.

"Walk about a half a mile down a trail. You can't miss it because it's the only thing that's out of the water this time of year. You'll find a pirogue tied there. Get in it, follow the white flags, and you'll get to the cabin."

He easily found the road between the two trees. Pulling a knapsack out of the backseat, he locked the car and set off down the path, which wound around huge cypress trees. It should have been cooler in the shade, but the heat seemed to be trapped by the bulk of the trees. By the time he had gone fifty yards, he was soaked with sweat. The path narrowed and ten minutes later played out completely.

He stared at the pirogue tied by a frayed cotton line and shook his head but moved toward it anyway. The small dugout was not much over eight feet long, not wider than three feet, and very shallow. He had seen the Cajuns stand up in them, skimming over the water like water bugs, in what they called their *pee-row*. But when he put the knapsack in the bow and gingerly lowered himself, the flimsy craft almost rolled over.

Ben caught his balance, knelt on the hard floor, and shoved off with the short-handled paddle. The boat tilted alarmingly, but soon he was able to paddle the craft along. "Thing moves easy enough," he murmured to himself. "Easiest thing to paddle I was ever in."

By now he was at least somewhat accustomed to the heat, but the rising hum of mosquitoes and gnats sang in his ears. He slapped at his neck, almost falling out of the boat, looked at the bloody mark on his hand, then shook his head and threw his back into the work. As the pirogue skimmed along, he became aware of the otherworldly silence. There was no sound save the drone of insects and the noise of his paddle gurgling through the murky black water. A dirty, weather-stained white rag caught his eye, and he steered the boat into what seemed to be a large canal. The sun flickered through the limbs of the cypress trees, resembling latticework, and he batted his eyes, watching for the next flag.

He missed it, for it was so water-dyed it was almost brown. Backpaddling, he awkwardly made his way through an even narrower channel—so narrow that he could touch both banks with his paddle. This lasted only a few yards, and he soon emerged into a body of open water, a small lake that must have covered thirty acres or more. Surveying the far shore, he saw a cabin sitting on stilts. A thin ribbon of white smoke was rising out of a round smokestack.

"Well, I didn't get lost anyway." Dead cypress trees withered to tall splinters poked at the sky like dead men's fingers, and he had to steer the craft carefully between them. Once he put out his paddle to shove off on a large black branch as big around as his arm—and the branch turned out to be a cottonmouth moccasin. He felt the tip of the paddle prod the firm flesh, saw the white of the widespread jaws, and jerked the paddle back, making a club out of it. But the snake slid into the water and disappeared beneath the black surface.

With a hand that was not entirely steady, Savage wiped the sweat from his face. "I'll be seeing you, old boy, in every little ripple in this blasted swamp." He was almost to the little finger of dry land that reached out into the main body when he made the mistake of standing up. He was coming in smoothly, and it was like riding water skis, which he did well. But the pirogue hit something that seemed to rise to the surface, and even as Savage fell into the water the thought screamed through his mind: *Alligator!*

He hit the water full length. Though his legs churned frantically, his feet sank into the muddy bottom, which seemed to pull him down. A mindless shout escaped him. He jerked his feet loose and in a desperate effort that was half swimming and half crawling reached the shore. He could almost feel the teeth closing on him as he got to his feet, made an enormous lunge, and fell facedown in the black mud.

A calm voice greeted him. "Hello, Ben."

He looked up, wiped the mud from his face, and saw Dani sitting in a lawn chair under the raised cabin. She was wearing denim shorts, a man's blue shirt, and a pair of dark glasses.

He stared at her, then waved back at the water. "Hit an alligator!" he gasped. "He nearly got me!"

Dani got up out of her chair, walked over in front of him, and looked at his mud-blackened face, then at the water.

"That's a log," she pointed out casually and walked back to take her seat.

Savage twisted his head and noticed a half-sunken log gently bobbing beside the pirogue. Not wanting to face Dani, he felt tempted to get in the pirogue and just leave. But he got up, waded out to the boat, picked up the knapsack, shook it off, then dragged the boat to shore, dropping it with a thud.

The knapsack was dripping wet, and he was sure that everything was spoiled. Still not looking Dani in the eye, he moved to dry land and began to unpack the contents.

She watched as he shook the water off the groceries and pulled out a pack of sodas. "What are you doing here, Ben?" she finally asked.

He shook water from a package of Snicker bars, then looked at her. "Oh, I was just passing by, you know? Thought I might as well say hello."

She stared at him. "There's a cold-water shower. Wash the mud off your face," she ordered. "You look like one of those old-time minstrels."

He glared at her, stomped over to the shower, a ten-gallon bucket with holes punched in the bottom, and pulled the chain that let fresh water fill it up. He washed the black mud off his face and hands, then took off his T-shirt and wrung it out, but left the pants and shoes the way they were.

She had her back turned to him. "Have you had breakfast?" she threw over her shoulder.

"No."

"I'll fix something."

Thirty minutes later they were sitting at the small table inside the cabin. The sides were mostly open but screened. He took a bite of ham and chewed it, watching the sun hit the bayou. Little streaks of fire seemed to run across it, and once a huge fish broke water, sending out a shower of silver drops. He ate the ham and eggs and put preserves on three pieces of toast. Dani sat and watched him, saying nothing. Finally he finished the coffee.

"Dad sent you, I suppose."

"Yep."

"I'm not going back."

"All right."

She stared at him. "I mean it, Ben!"

"Okay." He leaned back in his chair and stared through the screen. "After you go through the Lost World to get here, this place is pretty nice."

"Ben, I'm not kidding," she said. Her skin was brown from the sun, but she looked thinner.

"So you're not kidding. So you're not going back." He shrugged his thick shoulders. "I'm not going to drag you back by the hair. And I'm not kidding about that!"

She held his eyes, her shoulders very straight. A pelican flapped lazily across in front of the screen, and Savage watched with admiration as the bird suddenly folded its wings, made a dive, and came up with the silvery tail of a fish flopping wildly in his pouch.

"All right then," Dani agreed. She got up and washed the dishes. When she was finished, she commented, "I'm going fishing."

"I'll clean them." He nodded, not taking his eyes off the bayou.

She watched him through half-shut eyes, then turned and left the cabin. He pulled her chair over and put his feet on it. Lowering his chin on his chest, he promptly went to sleep.

♦ ♦ ♦

"That was good fish," Savage complimented Dani. "What kind was it?"

"Sacalait," she told him. "What some people call white perch or crappie." She had stayed away from the cabin most of the day, hoping he'd be gone when she returned. But she found him reading her copy of *Pride and Prejudice*.

He had cooked the fish on the gasoline stove, talking cheerfully all the while and appearing not to notice her silence. Now she walked onto the small deck that projected from the front of the cabin and stood there, holding her arms around herself. The odors of the swamp, mysterious and rank, floated up to her, and she somehow knew when he came outside to stand beside her.

A hoarse, wild, grunting noise erupted from the ground to their left. Savage turned sharply. "What was that?" he wanted to know.

"Bull gator."

He asked cautiously, "Can those things climb ladders?"

She opened her eyes and dropped her arms. "Ben, I know you're worried about me, that my family is worried about me. I'm sorry for that, but you can't help me." She turned to face the bayou, whispering, "Nobody can."

"God is dead, huh?" he demanded.

His reply angered her. "Don't you start on me, Ben Savage! You've always laughed at my faith."

"That's a lie," he said calmly. "I've always admired it—until now."

The guilt that had borne down on her spirit like a vast weight suddenly seemed to grow even worse. She clenched her teeth, shut her eyes, and hugged herself again. A moan escaped her lips. "What am I going to do? What am I going to *do*?" He said nothing, and she pressed her fists against her mouth until her lips hurt, trying to stop the words that rose. Finally she lifted her fists and struck the rail, crying out, "I did it all by myself! Oh, what a *clever* girl! How very wonderful I am!"

Savage stood in silence, watching her carefully. She held his gaze, then suddenly lifted her fists and struck him in the chest, her voice rising. "You don't understand! I'm the one who put her in prison for the rest of her life! She trusted me—loved me—and—and—" Her voice was choked with grief, and all the pent-up guilt and self-hatred erupted in a torrent of tears. Without realizing it, she leaned against him, and he put his arm around her. She grasped his shirt with her fists, burying her face against his shoulder. Great waves of grief rose and fell, and she swayed in his grasp, would have fallen if he had not held her upright.

An owl floated across the sky, framed in the full moon that seemed tangled in the branches of a cypress. His flight was noiseless, and so was the world he looked down on, except for the sobs of the woman, which floated over the bayou in a ghostly fashion.

Finally she grew still and realized he was holding her. Pulling back, she drew a handkerchief from her pocket and dabbed at her face. "What's happened to all of them, Ben?"

He told her slowly, "Jonathan Ainsley is making a mint. The play is sold out for the next year, and he'll star in the movie version. He sent a whopping big check to the Ross Investigation Agency. He's not sorry about what he did, though he is paying all the legal bills for Victoria. Trask will do maybe a year, with time off, Carmen less. The rest are doing their roles."

She said quietly, "You know whom I mean."

"Trial is set for next month. There's lots of sympathy for her. The old mercy-killing crowd is in full cry. Others want to see her die, but the governor won't allow the death penalty in his state, so you don't need to worry about that."

His words sent a shiver down her back, and she looked at him quickly. "Ben, what will happen?"

He said slowly, "Depends on her friends, I'd say." Then he gave her the tough look she knew so well. "And her friends hiding out in a swamp aren't going to be much help, are they, boss?"

She shut her eyes and turned away from him. But after a few moments she asked in a small voice, "What could I do, Ben? I'm the one who put her in jail!"

"No, you're not the one who put her in jail," he responded evenly. "She did it—and as she said at the hearing, she'd never have kept quiet about it. As for helping her, I can't think of anyone who could help more. It would be pretty tough for a prosecuting attorney to handle—the woman who took her in begging for her." He let that sink in, then added, "She sends you her love."

"What?"

"You heard me. I've talked with her three or four times. She always says, 'Give Danielle my love.'"

Dani stood absolutely still. Then a ragged cry escaped her lips, "Oh, Ben, I feel so rotten!"

"Here," he said, spinning her around. "Use this shoulder. The other one is soggy."

She glared at him. "You monster! To make fun of me while I'm—while I'm—"

When she broke off in helpless anger, he went on, "While you're out in your little ol' swamp feeling sorry for yourself?" She hit at him, but he caught her wrists easily and held her firmly.

She struggled, but his grip was iron. Finally she stood quietly, and far away a night bird called. Her eyes filled with tears, but he shook his head. "That's just the way it is, boss."

His grip relaxed, but she leaned against him. She looked up at him, and he bent his head and kissed her. He pulled back and stared at her.

The bull alligator roared again, making Ben jump, and she grabbed his hand. Pulling him inside, she cried, "Let's have dessert!"

Dani Ross Mysteries

Danielle Ross is a bright, attractive young woman whose future plans have been put on hold. Returning home to run her ailing father's detective agency, she immediately finds herself in a world she never imagined. From one challenging case to the next, Dani and her partner, Ben Savage, unravel each tangled web to identify the sinister minds behind the scenes, even as her faith—and her heart—are challenged.

BOOK 1: *One by One* BOOK 2: *And Then There Were Two*

THE CHRONICLES OF THE GOLDEN FRONTIER

Jennifer DeSpain's life used to be quiet and dull, but that was before a whirlwind romance and marriage—and a tragedy that left her a widow with only a defunct newspaper to her name. With hopes of a fresh start, Jennifer boldly moves her family to Nevada, where she will have to resolve the challenges of poverty, newspaper publishing, a reversal of fortune, parenting—and matters of the heart—all with the help of some colorful friends and the Lord above.

BOOK 1: *Riches Untold*
BOOK 2: *Unseen Riches*
BOOK 3: *Above the Clouds*
BOOK 4: *The Silver Thread*

ALL THAT GLITTERS

Standing alone in her mother's empty apartment, Afton Burns is startled by the ringing phone—and the voice of her father on the other end, inviting her to join him on the set of the movie he's directing. Still suffering from the loss of her mother, Afton knows she needs to be near him and reestablish a relationship that was broken long ago. But that tinseled, movie-star world is an alien place that turns even stranger when it becomes clear that someone doesn't want this film to be completed. There is only one person Afton can trust with her heart and her life—and it's the last person anyone would expect.